Praise for *Among the Departed*

"A rugged western landscape and modern-day Mounties make this a series to watch." —Dana Stabenow
Edgar-winning author of the Kate Shugak series

"Delany invigorates the cozy genre with an unsparing look at love in all its variations, including coming to terms with it the second time around." —*Kirkus Reviews*

Praise for *Negative Image*

"Delany...deftly sprinkles clues—and red herrings—without ever slighting her engaging characters." —*Publishers Weekly*

"Combines the crisp plotting of the best small-town police procedurals with trenchant commentary on such universal problems as love and trust." —*Kirkus Reviews*

"Delany adds fine layers of intricacy and depth to the crimes, investigations, pacing and characters of *Negative Image*, so that by the end, those virtues have put her well within range of the most sterling of smart, talented crime writers."
—*London Free Press*

"How she manages to...hold herself together in a time of crisis shows just how well Molly has matured....Keeps you anxious for more." —I Love a Mystery.com

Praise for *Winter of Secrets*

"Artistry as sturdy and restrained as a Shaker chair...with a denouement that's equally plausible and startling."
—*Publishers Weekly* starred review

"Delany effectively combines a cozy tone and a picturesque setting with plenty of action and procedural detail." —*Booklist*

"This series about Canadian constable Molly Smith has only gotten better." —*Contra Costa Times*

"Will satisfy the most demanding fans of the cottage-cozy genre...."
—*Globe and Mail*

"Tying the warmth of a cozy mystery against a traditional police procedural, this Constable Molly Smith series pits small town familiarity against cold police authority in a way that delights the reader." —*Salem Press Magill*

"*Winter of Secrets* is another outstanding police procedural from Vicki Delany. Anyone who enjoys small town police procedurals should try her book, set in eccentric Trafalgar." —*Mystery News*

Praise for *Valley of the Lost*

"Intertwined subplots, complex characters, and an easy prose style make this a great follow-up to...*In the Shadow of the Glacier.*"

—*Library Journal*

"Contrasts the beautiful British Columbia wilderness, vividly described by Delany, with the sober realities of contemporary crime."

—*Booklist*

"Delany explores the social dynamics of a small mountain community as well as deftly handling the plot's twists and turns as it builds to a pulse-pounding conclusion." —*Publishers Weekly*

"The plot is finely tuned and action moves at a fast clip with a climax that is worth the read. The characters are well fleshed out. Wouldn't mind knowing some of them. The village is a gem. Too bad it's a product of the author's very active imagination."

—Bookloons.com

"The author effectively integrates an engrossing whodunit within a social commentary on small town life. Her observations ring true primarily due to the credible characters she has created. The intricate, well-thought-out plot also helps, and will keep readers guessing until the surprise ending." —*Mysterious Reviews*

Praise for *In the Shadow of the Glacier*

"An exciting series debut from Delany...featuring complex characters with plenty of room to grow." —*Kirkus Reviews*

"An unlikely police officer but a likable lead character, Molly shows her mettle in this initial offering in a promising series set in the Canadian wilderness." —*Booklist*

"Delany carefully sets up the conflicts, resolving most but not all in anticipation of the next assignment, and begins what looks to be some extensive character development for...Winters and Smith."
—*Publishers Weekly*

"Writing in the quiet voice of a 26-year-old woman striving to succeed in a job of which her parents disapprove, Delany launches a new traditional series about Canadian small-town life that may appeal to fans of Louise Penny's Quebec cozies."
—*Library Journal*

"This new series promises to surpass Delany's previous novels and that is hard to do. Her characters are finely drawn as is the backdrop of Trafalgar. Tension mounts at a rather fast pace as an unscrupulous TV newscaster rankles everyone. The reader could easily learn to hate that man. The climax is surprising. Didn't figure that one out. Don't miss *In the Shadow of the Glacier.*" —*Bookloons*

Praise for *Burden of Memory*

"The striking setting, the picture of the Canadian social elite and several deftly handled subplots make for a richly textured and highly satisfying read." —*Publishers Weekly*

"Readers who favor leisurely puzzles steeped in family dynamics and flavored with descriptions of beautiful scenery may find this just what they're looking for." —*Booklist*

"Delany has done a great job with this book....This is, obviously, ideal reading for a weekend at the cottage....Read it under the trees and see every page come to life." —*Globe and Mail*

"*Burden of Memory* is enjoyable on many levels—rich historical fiction, a gradually unfolding mystery, and psychological suspense." —*Crimespree Magazine*

"*Burden of Memory* is one of the best books I have read in a long time. It has everything—suspense, history and geography." —I Love a Mystery

"Delany seamlessly integrates the parallel narrative of today and the wartime period. She also integrates the old lifestyle of the wealthy Ontarioites and their summer 'cottages' with today's necessities. The characters are interesting and alive. This is a very good second novel." —Reviewing the Evidence.com

Praise for *Scare the Light Away*

"*Scare the Light Away* is an exciting and suspenseful crime novel certainly. But more than that, it is an evocative account of the tenacious grip the past holds over us, and the pain and joy of reclaiming it." –Lyn Hamilton
author of the Lara McClintoch Archaeological Mystery Series

"This atmospheric novel deftly weaves a family's tragic and violent history with a horrific present-day crime that threatens to undo them. Through her superb characterization of a transplanted English war bride and her Canadian husband and children, Vicki Delany has created characters worth caring about and plunged them into a suspense-filled, nightmare scenario. Like her contemporary protagonist, Rebecca McKenzie, the author never takes the easy way out. Don't plan to sleep any time soon." —Mary Jane Maffini
author of the Camilla MacPhee mysteries

"Vicki Delany has created a formidable character in Rebecca McKenzie. Her statuesque size and smart mouth are at odds with her vulnerability. We come to understand that vulnerability through her British mother's diaries. Nothing is predictable here, not the rural Ontario dysfunctional family the mother is pulled into, nor the dramatic shift in the family that Rebecca finds when she returns home after an absence of thirty years. The isolated countryside is an integral part of Rebecca's character, as is her dog, Sampson, both lovingly described with a fond but unsentimental eye. Through deft characterization and some honest writing, Delany convinces us that people can change."

—Sylvia Warsh, author of *Find Me Again,*
winner of 2004 Edgar for Best Original Paperback

"The reader...is pulled into an engaging family drama that avoids cliché and illuminates small community life, good and bad. In this ...promising first novel, suspense takes second place to the larger mysteries of survival, love, loss and forgiveness."

—*The Drood Review*

Among the Departed

Books by Vicki Delany

Constable Molly Smith Series
In the Shadow of the Glacier
Valley of the Lost
Winter of Secrets
Negative Image
Among the Departed

Other Novels
Scare the Light Away
Burden of Memory

Among the Departed

A Constable Molly Smith Novel

Vicki Delany

Poisoned Pen Press

First Edition 2011

10 9 8 7 6 5 4 3 2 1

Library of Congress Catalog Card Number: 2011920300

ISBN: 9781590589243 Hardcover
9781590588895Trade Paperback

Poisoned Pen Press
6962 E. First Ave., Ste. 103
Scottsdale, AZ 85251
www.poisonedpenpress.com
info@poisonedpenpress.com

Printed in the United States of America

To Alex, Julia, and Caroline

Acknowledgments

As always I am extremely grateful for the help and support I get from police officers in Ontario and British Columbia. In particular I'd like to thank Staff Sergeant Kris Patterson, Sergeant Rene Menard, Sergeant Brad Gilbert, Constable Paul Burkart, Corporal Al Grant, Constable Nicole Lott, Constable Kyle King. Thanks to Constable Dan Joly who told me about living and working with police dogs, and to Diablo who demonstrated.

I try as hard as I can to get the policing right, but sometimes the story has to take precedence over the facts, so any and all procedural errors are strictly mine.

Thanks to my fabulous critique group: Dorothy McIntosh, Cheryl Freedman, Donna Carrick, Madeleine Harris-Callway and Jane Burfield, who read as fast as I can write.

Also to Carol Reynolds for details about artists and art galleries. When next you are in Nelson be sure to look up Carol and her art.

And to Tony and Herb for lending me their names.

"I hate you."

"That's too bad because I love you, but you still have to take a timeout."

"No!"

"Jamie, go into the tent and stay there until you're told you can come out."

"No."

"I'm going to count to three and if you are not in that tent, you won't be allowed out for hot chocolate. One..."

Jamie wanted to stick out his tongue but he didn't dare. That really made his mum mad.

Poppy pulled a face at him from behind their mother's back.

Poppy could stick out her tongue. Poppy could do whatever she wanted. It was her stupid fault he was in trouble. It was always her fault.

"Two..."

Jamie turned and stomped across the campsite to the tent, stamping his feet as loudly as he could. He stretched as he entered, but still didn't quite brush the top of the door.

Stupid tent. Stupid camping. Stupid Canada.

He wanted to go home.

He gave his sleeping bag a good satisfying kick before throwing himself onto it.

He wanted to cry, but at five years old Jamie Paulson was too old to cry.

This was supposed to be an adventure. Dad had said they'd see grizzly bears and hear wolves and catch fish and cook over a fire and live like Indians.

Yesterday they saw a squirrel.

He heard a wolf last night, after he and Poppy went to bed, when Mum and Dad were sitting around the fire, but Poppy said it was Dad trying to be scary.

Stupid girls. Ruin everything.

Fishing was boring. Dad stood on the side of the river and threw a line in and pulled it out again. So far he hadn't even had a bite, never mind catching enough fish to feed the whole family. And take some back to Granny, which is what he'd said he'd do.

When Jamie had thrown a stone into the water, Dad got mad and said he was scaring the fish away.

"Fishing is stupid."

"It's not the fish, Jamie," Dad said with that sigh that meant he was not happy, "It's the fishing. Peace, quiet, relaxation."

Peace and quiet were stupid. Jamie stared at the roof of the tent. He didn't know why adults wanted peace and quiet anyway. Dad wouldn't let them bring their new DVD player on the camping trip, and Poppy got in a snit when ordered to leave her iPod behind.

They were in Canada for a whole month, them and Granny, visiting Aunt Maureen and Uncle Henry. Jamie expected it would be more fun than this. He'd bragged to all his mates back home that they were going to be having adventures in Canada, riding horses and climbing mountains and staying in really big houses. Instead Aunt Maureen and Uncle Harvey lived in a middle unit of a townhouse row in Abbotsford, a home even smaller than Jamie's family's new bungalow in London.

He grudgingly had to admit that the mountains, some with snow still on the tops even though it was late summer, were pretty neat, and the Vancouver aquarium was brilliant, and so were the totem poles at the museum. He'd asked why no one was looking after the totem poles, just letting them rot and fall down. The museum guide said the Haida (Jamie said the word out loud, to hear it on his tongue) believed totems should have a natural life, like people and animals. Jamie liked that. His dog Rusty died before they came on this stupid trip, and Dad had told him death was part of life.

If Rusty had been here, this would have been a great vacation.

Dad asked Poppy to come down to the lake with him and get water to boil for coffee and hot chocolate. Poppy huffed and puffed, but Jamie heard branches break as she got up off her fat arse and followed him.

He smelled smoke and heard the pop and hiss of the campfire.

Mum wasn't a very good cook, nowhere near as good as his friend's Michael's mum who'd worked in a restaurant before she got married, but Jamie had to admit the food was pretty good cooked over a fire. They ate Canadian food like hot dogs and hamburgers, and before going to bed they drank hot chocolate and toasted marshmallows on sticks over the fire. He liked to let his marshmallow catch fire, and watch the flames leaping into the darkening sky. He couldn't eat them like that, burned black, and Mum said he was wasting food, but he still did it.

They had not caught and eaten any fish.

They had not seen grizzly bears or wolves.

Jamie pushed the sleeping bag aside and sat up.

If Dad didn't spend all his time trying to catch a fish, and Mum wasn't always reading and saying stuff like "It's so lovely and quiet" maybe they would have seen some bears. Bears aren't going to come to where people are making fires and talking. And Poppy used so much of her stupid perfume the bears wouldn't come within a mile of the camp.

He could find bears. They'd been told grizzly bears were dangerous and sometimes attacked people, but he was little so he could be really quiet. He'd find a bear fishing in the river and sit behind a rock and watch. Maybe the bear'd throw the fish onto the rocks and he could grab a couple to bring back to Dad.

He'd show them that he wasn't a baby to be sent to the tent for a time out.

Jamie rolled up his blanket and stuffed it into his sleeping bag, and then he put Pinky, his elephant, into the bag. He pulled off his cap and put it on the elephant and adjusted the toy so only the top of the brown head lay on the pillow.

Then he crawled to the tent door and peeked out. Dad and Poppy were down by the river and Mum had her head in the car's boot, searching for something.

Jamie dashed for the woods.

Chapter One

Adam Tocek held a match to a pile of crumpled newspaper and twigs. With a soft whoosh the kindling ignited, filling the room with an orange glow. He poked at the fire and placed a birch log on top. The scraps of newspaper burned quickly, and the fire jumped from stick to stick, chewing at the dry white bark. He placed a larger log on top of the growing inferno and settled back on his heels to admire his handwork.

"Am I getting old," the woman on the floor said, "or do we start using the fireplace earlier and earlier every year?"

"You're getting old."

"Gee, thanks."

"This place is at a much higher elevation than down in town and the nights get cold early."

He dropped down beside her and nuzzled her neck. She handed him a glass, and red liquid danced in the light of the flames.

The remains of their supper, barbecued ribs, potato salad, fresh greens, were on the coffee table in front of them. The big dog sniffed at the fire and made several circles on the rug before collapsing with a happy groan in front of it.

Tocek massaged the back of her neck. The woman sighed with as much pleasure as had the dog and settled back into his fingers. "Nice," she murmured.

His hand drifted down, down her neck, across her shoulders, down her upper back. His fingers found the clips of her bra. He put his wine glass down and brought his other hand up. The bra sprang free and she turned her face. Her blue eyes were soft and moist in the firelight, her lips open, the tip of her pink tongue trapped between her white teeth.

He leaned into the kiss, and then broke away to lift her T-shirt over her head. Her fingers moved toward the buckle on his shorts.

His phone rang.

Constable Adam Tocek was with the Royal Canadian Mounted Police, the dog handler for the Mid-Kootenay area of British Columbia. He was on call tonight, and so had restricted himself to one glass of wine with dinner.

He could not ignore his work cell phone.

Could he?

He stretched out a finger toward the dark nipple, flushed and hard with the anticipation of pleasure.

But she was a cop too, and Molly Smith pulled away with a laugh. She slithered to her feet and reached across the table for the phone. Her body was long and lean. Her breasts, small and round above a taut belly, moved and he almost said to heck with duty.

She handed him the phone.

"Yeah?"

He listened for a moment before getting to his feet and snatching a scrap of paper off the table. "Got it," he said, making a note. "Kid missing from a campsite at Koola Park."

By the time he turned around, Molly Smith had her bra fastened and was pulling her shirt over her head.

"Come on, Norman," she said, giving the dog a nudge with her bare toe. "You've got work to do."

She glanced outside. Rain spattered against the windows and it was fully dark. The timbers of the house shuddered in the wind. "Want company?"

"Always."

He pulled on a pair of jeans and his uniform shirt and jacket and got his gun out of the safe. By the time he was ready, Smith had Norman's orange search and rescue vest on him and was loading the excited dog into the back of the truck. Unlike Tocek, Norman was always happy to be going to work.

She got into the passenger seat; Adam started the truck and pulled onto the gravel road. This far out of town, high in the mountains beyond the range of the motion detector lights over the garage and shed, the dark was total.

"How old?" she asked.

"The kid? Five."

"How long?"

"Less than an hour."

"That's good, right?"

"Who knows, Molly. It's dangerous out there. Little guy, big woods, big animals. Fast-moving rivers, steep cliffs. We won't know 'til we get there, but it sounds as if they called soon as they noticed him missing. Every second counts."

He pulled onto the highway and sped toward Koola Provincial Park.

Chapter Two

The rain had stopped by the time they slowed to enter the park. Tocek flashed his lights at the waiting RCMP patrol car, and it shifted into gear and led the way.

"I haven't been here for a few years," Smith said quietly. "The park's changed. Looks more civilized somehow."

The campground was quiet, less than a quarter of the sites taken. Summer was over, most vacationers back at school or work. Days remained warm, but temperatures dropped sharply at night.

They followed the RCMP car down the dark, winding, narrow trail and soon came in sight of bright lights and groups of people standing in nervous clusters. Norman was edgy in the back; he knew work was ahead.

A van and a four-person tent in cheerful yellow were lit up as though for their Broadway debut. A park-issue picnic table holding the remains of the family's washing up, covered with a tea towel, was in the center of the clearing, a group of folding chairs loosely scattered around. The remains of the campfire, dark and wet, still emitted little curls of smoke. Large trees, heavy with lichen, crowded around the patch of civilization, waiting for the humans to pack up and return to where they belonged.

A man ran up to meet them, followed by a second Mountie, as soon as Tocek pulled the truck to a stop. He was bald-headed, with a square body to which his head, arms and legs seemed to have been attached by afterthought.

He thrust his hand out and Tocek shook it while Smith led Norman out of the truck. "Nigel Paulson. Thank God, you got here so quickly." His accent was working-class English, swallowing about half the words.

"I'm Constable Tocek and that's Constable Smith. What have you done since your boy went missing?"

The man pulled at his hair. He spoke to Tocek but his eyes darted from side to side, seeking a glimpse of his son lurking outside the circle of light. "I sent my wife up to the highway with the cell phone to contact you people, and my daughter and I have been up and down the road calling and calling, checking the other campsites." He gave them a small, tight smile. "I'm a copper myself, back home in London. I know too many people can ruin things for the dog."

"Good man," Tocek said. He took Norman's lead from Smith.

"My wife started into the woods, but I told her not to. I hope that was the right thing to do. I warned her not to venture much further than the edge of the campsite. It's dark and we don't know these woods at all. You don't want to be searching for us as well."

"It was the right thing to do," Tocek assured him. "When did you notice your son missing?"

"Ten, a few minutes after ten. I checked my watch."

"When had you seen him last?"

"Two hours before, maybe. He was cheeky to his mum so she sent him to the tent. About ten minutes later she went to tell him he could come out for hot chocolate. He'd stuffed his blanket and toy elephant into the bag so it looked like he was in it. We watched a movie a couple of weeks ago where someone did that, and I guess he remembered. Too damn smart for his own good sometimes." Paulson wiped at his eyes. "Emily called his name, and when he didn't answer she assumed he'd fallen asleep and left him. It was only when Poppy, our daughter, went to bed she realized Jamie wasn't there."

He looked down at Norman, sitting by Tocek's leg. "Looks like a good dog. He'll find my son, right?"

Tocek spoke to the Mountie standing with the family. "Where have you searched?"

"All the other campsites. No one's seen him. We went down to the river. I know not to disturb the scent, but," he glanced at Paulson, "couldn't chance the boy having fallen in and be stranded on a rock or the far bank."

"Right."

Molly Smith wasn't here to do anything more than stand out of the way. She wouldn't have normally been allowed to come along to watch Adam and Norman at work, but as an officer with the Trafalgar City Police she was well known to the area's Mounties, and no introductions had been necessary.

The mother, a delicate fine-boned blonde, stood off to one side beside the dead campfire, her arm around her daughter.

Smith went over to the women and introduced herself. "Your son hasn't been gone long. That's good."

The woman nodded, unable to smile. Her eyes and nose were red and her pale face pinched with fear. She clutched a stuffed pink elephant to her chest. "I'm Emily, and this is my daughter Poppy." She spoke with the same accent as her husband.

The girl had a startling shock of purple hair, cut very short with one long section hanging over her right eye, but her skin was good and she'd avoided, so far, piercings any more outlandish than through her earlobes. Both arms were wrapped around her mother.

"What's Jamie wearing?" Smith asked.

"Long brown trousers and a white jumper. A sweater," Emily said. "It's not a heavy jumper. He'll be cold."

"Red's good," Smith said. "The color'll stand out in the woods."

They watched Tocek and Norman walk around the campground, Norman's nose moving across the ground. People had gathered, attracted by the commotion and the police cars. Norman started to move into the woods.

"That's the trail to the river," Nigel Paulson said. "Jamie wouldn't have gone that way. Poppy and I were getting water when he must of snuck away."

"We checked there already," the Mountie added.

"I'd like to see what Norman's interested in. If you'll stay here, sir. The less activity the better for the dog." Tocek glanced behind him. "Constable Smith?"

Pleased to be asked, she started to walk toward him. Then she turned back to Emily and Poppy. "Would you mind?" She gestured to the elephant. "Jamie will be lost and frightened. If… I mean, when we find him, it would be nice to have something familiar."

The woman gave her a ghost of a smile. "What a lovely idea." She held the pink bundle close for a heartbeat and passed it over.

"He's been taught," Paulson called after Tocek, "over and over, if he's lost he's to stand still and wait for us to come for him." His voice broke. "Please God, he hasn't forgotten."

A Mountie handed Smith a flashlight and, armed with a pink elephant, she followed Tocek and Norman into the woods.

Almost instantly the light and sounds from the campsite faded away. Up ahead they could hear the creek running over stones and splashing against the bank. Clouds drifted across the sky, but a thin line of white light from the waxing moon shone through the trees.

"Poor kid," Smith said, "he must be terrified."

"Shush," Adam said in reply.

They soon reached the creek and Norman cast around, following who-knows-what. Tocek said nothing, and Smith stood out of the way, watching, holding the light.

Finding nothing of interest, the big dog abruptly turned and headed back to the campsite.

Smith could see the look of hope flash across the Paulson family's faces, and then die when they saw the boy wasn't with them. The girl, Poppy, gave a low sob and her mother gathered her close.

Again, Norman sniffed the ground. He spent a lot of time at the tent entrance. He was a German shepherd, a big one, with ears the size of satellite dishes, a long sweeping tail, and he walked with a lope, hips low to the ground. Norman was six years old and had lived and worked with Adam Tocek for five.

Molly Smith knew Adam loved her, but she sometimes thought if it came down to a choice between her and Norman, the dog would win. She smiled at the thought.

Everyone else, family, police officers, onlookers stood quietly and watched. They'd let the dog try first, and only if he didn't come up with anything would police begin an organized search.

No one but the dog could do much until light.

Norman, Smith knew, didn't follow a specific scent. No shirt or socks waved under the dog's nose and a dash straight for the missing child. That was TV fantasy. He'd cast around, in larger and larger circles, seeking something that didn't fit, following the freshest trail, a scent that broke away from all the others.

Which was why it was so important that everyone and their proverbial dog hadn't rushed into the wilderness in search of Jamie. With numerous trials to follow, all crossing back and forth over each other, Norman wouldn't have a chance of picking out the scent of one small boy.

"Good man, Paulson," Tocek mumbled, in answer to her thoughts. "Kept his head and helped his wife keep hers."

Norman plunged into the woods. Tocek and Smith followed, flicking on their flashlights. Fortunately, the Paulson family campsite was situated at the edge of the campground, the last one on this road, before the dark forest closed in. Not too much foot traffic would have come through here in the last couple of days.

"Call his name," Tocek said. "Keep calling it. I figure a child's more likely to find a woman's voice unthreatening. It's sexist, I know, but that's why I brought you along."

"I'm good with that," she replied. She raised her voice. "Jamie!"

Norman had a scent now. He didn't hesitate but moved forward at a steady loping clip. Tocek and Smith jogged behind him. She tried to keep her eyes on the ground and at the same time peer into the woods for any sign of the child. This was not a trail; the forest floor was rough, covered with broken branches and rocks, thick with undergrowth. No one needed a sprained ankle right now. Light caught the reflective strips on Norman's vest, making him look like something otherworldly moving through the black night.

Jamie must have been lost from the moment he stepped into the woods. A couple more steps and he wouldn't have been able to see the light from his family's fire or the other campsites. Frightened and disoriented, he would have panicked, blundering further and further into the forest. It was getting noticeably colder. All Smith wore was a sweater; she hadn't planned on going for a walk in the night woods. Jamie, according to his mother, wasn't wearing much more. If Norman couldn't find him the child would spend the night out here. A more effective search would have to wait until morning.

He couldn't have gone far, she told herself, not in the dark, with no path to follow, on short five-year-old legs.

Norman moved quickly, not having to cast about for traces of the scent. *That was good. Wasn't it?*

She could only hope he was following Jamie Paulson, not a hiker who'd been out this afternoon and was now resting at home, feet up, beer in hand, watching cop shows on T.V.

As a police dog, Norman took the same approach when following a suspect, but the communication between Adam and Norman was such the man would have let the dog know that when they found the little boy he was not to be treated as if he were an armed criminal.

Norman stopped so suddenly Smith almost crashed into Adam. The dog barked, just once, and turned his head to look at his handler. Smith might have seen a satisfied smile cross the animal's face. "Jamie," she called. "Jamie, where are you? Your mom and dad sent us to look for you. The dog's very friendly, he won't hurt you."

Tocek patted the Norman's flank and whispered something. Norman walked around a large Western Red Cedar and barked once more.

Smith heard a sob and saw a flash of white.

A little boy was crouched at the base of the old cedar, his arms wrapped around the dog's head and his face buried in the soft fur.

Smith squatted in front of him. "Hi, Jamie. I'm Molly and this is Norman. Look what I brought you."

He lifted his head. A scratch on his cheek leaked blood. Tracks of tears flowed through the dirt, blood, and snot covering his face. The right knee of his pants was torn, the cloth streaked with blood. He'd lost one shoe and had holes in his sock. She held out the pink elephant and he grabbed it, the other hand still clutching Norman's fur.

"I wanted to see a bear," he said, in a very soft voice and a cute English accent. "I'm sorry I ran away."

"You're lucky Norman found you and not a bear," Adam said. "Can you carry him, Molly?"

"Sure I can. Come on, little buddy, let's get you up and back to your mom and dad."

The tree's huge roots had carved a depression in the forest floor and time had filled it with leaves, needles, branches, and small stones. The ground was muddy from the earlier rain. As Smith shifted her weight to stand and pick up the child, her foot, clad only in running shoes, slipped. She fell backwards, crashing hard to the ground, giving a startled cry.

Tocek dropped the dog's leash and ran to her. "You okay, Mol?"

"Just startled. Help me up, will you?" She held out her hand and he hauled her to her feet. They smiled at each other.

"We done good," she said.

"Let's get this guy back to his family."

She bent over the child. "Up you get, Jamie. You look like a big boy, but I think I can manage you." He clambered to his feet and raised his arms, clutching the pink elephant. She lifted him up, marveling at how small and fragile he was.

"What the hell?" Tocek said.

Norman scratched at the patch of ground where Smith had fallen. The earth had been disturbed by her scrambling feet, uncovering the round end of a smooth beige log. The dog gave his boss a glance and began scratching again.

"What's he doing?" she asked.

"That's his signal when he's found someone de...," Tocek glanced at the child, "...among the departed. Shine that light over here."

Chapter Three

Eliza Winters pulled off her boots with a contented sigh. The scent of dinner being prepared wafted out of the kitchen. "Good heavens," she said, "is my man actually cooking?"

He was in the kitchen, peering into a pot when she came in. Tangy spices and warm food filled the air. "Someone has to."

"Ha, ha. What are you making?"

"Chicken curry." He pointed to a colorful book, open on the counter. "Supposedly a simple recipe that anyone can make."

"Smells good. Sorry I'm so late."

"Payback time, I guess," he said, "Fortunately this keeps fine on the stove."

"I want to get out of these clothes. Be right back." She went upstairs, pulling off her blouse and unzipping her skirt. It was nine-thirty and she didn't want to eat; she wanted to read for a while and go to bed. But he was making an effort, trying, and so she would try in return.

The chicken was excellent, although the rice overcooked. Not that Eliza had grounds to complain. Her husband was a better cook than she was. Anyone was a better cook than she was.

"What's the verdict?" he asked, after they'd taken a few mouthfuls.

"The food is good. The art even better."

"You think so?"

"I do. His talent is indisputable. His subject matter is not necessarily to my taste, but I'm not looking for something to buy for myself. For us, I mean."

"What don't you like about it?"

She chewed and thought. "The colors are brash, harsh. Angry almost. I sense an underlying trace of violence."

"Do you think he's violent?"

"You're thinking like a cop." There was a spurt of anger behind the words and she saw him react. She didn't apologize. "He's no more likely to be violent than a middle-aged woman with three kids living in the suburbs who writes novels about serial killers and dismembered hookers. I only mean that I see violence in his work and it isn't aesthetically pleasing to my eye. But, as I said, I don't have to like it. I just have to think other people will like it."

Last year Eliza had taken an extended trip to Vancouver. She owned a condo in order to have someplace to stay when both work and the need to be in a busy city took her there. She was a model, had been internationally known at one time, and although she still got work, age was catching up to her, fast. Approaching fifty, she found there were far more women of her age, every bit as good as she, than there were jobs. She'd spent some long, boozy nights with her agent and good friend, Bernadette, reassessing her life, her work, her marriage. She came to the conclusion that what she wanted most of all was what she had: her home in the mountains outside Trafalgar, her twenty-six year marriage to John Winters.

Without modeling, what could she do? What was she?

She was an amateur financial whiz; almost everything she touched in the way of investments turned out well. But finance was work and she found no passion in it. She managed her money with care because she trusted no one else to do it for her. Not something she had an interest in doing as a business, certainly not for other people.

One night she'd gone with Bernadette, whom everyone in the fashion business called Barney, to an industry party. She'd sat with Tony and Herb, a couple in their early nineties who owned art galleries in Vancouver, Victoria, Whistler, and Seattle. They'd worked hard most of their life building Herb's father's local newspaper into a multi-million dollar corporation. When they turned seventy, they sold the business and, with no family to make provision for, began seriously investing in art.

Art had become their hobby, then their obsession, and finally their business as well as their life. Their wrinkled and liver-spotted faces lit up with joy at discussing their passion. They invited Eliza to lunch the next day and for a visit to their gallery in Kitsilano.

She knew she'd never reach the excesses of obsession the two old men had, but as she walked through their gallery, enjoying the major exhibit, stunning watercolors of the derelict Downtown Eastside, and listening to them talk, finishing each other's sentences like the married couple they were, she started thinking.

She stayed in Vancouver for another month, and by the time she went back to Trafalgar, to her home, her husband, her marriage, she had signed her name on the lease of a small storefront space in Kitsilano, near Tony and Herb's.

A year later, after rent and staff wages, the gallery was bleeding money, but she could afford it and could make use of the tax loss.

Three months ago she opened a gallery in Trafalgar. A lot of artists lived in the area and the nearby town of Nelson was home to the Kootenay School of the Arts, bursting with talent. Her current show featured paintings of the area, beautiful art of the sort tourists buy. For November, she was preparing a selection of small-piece artists, in paint, fabric, and metal work, for the pre-Christmas period.

Last week she was told about an artist who lived in Upper Town. Only in his thirties, he had a reputation as a recluse and eccentric. Far from being eager to meet her and show her his art when she phoned to ask for a meeting, he said he only allotted one hour a day to interacting with people from the art world. He would see her on Monday evening. Take it or leave it.

She'd loved his work and they'd spent another hour talking about the direction he wanted his art to take.

John scooped up curry sauce with a hunk of naan. "Are you going to take him on?"

"I'm not sure. I love his talent, yes, but I'm looking for someone to exhibit next summer and I can't see his stuff being popular with tourists. And, well, to be honest, I don't know if I like him."

"Does that matter?"

"The galleries are a business, John, but nevertheless I am in it because I love it. The art, the artists, their world. He's just… odd."

"Aren't all great artists odd?"

"Not at all. Many are quite mundane, they only express themselves on canvas. This fellow, his name is Kyle Nowak…"

"Nowak, I've heard that name."

"Where?"

"On the job." She could see him sorting through his memory banks. "Don't remember. Probably nothing. Might not even be him. Does he have family in the area?"

"I don't know anything about him. He barely talks. Perhaps that's why I don't like him. He didn't say much, just sort of stared at me."

"You're always worth staring at."

She smiled and dug into her meal, pleased at the small compliment.

◇◇◇

Molly Smith balanced the child on her hip and turned the beam of her flashlight onto the ground in front of the dog. Adam Tocek crouched down and used both hands to pull away the loosened dirt. Norman settled back on his haunches, job done.

Tocek held up the small light brown object they'd first taken to be wood. "Wow! This is a bone."

She peered over his shoulder. "Human?"

"Could be a bear. They can be hard to tell apart. But this looks like part of a hand to me."

Jamie squirmed in Smith's grip. "Let me see."

"I don't think that's a good idea," she said. He seemed to have recovered from his ordeal in the woods mighty fast.

Carefully, Adam placed the object back where he'd found it. He got to his feet and began unfastening Norman's vest.

"What are you doing?"

"First we have to get Jamie back. I'll call this in and suggest someone come out and have a look in the morning. We'll have to find this spot again. If it's a bear, we'll leave it alone. If not…" He tossed the orange vest over the branches of the cedar. "Get ready to leave markers all along the trail."

Norman and Adam led the way and Smith followed. She peeled off the child's remaining shoe and socks, and Adam pulled gloves out of his uniform jacket. He even left his handcuffs, dangling from a brown, broken tree, one of many killed by mountain pine beetles.

The child had almost immediately snuggled his head into Smith's shoulder and fallen asleep. He smelled nice, of shampoo and warm breath. She looked at his face. His eyes were closed, the long thick black lashes resting on his cheek. He had a trace of freckles scattered across his nose and a lock of blond hair fell over his forehead. She was only twenty-eight years old and hadn't given any thought to having children. *Was it time?* She looked at Adam, walking ahead of her, his six-foot four bulk outlined in the beam of his flashlight. She cleared her throat. "Anyone wandering in the woods tonight will think we've had quite the wild romp."

"Don't remind me," he groaned, "of what I missed because of this little guy."

They returned Jamie to his relieved family and applauding onlookers. Norman got the lion's share of the attention, which was fine with Smith. He'd done all the work.

After the dog had basked in the fuss and excitement, Tocek put him in the truck and pulled the Mountie who'd stayed with the family aside.

The man's eyes opened wide. "You are kidding me?"

"Nope."

"I'll call it in."

"What happens now?" Smith asked.

"Ron or Alison will come out in the morning, there's not much of a hurry, and take a look. They'll send it off to an expert somewhere for analysis. If the bones aren't human they'll call me nasty names. If they're human but more than fifty or so years old, they'll take them for a proper burial. And if not, then someone has a case. Are you, uh, coming back to my place?"

"Drop me at home, please. I'm bushed. That was emotionally draining." She gave him a small grin. "Do you mind?"

"Yes, but tell you the truth, I'm done for too."

"Officers." Mr. and Mrs. Paulson came up to them. The purple-haired daughter, Poppy, with them. She ignored Smith and gave Adam a huge smile, ruined by the row of braces across her teeth. "We can't thank you enough." Emily carried Jamie so tightly she might have feared if she relaxed her grip he would disappear in a puff of smoke. He clutched the pink elephant.

"You saved our son," Nigel said.

"It was our pleasure," Smith said.

"He'll be able to tell his friends at school about his great adventure," Tocek said, trying to ignore the purple-haired girl's adoring eyes.

"No more adventures for this family." Nigel held out his hand, and Tocek and Smith shook. "Give that dog a big fat bone from us, will you, Constable?"

"Sure. Take care."

"Nice to be thanked for doing our job for a change," Smith said, buckling her seat belt.

Tocek put the truck in gear. "Yeah. I'll let you know what they find out about those bones, if you're interested."

"I am."

Chapter Four

Smith looked up at a tap on the door to the constable's office. It was coming up to one o'clock and she was finishing her sandwich while doing paperwork before heading back out to the street.

"Hey, John," she said.

"Heard you had a bit of off-duty excitement last week and went for a tromp in the woods," Sergeant John Winters said.

For a moment she wasn't sure what he was referring to. "Oh, right. Adam and the dog got a call for a little boy lost in Koola Park. Left his parents' campsite to go looking for grizzly bears. It was incredible watching Norman work. He and Adam, sometimes it's like they're communicating telepathically."

"Never fails to impress me, either. You were there when they found the bones?"

"I didn't get much of a look, but Adam thought they might be human. Have you heard anything more?" She pushed her chair away from the computer and got to her feet.

"Ron and Alison are heading out there now. Ron got a call this morning from the forensic anthropologist at Simon Fraser University where he sent the bones. A preliminary test shows they're human. I'm going out to have a look. Want to join me? Won't be long. I have nothing to contribute at this stage."

"Sure." Walking the afternoon beat on Front Street in Trafalgar, British Columbia was one of the most boring jobs on earth. Until the bars got busy, and on a Tuesday they'd be quiet now that university students and summer visitors had headed back home. The most exciting thing that might happen would be a little old lady trying to parallel park her little old car and scratching the parking meter.

They took the detectives' van and headed out of town. It was still summer in Trafalgar, but as they climbed into the mountains the few deciduous trees scatted among the evergreens began turning yellow and the temperature dropped. "Why did the Mounties call you? Do they think these bones have something to do with the city?"

"Just a courtesy. The person could have originated in Trafalgar."

They parked at the same spot she and Adam had the previous week. She recognized the van belonging to Ron Gavin, the RCMP's head forensic investigator for the area. The campsite was deserted, Jamie and his family long gone. She hoped they hadn't given up on camping or the B.C. wilderness.

A line of yellow police tape had taken the place of discarded clothing, dog vests, and handcuffs leading to the bones.

Winters called out as they got near and Ron Gavin shouted in reply. Smith followed the sergeant to see a scene considerably different than the previous time she'd been here.

Although it was daytime, lights had been set up to break the forest shadows. The spot where they'd found Jamie was at the bottom of the mountain. A trickle of water wound its way down the slope, around rocks, leaking into the ground at the depression at the base of the red cedar. It had been a hot dry summer, and the stream was little more than a patch of wet ground. In spring it would be a fast-moving creek.

Corporal Alison Townshend, Gavin's partner, knelt in the mud several feet up, her more than adequate butt greeting them. Her curly gray head was close to the ground and she carefully scraped at the dirt with a small trowel. She grunted something that might have been a greeting without bothering to look up.

"Human all right," Gavin said. "Not ancient, either. On sight, old bones look much the same as more recent ones. It mostly depends on the environment they've been in. The people at the lab did their thing and that's what they tell me. Adam pulled up part of a hand. We found three finger bones close by, and further up," he gestured to his partner, "part of a long bone that might be from a leg."

"Not much," Smith said.

"We've got a lot of ground still to cover. We're setting up a grid pattern and we'll pretty much take this mountainside apart. At a guess, I'd say the excessive amount of snow we had last winter caused more flooding than normal and the bones washed down. So far they seem to be scattered up the hillside."

"Age?"

"Adult, or near enough. Can't tell gender, with nothing more to go on."

Townshend grunted and straightened up. She leaned back on her knees. "Been dead for less than fifteen years."

"Wow," Smith said, starting up the hill. "You can tell that from the bones?"

"Hold it, Constable," Gavin snapped. "Don't take another step. You don't know what's under your feet."

"Sorry," she said, face burning. She retraced her path carefully.

"What you got, Alison?" Gavin asked.

She studied the objects in her hand. "There's a bit of rotting cloth here, might be part of a pocket judging by the stitching. Doesn't have to be from the same person of course, but it was caught on an edge of broken bone. In the cloth, I found this." She held up a small, round brown object. "One Canadian cent. Issued 1995."

"You might well have a case," Winters said.

"I'll assume that, until I get evidence to the contrary. I can't get a signal in here, so can you call this in when you get in range, John?"

"Sure. Come on, Molly. Back to work."

"What now?"

"You, to the streets. Me, into the dust of the missing person files."

◇◇◇

Lucky Smith had never been fond of the police. Sure, they were necessary to keep the peace, to keep people like her safe in their homes and businesses, knew they worked hard at a difficult job with few thanks and not a heck of a lot of money.

But she was an old hippie at heart and had never forgotten, nor forgiven, the mean bastard of a Chicago cop who'd smacked her across the back of the neck with a truncheon, with no provocation whatsoever, and tossed her into a paddy wagon after the police ran amuck at the Democratic convention in 1968. Or even here in peaceful Trafalgar, the ones who arrested people for merely sitting on public benches, smoking a joint. Or burned out a crop of healthy plants that were intended to be turned into a product which did a lot less harm than alcohol or cigarettes.

And when she heard about police officers using Tasers on innocent civilians, sometimes even children, it made her blood positively boil.

But today, when the police officer came into her shop, dressed in the dark blue uniform, bulky Kevlar vest with POLICE in big threatening words across the back, the overloaded equipment belt jangling with the menace of physical force, it was hard to get too angry.

Lucky leaned over and accepted a kiss on the cheek. "You look tired, have you been getting enough sleep?"

"I'm fine, Mom." Molly Smith pulled off her hat and rubbed at her hair. Lucky was pleased to see that the short spikes were growing out. Before too much longer her daughter would have to tie her blond hair back into a pony tail. "Had a bit of excitement last week when Adam and the dog were called out to search for a missing child."

"Oh, dear, poor thing. Did they find her?"

"It was a boy. Norman found him safe and sound, disappointed he hadn't seen a grizzly."

"That dog does such a good job. Too bad about the time he bit that man who was..."

"You mean the man who was threatening to slice up his former boss with a chef's knife? Give it up, Mom. Norman does a good job period. As does Adam and as do I."

Lucky mumbled her agreement.

"I swear, Mom, ever since Dad died you get more and more sentimental about the golden olden days when you and Dad were against the world and the fascist police were on the other side."

"I do not."

"I came to take you on a trip down memory lane. Do you have a few minutes?"

"Pull up a seat." It was almost closing time during the shoulder season between summer hiking and kayaking and winter skiing. Unlikely anyone would be coming into the store. Lucky flipped the sign hanging over the door to closed before heading for the stool behind the counter. Her daughter glanced at a skiing magazine, and Lucky smiled to see traces of longing cross Moonlight's pretty face.

Moonlight was the girl's name. A beautiful, soft, romantic name that she'd decided wasn't suitable for a police officer, and thus started calling herself Molly.

"Only a couple more months," Lucky said, tapping the face of the magazine with a badly chewed fingernail. "And you'll be back on the slopes."

"Don't know if I can wait that long. Tell me what you remember about Brian Nowak."

"Good heavens, that is a trip down memory lane. You were friends with his daughter, what was her name?"

"Nicky."

"Yes, Nicky. What's she doing now?"

"She quit school before graduation and left. I lost contact."

"I see Marjorie sometimes, in town. She's like a ghost of her former self. I tried to encourage her to keep coming to the youth center or to join the African grandmothers' group, but she seemed to want to fade away."

"You weren't friends though, not that I remember."

"No. I tried to make friends after, but she rebuffed me. Come to think of it, it's been a long time, more than a year at least, since I've seen her. I wonder if she's still in Trafalgar."

"Nicky had an older brother, didn't she?"

"Kyle. People still talk about Kyle. He's an artist who almost never leaves the house, except at night."

"We, the police, know him. I'd forgotten he was Nicky's brother until today. He hangs around the streets at night like you said, but never gets himself in any trouble."

"Why are you asking? Has something new been discovered?"

"Perhaps. Mr. Nowak disappeared in '96."

"I don't remember exactly, but that sounds about right."

"Don't gossip about this Mom, okay? It will be in tomorrow's paper, so keep it under your hat until then."

Lucky nodded. As if she ever gossiped.

"The night we found the missing boy, Norman dug up some bones, human bones."

"You think..."

"We don't think anything, yet. It might be that the bones are from someone who was alive in 1995. Obviously, the forensic guys have work to do to be sure, and so far we've only got a few hand bones and part of a leg, which isn't much. John Winters has sent over to city hall where they keep the old boxes of statements and case notes, and is probably down in the basement now digging through old evidence files. I thought of Mr. Nowak right away. I was in grade eight, so it would have been in '96 when he disappeared."

Chapter Five

"Why would a daddy leave home?" Moonlight asked between spoonfuls of homemade granola. At Nicky's house they ate store-bought cereal. Count Chocula and Fruit Loops and Sugar Puffs. Good stuff that turned the milk all sorts of yucky, fun colors. At the Smith house they ate granola made by their mother and never got store-bought cookies, either. And no matter how much Moonlight begged, Mom refused to buy chocolate milk.

She looked up in time to see her parents exchange a glance. "Well," she demanded. "Why? Mr. Nowak ran away from home. I thought only kids did that."

"Mr. Nowak's a jerk," her brother said.

"Samwise," Mom snapped. "Don't talk about things you don't understand."

"Is that what they're saying at school?" Dad asked. "Mr. Nowak ran away?"

"Meredith told everyone Mr. Nowak ran away because he couldn't stand being Nicky's father any more."

Sam laughed so hard he almost sprayed milk across the kitchen.

"Meredith Morgenstern is a common-or-garden gossip," Mom said. "Not to mention a troublemaker. That's pure nonsense."

"No one knows what's happened to Mr. Nowak, Moonlight." Dad got up from the table and gave his wife a kiss on the top of her red curls. He was tall and Mom was short. Moonlight was only in grade eight, but she'd already passed her mother's height, and Sam at seventeen was almost as tall as Dad. His running shoes were the size of boats. "See you at the store, dear. You kids have a good day at school."

"As if that ever happens," Sam said, rolling his eyes.

Dad took his keys down from the hook by the door. Jerome, the big shaggy retriever, sensed someone was leaving the house. He lumbered to his feet, but Mom said, "No," and Dad shut the door behind him.

"Finish your breakfast. The bus will be here in ten minutes."

"Why can't we live in town, like Nicky does?" Moonlight asked. "So I can walk to school."

"You know what, Moon," Sam said as a sudden light came into his eyes. "If Mom would let me use her car, I could drive you to school every day."

"Don't put ideas in your sister's head." Mom poured the last of the coffee into her mug and switched off the pot. "You know that's not going to happen."

"So, where's Mr. Nowak?" Moonlight said. "If he isn't home?"

"He's missing, dear. No one knows where he is."

"That's what missing means," Sam explained.

Jerome lifted his head and barked, and moments later they heard a car coming up the long driveway. Lucky turned to look out the window. "Your father must have forgotten something. Oh."

Moonlight jumped to her feet and ran to the window. "Neat. A police car."

Mom was standing in the doorway, hands on hips, guarding her threshold by the time the car pulled to a stop and a man got out of the passenger seat. To Moonlight's disappointment he wasn't wearing a uniform or carrying a gun on his hip.

"Sergeant Keller," Mom said. "What are you doing here? The judge said I didn't…"

"I'm not here about that, Mrs. Smith. Is your daughter still at home?

"Moonlight? Yes, but the school bus will be here in a few minutes."

"It won't take long."

Mom stood back and the man came into the kitchen. He said hi to Moonlight and Samwise but looked at Mom.

"Samwise, go upstairs and get ready for the bus."

"But..."

"Now."

Sam left. Mom planted herself against the kitchen counter, arms crossed over her chest, a scowl on her face. Moonlight wondered why she didn't offer to make the visitor coffee or bring out cookies. Uninvited, the man sat in Dad's chair.

"Moonlight," he said. "I'm Sergeant Paul Keller, with the Trafalgar Police."

"I know."

"I need to ask you some questions about your friend Nicky's father, Brian Nowak." He glanced over his shoulder. Mom's face relaxed a bit. "Go ahead," she said. "Bad business to be sure."

"Okay," Moonlight said.

"You were at the Nowak house last week. Having a sleep over, is that right?"

"Yes," Mom said. "Saturday night."

"If you don't mind, Mrs. Smith, I'd like Moonlight to speak for herself."

Moonlight hid a grin behind a glass of milk. Mom did sometimes think she could answer for her children. Even now that Moonlight was thirteen—a teenager!

"I slept over, yes."

"Was Mr. Nowak at home?"

"I think so."

"Are you sure?"

She thought. "Yeah, he was there."

"Bye, Mom." The front door slammed as Sam left for school. Moonlight hoped she'd be talking to Sergeant Keller long enough that she'd miss the bus. Maybe she'd get a ride in the police car. Wouldn't that be great; they'd turn the lights and sirens on and all the kids would see her getting a ride as if she was a celebrity or something.

"We were listening to Alanis Morissette and Mr. Nowak yelled at us to turn it down. Nicky said she could hardly hear the music it was so low, and her dad came into her room and said if she didn't turn it town, I'd have to go home. She got mad and turned the CD player off." Moonlight shrugged. "It wasn't much fun after that. Nicky was mad and didn't want to do anything. I wanted to play the CD, even if it had to be on low, but she said no."

"Do you remember what time this was?"

"We watched 'Dr. Quinn, Medicine Woman', and then went up to Nicky's room to listen to music."

"Did you see Mr. Nowak the next morning?"

"He was at breakfast. We had pancakes and pop tarts and chocolate milk." Moonlight didn't look at her mother. "Then Mom came to pick me up 'cause Nicky was going to church."

"Thank you, Moonlight. That's been a help."

"What happened to Mr. Nowak anyway? Did he run away from home?"

"We don't know at this time. Lucky, I mean, Mrs. Smith." The policeman's voice changed when he spoke to her mom. Kinda gruff and soft at the same time, as if he wasn't sure what he was supposed to be saying. "Did you see Brian Nowak when you picked up Moonlight?"

"No. I didn't go inside. I phoned before I left home and Moonlight knew to be waiting. I beeped the car horn and she came out almost immediately."

Sergeant Keller got to his feet.

"Was that important?" Mom said, in a low voice as if she didn't want Moonlight to hear.

"Aside from his family, it seems that Moonlight might be the last person to have seen him."

"Do you know what happened?"

"He's simply disappeared."

"Did he take anything with him? Clothes, money, credit cards?"

"Sorry, Lucky, Mrs. Smith, but I can't comment at this time."

"I've missed the bus," Moonlight said.

"I'll drive you to school, if your mother will let you ride in the police car."

"Certainly not," Mom said. "I'm not going to have my daughter arrive at school under armed guard as if she were a common criminal." She turned and tossed the remains of her coffee into the sink. Sergeant Keller gave her a long look that Moonlight couldn't interpret.

Chapter Six

John Winters did not want to come anywhere near a case that had even the slightest possibility of touching his wife. They'd been through that a year ago, when Eliza's former photographer had been murdered, and the strain had almost broken their marriage. Even now fissures remained, patched over, but still there, lurking under the surface.

She'd gone to Vancouver, to do some thinking she said, and he'd spent months of restless nights worried that she was thinking about whether she wanted to remain married to a man who could think her capable of murder.

She came back to Trafalgar because, she said, she loved him, and realized she also loved this quirky town. She'd thrown herself into the art gallery business and seemed to be happier than she had for a long time. It was hard for her, he suspected, even though she'd never admit it, to see her career as a model so prominent she'd been on the cover of *Vogue* and walked the Paris runway for Chanel, morphing into gigs shilling for dishwashing detergent and minivans.

Whether he wanted a case to affect Eliza or not didn't matter one bit. It was possible that Kyle Nowak, Eliza's prospective client, might be the son of the owner of the bones.

Molly Smith had told Winters about Brian Nowak on the ride back to town. "Obviously, it could be anyone. A guy went hiking sometime back in the seventies and not a trace of him was ever seen again. My dad told us about him when he taught Sam and me to live in the wilderness. Anyone who was kidnapped from any place in B.C. or Washington might have been dumped on the mountain. But there was this one case in particular, a guy who just up and disappeared when I was in grade eight. I knew his daughter. Keller was the detective at the time."

"You mean the chief constable?"

"Yes. He was with the TCP for a number of years before he went to Calgary."

"Did he suspect foul play?"

"I can't say. I didn't know what the police thought or not, but the man was never found. It comes up every once in a while. People say, I wonder what happened to…"

"Name?"

"Nowak. Brian Nowak."

Nowak. Eliza had mentioned that name recently.

"Did he have a son?"

"Two kids. My friend Nicky and her brother Kyle. Nicky's left, but Kyle still lives in town. If he's the person I'm thinking of."

Winters opened the box that had been sent over from the basement of city hall. A cloud of dust rose up to greet him. It had been a long time since anyone had showed any official interest in the disappearance of Brian Nowak.

A quick glance revealed the chief constable's handwriting all over the files. Winters flipped through the pages.

Brian Nowak had last been seen by his wife when she returned from church on Sunday morning. Their son, Kyle, was with her but the daughter, Nicky, had stayed to play baseball with the young people's group and would be brought home by one of the parents. Shortly after, Nowak had gone to the corner store to buy cigarettes.

He neither arrived at the store, nor returned home.

He had not been seen or heard from in the fifteen years since.

Other than members of his family, the last person to report seeing Nowak was a thirteen-year-old girl who'd spent the previous night at the Nowak home and said Mr. Nowak had been at breakfast Sunday morning.

Her name was Moonlight Smith.

Kyle Nowak wasn't a common name; chances were good the artist Eliza met was the son. Winters flicked through the files for the wife's name. Marjorie.

It was still too early to reopen the Nowak case. As Molly had said, the bones could belong to just about anyone, and the penny could have fallen out of a hiker's pocket and lain on the ground until snowmelt washed a few old bones downhill to come to a rest on top of it. Before getting any deeper into this, he'd have to wait for a forensic analysis of the age of the bones, and any other details they might be able to pry out of the scatterings of a skeleton.

As a courtesy, he'd pay a visit to Mrs. Nowak, let her know they had a possible lead. If the finding did turn out to be the remains of her husband Winters would have an investigation on his hands.

He reached for the phone on his desk and asked, "Barb, is Paul free?"

"Yes."

"Tell him I'll be right there." Winters picked up the file box and headed down the hall. Barb Kowalski, the office administrator and chief's assistant, was struggling to get her right arm into her coat. She glanced at the box in his arms. "Paul has a dinner meeting with Rotary at six. Don't let him get so wound up in old cases he forgets."

"I heard that," Keller shouted from his office. "I have a wife, thank you Barb, I don't need a nanny also."

"Yes you do," she called back. "See you tomorrow."

She grinned at Winters and left. Barb had been with the Trafalgar City Police for almost thirty years, much longer than anyone else. Everyone, including Keller, knew who really ran the building.

Winters went into his boss's office. He put the box on the desk and Keller eyed it with interest. "Cold case?"

"Perhaps. Does the name Nowak mean anything to you?"

Keller leaned back in his chair. "It certainly does. I was the detective sergeant here at that time. It was my case, and it's one of those ones that still rankles. Don't tell me you found the old bugger?"

Winters explained what had been found. "There's a guy in town name of Kyle Nowak, would that be the son?"

"It is."

"The wife? Marjorie?"

"Still living in the old house. Marjorie rarely steps outside her garden gate any more, and I hear the boy is reclusive himself. It was hard on them. Husband and father simply vanished. Not only did he up and leave his family, but Marjorie had no means of support. The family's assets, limited as they were, were frozen. She ended up on welfare."

"What do you think happened?"

"Unofficially, I think the guy walked out. There was never the slightest indication of foul play, and no reason to believe anyone would want him gone. He wasn't the type to have the mob as enemies and I didn't find any trace of hidden vices such as gambling debts or drug addiction. He didn't take anything with him and that looked odd, I'll admit. Other than his wallet, which he had on him when he supposedly went to the store for cigarettes."

"Wouldn't a man leaving home take at least some clothes, shaving kit?"

"You'd think. The wife, of course, insisted that Nowak was a happily married family man who had no reason whatsoever to contemplate leaving them. They were church-going. Catholic. The picture of domestic bliss. Not that that matters, in my experience."

"You must have had a reason to suspect he walked out."

"Gut instinct. Not that that's worth much either. Perhaps I just didn't like Marjorie, the wife. Weak, whiny little thing, I thought. I wondered at the time why anyone would want to live with a woman like that." Keller shook his head and took a long pull on the can of Coke by his elbow, one of many he consumed over the course of a day. The scent of tobacco was an invisible cloak clinging to the man's clothes and skin. His eyes drifted away. "'Course you never know what attracts one person to another, do you? Or what goes on in other people's marriages.

"I'm glad Eliza's back," he said, apropos of nothing.

"She was only in Vancouver," Winters replied, defensive hackles rising. "She needed a break."

"Sorry. Back to Nowak. I uncovered one piece of evidence in all the time I spent on the investigation. Only one thing that possibly had any bearing on what happened to him."

"And?"

"Three weeks before he disappeared, he sold ten thousand dollars worth of Royal Bank stock. The cash sat in his bank account for one week, and then it was gone."

"Gone?"

"Gone. He withdrew ten thousand in cash. And didn't use any of it to buy cigarettes."

"Did his wife have an explanation?"

"Says she didn't know about it. He'd inherited some money when his mother died about five years before. He told Marjorie he was investing it, but she didn't know what he did with it. She didn't seem to know, or care, anything about their finances. The money didn't go through their joint account, and she didn't know he had a personal one. Which, I might point out, he'd only opened in time to store the money."

"I assume the cash was never located."

"Right on that."

"Looks suspicious."

"Talk was rampant around town, as you can imagine. Nowak and Marjorie had the usual sort of friends, neighbors, people from church, his work. But the man himself didn't seem to have any real buddies. Anyone he'd talk to. I mean if he was considering running off."

"Lots of men of that generation don't have good friends of their own. Our generation, I guess."

"True."

"You checked with his family? Extended family?"

"Yup. Parents both dead, one brother. The brother claimed he hadn't seen Brian since Christmas the year before the previous one, nor had he any idea where he could have gone."

"Did you think about suicide or getting lost? A walk into the mountains, not able to find the way out?"

"Sure. Except for one thing—he didn't take his car. He didn't get a lift, least not with anyone we were able to locate. No one reported seeing him walking along the highway heading out of town. We did a search of the mountainside near his home and came up with nothing. Even had a psychic show up one day about a month later, saying he could lead us to the grave. It was a grave all right—where someone had buried their damned dog in a quiet spot in the forest overlooking town."

"I'm going to wait until tomorrow and see if Ron comes up with anything more. I should pay a visit to Mrs. Nowak. She deserves to know we might be reopening the case. If we do have to reopen it, I'd like to get a feel for her."

"Agreed."

"Want to come?"

"You bet."

"He had a daughter, Nicky. Know anything about where she is these days?"

"She was a pretty little thing, friends with Molly Smith, I remember. She's not in Trafalgar, but I don't know where she ended up. Better than her mother and brother, I hope."

The man stank.

Most of them stank, but on a scale of one to ten, this one was a ten.

He grunted and rolled off her, letting rip with a huge fart. He sat on the edge of the bed and pulled on his socks. "Good one."

"You're the best, babe," she said, trying not to breathe.

He got to his feet with a groan and went to the bathroom. He didn't bother to close the door, and she could hear the sound of urine splashing into the toilet and water in the sink. He came back, his belly so big and his cock so small it was almost invisible, and pulled on his clothes. He slapped a couple of bills on the bedside table. "Next week?"

"I'm already dreaming about it," she said with a soft purr.

He slapped her naked rump and left.

Pig.

She rolled out of bed. She needed a shower, but first things first. She checked the notes.

An extra hundred bucks.

If she had to be a whore, she might as well be a good whore.

Nicole Nolte stood under the shower for a long time. She imagined she could fell the man's sweat running off her body, swirling around the drain, disappearing into the sewer.

She stepped out of the shower, dried her hair and made up her face. She studied herself in the mirror. Time to change the hair color, maybe. Shake things up. Perhaps she should go blond. She ran her fingers across her flat belly. Not an ounce of flab.

The bedroom door opened and footsteps crossed the floor.

"Don't you ever knock," she said, coming out of the bathroom.

He stood at the dresser, counting the money. "Anything more?"

"No. Not that I'd tell you if there was."

"You're getting a real mouth on you, Nicole."

"So the customers tell me. Particularly when we play Christmas candy cane." She licked her upper lip, stood naked in front of him, and held out her hand. "Give it to me."

He handed her a paper packet. She held it to her nose and breathed deeply. She wouldn't take it here, not in front of him.

"I got into his wallet," she said. "First time I was able to convince him to take a shower before coming to bed."

"Good girl. What'd you find?"

"Driver's license, of course. With address." She opened the dresser drawer and pulled out a scrap of paper. "It's all here. Also a picture of a scrawny broad who's had her face done and two kids. A couple of school pics of the same kids."

"Where's he live?"

She tossed her clothes onto the bed, stepped into her thong, and fastened her bra behind her. "West Vancouver. Nice area. Big houses." She sat on the edge of the bed and pulled on pantyhose. She put on a white blouse and gray suit with skirt cut just above the knee. It was the middle of the day, lunchtime, and she had another appointment when the offices downtown closed.

Her partner called himself Joey Stewart. He was a rat-faced Scotsman with bad skin and a worse accent. She didn't like him much, didn't trust him at all, but she needed him and he needed her and they kept their eyes on each other.

She'd told him from the beginning that he wasn't getting any extra benefits from their business relationship. Sometimes he tried to play the tough guy, as if he were some kind of pimp. She slapped him down fast enough.

If he thought he could walk in on her anytime he liked, then he'd just have to watch her strut around the room and wiggle her butt and know he wasn't getting any. Ever.

Nicole Nolte, once named Nicky Nowak, wasn't a whore.

She was a businesswoman.

She and Joey ran an escort service. With a difference. They had only one escort—Nicole. Joey advertised in the seedier papers and on the Internet with pictures of beautiful, sexy women. The customers only ever got Nicole. Not many were dissatisfied.

Some of them wanted dates and she could do glamour. Some of them just wanted a fuck and she could certainly do that. Joey tried to weed out the one-timers, but some always got through, a waste of time and effort although it paid well. They made their real money off the ones who wanted a regular encounter. Wednesday lunchtime, Tuesday and Thursday before work, Friday for drinks. This one, the fat banker with a flatulence problem, called himself Matt Jones, real name Matthew Packer, visited her every Wednesday from twelve to one. He'd been coming for two months, and today for the first time she'd been able to get into his wallet and obtain the information she needed.

Joey rented this apartment, small but in a fashionable building downtown, and had mounted cameras in the ceiling and the headboard of the bed.

It was unlikely Matthew would be showing up next Wednesday. Nicole had pinched a business card on their first date—no point in continuing if he were a shop clerk or something—and the day after tomorrow he'd get a package in the office mail. A couple of pictures of him in action, Nicole's face blanked out. She made sure to change the color of the sheets from one assignation to the next, so it would be obvious the pictures were taken on different days. The package would include a photo of his house, taken by Joey. Even better if he could snap the wife or one of the kids. Twenty thousand dollars and he'd never hear from them again.

He'd pay up; they always did.

He never would hear from them again.

No need to be greedy. There were plenty more suckers where he came from.

Chapter Seven

"An adult, between five foot seven and nine. Unlikely the bones have been in situ for more than twenty-thirty years."

"Could be a lot of people."

"They have lots more tests to do down at the lab, but this isn't a priority so we'll have to wait. They won't be able to tell us much more unless we can locate additional bones. A skull would be good, teeth even better, if we want to make an ID."

Winters shifted the phone on his shoulder and looked past his partner's desk out the office window. Trees on the mountainside were turning yellow, and the snowline on Koola Glacier was lower than last week. "You can get DNA samples from bones, right?"

"Sure," Gavin said. "Mitochondrial DNA. But DNA doesn't give us anything without something to match it with."

"Are you going back up today?"

"I'm in the van. About to lose the signal. Alison's waving her fingers hi."

"Hi back. You'll let me know what you find up there?"

"No, John, I won't. I'm going to keep it secret."

Winters chuckled. "Have fun."

"Over and out."

"That Gavin?"

Winters swung around to face the door. The boss stood there, pulling a jacket over his neatly-pressed white uniform shirt.

"Yes. They've found nothing to eliminate Nowak, nothing to prove it either. We can ask the son for a DNA sample. They have enough bone to compare."

"Do they know we're coming?"

"I called Mrs. Nowak a few minutes ago."

"How'd she sound?"

"Not particularly interested. I'd have expected her to at least ask if I'd found anything new. She said she'd be at home this morning. *At home.* Made it sound as if I'm a gentleman caller."

They headed out back to get a car.

"What was your take on her, Paul?"

"Let's talk later. I don't want to give you any impressions before you meet her."

Marjorie Nowak lived in a small modern house in Upper Town. Trafalgar was situated in a river valley surrounded by mountains so steep that houses at the higher elevation not only had a great view, they were sometimes in a different season. The yard was neat, grass cut and raked, a few clumps of well-cared for perennials still in bloom. The mountainside dropped away at the back of the property, and the rear of the house stood below street level, opening onto an alley. The woman who answered the door bell wore a pale blue housecoat, tossed over pink pajamas and white slippers.

She'd known they were coming. Couldn't she at least get dressed?

"Mrs. Nowak, it's a pleasure to see you again. Do you remember me, Paul Keller? How are you?"

"Fine, thank you."

"I'm Sergeant Winters. We haven't met before." Winters held out his hand.

She took it. It was like holding a three-day dead fish.

"May we come in?" Keller said.

"Of course." She stepped back and led them into the living room.

The house was as neat as the garden. White doilies sat on piecrust tables and a line of delicate tea cups with flowers of pink and blue were displayed in a china cabinet. A large photograph sat on the mantle. A stiffly posed family. Man, dressed in suit and tightly knotted tie; woman, stiff hair and pale blue blouse with a bow at the neck; boy and girl, early teenagers. The room was gloomy, thick curtains on the back wall shut against the light of the day.

Winters picked up the picture and studied it.

"My family," Mrs. Nowak said. "That picture was taken for the church directory a year before Brian went away."

"Do you know where your husband went?" Winters asked.

"Isn't that why you're here? To tell me?"

Winters glanced at his boss.

"Marjorie," Keller said. "Human bones have been found up at Koola Glacier Provincial Park."

She was exceptionally pale, but at his words the last of the blood drained from her face. "Brian's bones?"

"We don't know at this time. There's no clothing, or other items that we've found yet. Identification has to be done and the search is continuing."

"You think it might be Brian?"

"We don't think anything yet. We wanted you to know, that's all. It will be in today's paper and I didn't want you to read it there first."

"I don't get the newspaper. Scurrilous rag."

"It is possible the bones belong to your husband, but it is also possible they do not."

Winters shifted from one foot to the other. Mrs. Nowak hadn't offered them a seat nor taken one herself.

"Thank you for coming, Sergeant Keller," she said.

Keller didn't bother to correct her. She obviously didn't read the paper, Winters thought, if she didn't know the man was now Chief Constable. She didn't even ask him what he'd been doing over the last fifteen years.

"Is Kyle around?" Keller asked.

"Yes."

"May we speak to him?"

"No need. I'll let him know what you've told me next time I see him."

"Next time? Isn't he still living here?"

"He has an apartment downstairs. After Brian left Kyle turned the lower level into his personal space. He has a small kitchen and I believe he set up a studio for his painting."

"You believe? When did you last see Kyle, Marjorie?"

She thought for a few seconds. "A month perhaps. He helped me dig up a dead bush that had to be removed."

Keller gave Winters an almost imperceptible shrug. "I'd like to talk to Kyle. Can we get there from here, or should we go around the house?"

"You'll need to go around. He uses the stairs to store his paintings."

"Thank you for your time, Marjorie. Sergeant Winters is in charge of the case and he'll let you know what's happening."

She nodded at Winters and held the door open for them.

He let out a long puff of air once they were standing on the sidewalk. "Did that seem a bit odd to you, Paul?"

"Odd? She was positively overflowing with good humor compared to when I was working her case. She showed remarkably little interest in how the search for her husband was going. She insisted he would never have abandoned the family and that he had been snatched off the street by a, quote, sadistic sexually perverted killer."

"What did she have to say about the ten thousand missing dollars?"

"He must have been planning a surprise. A vacation for their anniversary or something."

"Was that possible?"

"Unlikely. They weren't well off. Their checking account was in the red as often as not. Nowak missed a couple of payments on his car. The teachers at the kids' school said they had the impression the family just scraped by."

"What work did he do?"

"Insurance. Sold insurance for a company that isn't around any more. Let's talk about this back at the office. We're creating gossip standing out here on the sidewalk. Those stairs look none too steady. Let's drive around and see what young Kyle is up to."

"Is he as odd as his mother?"

"He wasn't back then. Who knows what the years have done to him."

Winters was driving the van. He maneuvered it to do a U turn on the narrow street and turned left, down the mountain, and left again into the back alley that ran behind the houses perched on the hill.

The Nowak house had been the fourth from the corner. Winters counted back lots as he drove.

A deck jutted out from the upper floor of the house, casting a thick shadow over the back entrance. No lawn or garden, just a bunch of weeds sticking out of cracked and faded concrete. A car was parked under the deck, close to the door.

"Oh no."

"What?"

"See that red car."

"What about it?"

"Eliza."

Chapter Eight

The watercolor showed an alpine meadow on a spring morning. A yellow sun in a soft blue sky, traces of clouds fluffy and white. Grass and flowers were drawn in perfect detail, every petal exact, drops of fresh dew glistening on leaves.

The flowers were not yellow and white and orange, they were black, brown, dark purple. The dew was not clear and pure but opaque and blood red. It was a highly troubling picture.

When she'd seen his art previously it had disturbed her. Yet she kept thinking about it, and this morning decided she had to come back and see more.

"Go to the craft gallery," he'd said the first time she ventured down the cracked and wobbly cement stairs into his basement apartment, "if you want to buy a pretty painting of pretty flowers and pretty little girls playing with pretty puppies."

Eliza had put the picture down and selected another. The scene was similar, this time showing the beautiful lake far below where a sailboat drifted over the waves. The colors were equally angry. It was the jarring contrast of the hideously ugly flowers with the beautiful scenic background that disturbed her so much. Trouble in paradise? The fall of man?

In the right corner she noticed a small object, almost invisible, behind a black flower. She looked closer: a pile of feces.

She looked back at the first picture, and saw what her eyes had missed, although her subconscious had recorded. Tucked away in a corner, behind a bush that was more thorn than flower, he'd painted the bottom of a small foot. Five tiny toes, neat nails, clean, unmarked skin. The foot was pale white, with a slight blue tinge. The color of death.

She shuddered.

He laughed. "Exactly. You see, Mrs. Winters, the purpose of my art is not to make the viewer feel warm and cozy. We live in a world of death and disease. Violence and disaster. Only by facing it, acknowledging it, can we hope to handle it."

She said nothing and moved on to the next work, and the next. She rifled through paintings piled against walls and heaped on shelves. There were more in the other rooms and stacked behind doors. They were similar; stunning scenery, ugly dramatic colors, a small token hidden somewhere, a reminder that life wasn't always beautiful. She turned to look at him. He leaned up against the wall, surrounded by unframed art, his arms crossed over his chest, no expression on his face.

She wondered what had happened in his life to make him see the world this way. He was pale, disheveled, verging on dirty. His brown hair was thin and lifeless, cut badly, his beard long and scraggly. He appeared to live in the basement of this house, rarely left it, and accepted visitors grudgingly.

"Your talent is extraordinary," she said. "Do you ever do anything more, shall we say, pleasing?"

He shrugged. "What you see is what I do. It's what I am, Mrs. Winters." His mouth was crowded with teeth. They crossed over each other, as if they'd fought to a draw for prominence.

"Thank you," she'd said. "I'll be in touch."

"Whatever."

She came back this morning. He opened the door with a lop-sided grin, almost as if he'd known he'd find her there. Standing on his step. He crossed his arms and waited for her to speak first.

"Do you want to work with me?"

"No. Do I want you to show my art? Yes. It's time."

"Time?"

He stepped back and bowed her into the apartment. The main room was his studio. Brushes, paint, sketches, half-finished canvases. The kitchen alcove was piled with dirty dishes, but there were no dishes or food in the studio. She could see into the bedroom, a small unmade bed, a computer on a cheap wooden desk, clothes tossed everywhere. But no pillows nor discarded socks or papers cluttered his art space.

A man who could compartmentalize his life.

He unfolded his arms and extended them. He gestured to the room around them. "Time to let my work see the world."

An interesting expression. Not to let the world see his work.

"Besides," the arms fell and he shrugged, "I need the money."

"What do you do for a living?"

"My life is art, and art is my life. I do nothing *for a living.* I do some web design stuff if and when I need the cash."

Despite being in a basement, the apartment could have been bright and sunny. It faced south-east with an unencumbered view all the way down to the town, the river, the mountains beyond. But the deck upstairs loomed over the windows, cutting off the sun. She wondered if he'd produce more cheerful work if the light were better.

Probably not. His art came from inside him.

"I'm interested in exhibiting your work, Kyle. I'm currently planning a summer show, but I think your paintings might be a bit too… unconventional for the sort of people who pass through over the summer."

"No kidding."

"Your work suits November. I find November to be a sad month, all rain, dead plants, dark clouds, the threat of snow."

"If that's what you expect, Mrs. Winters, you might get little puppies and pretty blond girls with hair ribbons after all."

Eliza studied him. Artists were supposed to be an unconventional bunch, uninterested in mundane things like money, strictly concerned with the development of their artistic vision. But most, she'd found, were very interested in mundane things like money, and ready to compromise if she would put their art in her gallery.

She suspected "compromise" was not in Kyle Nowak's vocabulary.

"I am interested, but I have to be sure you're going to be able to meet the demands of a professional show."

"What sort of demands?"

"The number of paintings I require, of the quality," It was her turn to spread her arms to encompass the art in the room, "I have seen here. They will have to be framed, and you have to put them up and take them down, or at least arrange to have that done, under my supervision."

"You can pick the pieces you want to use right now."

"I'm not making you an offer yet, Kyle, although I'm considering it. I have a friend in Vancouver who has a better idea of the art world than I do, and I'd like to consult with him first."

"I don't fit into the *art world*."

"My friend will not be making the final decision, I will, but I rely on his advice. With your permission of course, I'd like to send him photographs of samples of the work. If I go ahead, I'll want some of these paintings, yes, but I'm confident you will be producing more between now and then, and we both want to exhibit the best. If we decide to proceed with the show, that is."

"Sure."

"You'll have to appear at the gallery several times over the period of the show. Opening night for sure, any special evenings I decide to put on."

"I don't like talking to people."

"It's a condition of having a show. Prospective buyers like to meet the artists."

"If you were showing Vermeer they wouldn't expect to meet the artist."

"If I were showing Vermeer, I'd be charging a lot more."

He shrugged again, not much caring one way or the other. "I guess I can manage that."

"I'll be in touch again in the next...."

They heard footsteps on the stairs, and then a knock.

Kyle looked surprised at the interruption and went to open the door.

Two men stood there. One dressed in casual pants, pale blue shirt, and a loose jacket, the other in the uniform and white shirt of a senior police officer.

Chief Paul Keller said, "Mr. Kyle Nowak?" Sergeant John Winters gave Eliza an apologetic smile.

"That's me," Kyle said. "I heard you were back in town, Mr. Keller. Chief of police now. Should I congratulate you?"

"This is Sergeant Winters."

Kyle's eyes registered the name and flicked toward Eliza.

"My husband," she said, heart in her mouth. She did not want to be involved in another police investigation. "Are you looking for me, John?"

"Sorry to bother you, Eliza, but we'd like to talk to Mr. Nowak. Won't take long."

"Have you found my dad?" Kyle asked.

Eliza hesitated. She should be leaving, but Paul had closed the door behind him.

"Perhaps," John said.

"What does perhaps mean? Did you find him or not?"

"If you'll let me explain. Human remains have been found in Koola Park. They've been sent to the university labs for testing, but the age looks to be right."

Kyle swayed and Eliza grabbed his arm. "You need to sit down."

"I'm okay." He had been pale before, now he was the color of the foot in the painting which had simultaneously repulsed and attracted her.

"No you're not." She guided him to a chair, and he fell into it.

"I know this must be very disturbing for you," John said, "but we thought you and your mother need to know."

"My mother. Have you told her?"

"We've just left her."

"It might be a good idea for you to go up and be with her," Keller added.

"Maybe," Kyle said. He began to chew at the nail on his right thumb. "What happens now?"

"I'd like you to come in and give a DNA sample," John said.

Kyle shuddered. "I don't think I can do that."

"Why not? We can compare your DNA to that in the bones."

"That would be a violation of my body."

"Not at all. All they need is a hair follicle, a swab from inside your mouth perhaps. Nothing invasive."

"It would be invasive to me."

"If you'd rather not come in, we can arrange for a technician to meet you here."

Kyle lifted his head. He looked at John. "What part of no didn't you understand?"

"Don't you want to know if this is your father?" Keller asked. "You were what, sixteen when he disappeared? I know the years have been hard on your mother…"

"You know nothing."

"Perhaps your sister would be willing to help us," John said. "Do you have an address for her?"

"Not a clue."

"You don't know where she lives?"

"I haven't seen or heard from Nicky since she left town years ago."

"I can ask your mother."

"She won't know. Nicky's gone and we don't keep in touch. Nor do we want to."

Eliza felt like she had walked onto a stage to find herself in the midst of a play in rehearsal. "I think I'll be going," she said quietly, to no one in particular.

"Mr. Nowak," John said, in that calm low voice she recognized as him getting angry. "I'm surprised at your resistance to possible new evidence in this investigation."

"I don't want to live through it all again, get it? It's over. He's gone and he's done enough damage to me. To my mother, I mean."

John said nothing; he let the words fill the room. His phone rang. He put his hand in his pocket and checked the display. "Ron Gavin," he said to his boss. "I'll take it."

Keller looked around the room. "You're a painter, are you Kyle?"

"I'm not going to come 'round to slap a fresh coat of paint on your kid's bedroom wall, if that's what you're asking. I'm an artist and my medium is paint and canvas."

Eliza studied Paul Keller as he studied the paintings. She saw him struggle to make sense of what he was seeing. She'd been to the chief's home a few times for dinner or cocktails. He liked pictures of mountain scenes. An avid fisherman, he had some paintings of rivers or streams. He and his wife Karen had a couple of Robert Bateman limited edition prints: wild animals and woodlands perfectly rendered.

He looked at Eliza, confusion written all over his face. "Never seen a daisy quite that color. It's not very pretty," he added lamely.

"It's not meant to be fully representational." Eliza decided on the spot to offer Kyle Nowak a showing at her gallery in Vancouver although that had not been her intention in approaching him. She wanted to promote local artists, locally, and hoped to attract bigger names, with bigger prices, to the main gallery in Vancouver. Kyle's art attracted feelings and emotions, not many of which would be positive. A bit of controversy would get her fledging gallery noticed. She'd devote the smaller Trafalgar gallery to tourist-attracting and gift-buying works.

"That was the RCMP officer at the scene," John said, putting his phone away. "They've found part of a jaw. With teeth. We might not need your DNA after all, Mr. Nowak. I'll be in touch."

The two police officers headed for the door. Eliza debated remaining behind to tell Kyle her decision. She took one look at his face and followed her husband and his boss outside.

Chapter Nine

"You wanted to see me, sir?" Molly Smith stood at the chief constable's door.

"Yes, Molly. Come on in. You can leave the door open. Take a seat."

She perched on the edge of a chair, cradling her hat in her hands. She'd been driving back from a minor car accident on Station Street when Jim Denton, the dispatch officer, told her to come in and meet with the chief. Her heart had been in her throat the whole way back as she tried to figure out what she'd done wrong. She'd been a police officer for three years, but she still felt like an imposter. A little girl playing cop; someday the grown-ups would tell her she couldn't play any more.

She loved being a police officer and couldn't imagine what she would do if they took that way from her. She'd killed a man last year, shot him. It was kill or be killed and although she played the incident over and over in her mind, particularly in the dark of night while Adam breathed lightly beside her and Norman snored on the floor, she knew it could have ended no other way.

An open door to the chief's office was a good sign. He didn't fire officers when everyone in the station could overhear.

Did he?

Instead of reaming her out, or even praising her for a job well done, he surprised her.

"How's your mom doing, Molly?"

She had been called in to be asked about her mother?

"Uh, fine."

"She's managing the store all right?"

"Yes."

"Glad to hear it." He reached toward the bar fridge behind his desk. "Want one?"

"No thanks."

He pulled out a can of Coke and popped the tab. He took a long drink and she shifted in her seat. "Making a go of the store on her own is she?" Keller asked at last.

"It seems to be fine."

"Glad to hear it. Have you heard that the remains you and Tocek found might be those of Brian Nowak?"

"Yes, sir. Sergeant Winters told me."

"Nowak disappeared two months before I moved to Calgary. It's always bothered me that I had to leave that case unresolved."

"Yes, sir."

I came around to your house to talk to you about it, Molly. It was a long time ago."

"I remember."

"You were having breakfast. Your mom was there but your dad had left for work. Are you still in touch with Nicky, Nowak's daughter?"

"No, sir. The family changed after Mr. Nowak left. Nicky had to go home right after school and she couldn't have any friends around. She dropped out of the baseball team and gave up all her other activities. She quit school before graduating, left town, and I never saw or heard from her again."

"Why do you say Mr. Nowak left? Not disappeared?"

She shrugged. "Just an expression? No, more than that. Middle-aged men don't get snatched off the street by sexual predators or serial killers. Children certainly, women, sometimes. But men? With bad comb-overs and beer bellies? Doesn't happen. If he'd been in an accident he would have been found, somewhere, by someone."

"Good point," Keller said, and she was pleased with the praise.

"Thought I might drop in on your mom later. See what she remembers about the Nowaks. Do you, uh, think that would be okay?"

He was asking permission to speak to her mother? Lucky Smith and Paul Keller had known each other for a long time. Keller had spent the middle of his career in Trafalgar, coming as a new detective constable, being promoted to sergeant before going to Calgary where he climbed the ladder and ended up head of homicide. He came back to Trafalgar a few years ago to take the position of chief constable. Lucky Smith had always been known, as the expression went, to the police. Not because she was a criminal, but because you could just about guarantee that if any controversy was brewing in Trafalgar, British Columbia, Lucky Smith would have a spoon in the pot. Constable Smith herself had stood between two opposing groups of protesters a couple of years ago, her mother on one side, refusing to back off.

When she'd applied to the Trafalgar City Police, Smith had been afraid the chief would take one look at her last name and toss her application over his shoulder into the trash.

Lucky's husband Andy, Molly Smith's father, had died seventeen months ago. The death had been sudden, totally unexpected, an enormous shock to everyone. Lucky had been desolate, but in typical Lucky fashion she'd thrown herself even deeper into her political action groups—Molly had grown up edging around clusters of earnest people gathered around her kitchen table—her social advocacy, the store that was their family business.

The sadness filling her eyes and pulling at the skin on her face was slowly starting to lift.

"Sure," Smith said to her boss, thinking this was likely to be a bad idea. Lucky would not be happy at being questioned by the police. Particularly the chief constable. "Mom's at the store most days. She usually takes Sunday and Monday off."

"Thank you, Constable Smith," he said. "That'll be all."

◇◇◇

Lucky Smith studied the arrangement on the new rack. She moved a gardening book to the center of the display, reconsidered and put it on the bottom. The bell over the shop door tinkled and she turned, professional smile in place.

"Paul. This is a surprise. I don't think I've ever seen you in my store before." She gave him a real smile. He looked nice, she thought, in his white uniform shirt and blue hat with the blue band.

He colored slightly. "My oversight."

"Are you looking for something? A gift perhaps?"

"No, nothing. Well, maybe." He looked around. "Do you have any fishing rods?"

"Sorry, no. Here you are for the first time in the what, twenty years we've known each other, and I don't have what you're looking for. We've never had much call for fishing stuff. Although that might have been only because it wasn't an interest of Andy's."

"Tell you the truth, Lucky, I'm not really looking for a rod. Although I'm always looking for a rod, come to think of it. I mean, I'm always looking for…"

"I understand. Fishing is your hobby is it?"

"Yes."

Every man needs a hobby, she thought. *Keeps them from getting underfoot all the time.* Although, now that her own husband was no longer underfoot, she missed him so dreadfully.

She glanced at the large photograph she'd hung on the exposed-brick wall behind the counter. It showed a group of kayaks pushing off from the shores of a lake. A man was caught in the act of jumping into his boat while two others headed out to the open water. The lake and sky were a brilliant blue, the mountains dark green, the surface of the water so still the background was reflected as into a mirror. Only the smooth wake of the red kayaks and the dip of paddles slicing through water disturbed the surface.

Moonlight and Samwise. Andy taking the kids out in early spring to re-train them on kayak rescue. Lucky had been standing on the shore watching them go and snapped the photograph. She'd found it when going through old boxes looking for pictures to use at Andy's visitation and had it blown up and mounted.

She looked back at Paul Keller. He had turned a strange color, and shifted from one foot to the other, his hat tucked under his arm as if he were calling on a date. She smiled at the thought. No one would mistake Chief Constable Paul Keller for a young man. He'd been handsome once, but the years had taken their toll. He'd put on weight that didn't suit him, particularly around his face, giving him pudgy cheeks and flapping jowls. He didn't have all that much hair left, but at least he didn't try to cover up the fact with a comb-over. He kept his mostly gray hair trimmed short.

Of course, Lucky herself wasn't exactly a hot young babe. Not that she'd ever been particularly hot, although Andy seemed to think so.

Andy.

Everyone expected her to sell Mid-Kootenay Adventure Vacations when he died, but she hadn't even considered it. She needed the job. Not the money, but the work. She needed to be busy. She could retire, spend her time doing good works, but she and Andy had worked side-by-side in the store for so many years.

She'd cut the business back a bit, promoted Flower, the part-time assistant, to full time, hired a new part-timer. She brought in some different stock, books mostly, not just tourist guides but to do with nature and the environment. She didn't offer guided hiking and kayaking trips into the wilderness anymore. Andy had done that himself for many years, then he trained Moonlight and Samwise to lead the excursions, and when the kids left home he'd hired guides. She didn't have the expertise, and didn't have the time either, to continue with her part of the business, managing the money, the staff, the inventory, as well as take on all Andy had done.

No matter. She had an arrangement with a guiding company up the valley to send prospective adventurers their way in exchange for a finder's fee.

It had been a hard year, emotionally most of all. She was beginning to get some of her equilibrium back and found that she could occasionally pass as much as an hour without thinking of Andy. Before looking up from her computer to shout out something she'd discovered, or ask him if he wanted to go out for dinner.

Then that hollow feeling in her heart, when she knew she would get no answer.

She fought to keep sadness off her face and gave Paul Keller another smile.

"I'm not here to talk about fishing," he said. "Although I can always talk about fishing. We've had a possible development in the Brian Nowak case. Do you remember it?"

"I certainly do."

"I… Would you like to go for a coffee or something?"

"Coffee?"

"Or tea. Have you had lunch?"

"No, I haven't had lunch."

"Let's talk over lunch then. My treat. How about Feuilles de Menthe? The patio is open, and the rain should hold off for a while yet."

She opened her mouth to say no. It was the middle of a business day; she was working. And Feuilles de Menthe was quite expensive, even for lunch. And she didn't want a big fancy lunch anyway; she'd had a morning snack of a bran muffin, a big one, from the bakery. And… and… she really couldn't go to lunch with Paul Keller.

"Okay," she said. "That would be nice. We can't be too long, mind. Flower's in the back. I'll tell her I'm going out for a bit."

Chapter Ten

Old bones, long buried, have lost all their magic, John Winters thought. Hard to even imagine this was once a person. A human being with a life, a family, a job, friends, lovers, likes and dislikes. Enemies perhaps.

"Not much," Gavin said, "but it gives us something to work with."

It was a jaw bone, teeth still attached. These weren't ancient bones: silver fillings, dull and worn, gave off no sparkle in the fading afternoon light.

"Can you tell anything about age of the owner? The gender?"

"Gender, no. Adult or near-adult for sure, and judging by the amount of dentistry probably not young. That's about the extent of my knowledge. I'm not a bone guy, John. These will have to go to our labs so people who know what they're doing can have a look at them. They can tell a lot about a person from his or her bones. As to how he died, I'd say we need more than the bits we have to figure that out."

"We can use the teeth to identify him though, right?"

"Teeth are only good for matching with a definite suspect. Someone whose dental records you have. You've got someone in mind?"

"I have a cold case that might be ready to heat up. I checked the file before I came over. Guy's dentist was Tyler, who's still practicing in Trafalgar. I called him and he's okay with sending the suspect's records to Shirley Lee, the pathologist. Not her field, she said, but she has a forensic dentist friend she can consult. They'll do the comparison soon as we get the pictures to her. She told me that working from photographs won't make a positive identification, and might not hold up in court if that were necessary. But it will be enough to let us know if we're on the right track, or if this is someone completely different and I can pack my bags and go home. When the stuff gets to the labs the big brains will do the detailed comparisons."

Gavin held up his camera. "I'll send them off."

They were clinging to the hillside about ten yards above the bottom. More bones had been uncovered as investigators climbed the slope. Trenches had been dug through the dirt and there were patches of bare earth where leaves and branches had been lifted and carried out of the way. It was heavily overcast, rain threatening. The air was full of the ripe scent of long-decaying leaf mulch, now disturbed. Everyone's boots and pant legs were thick with dirt. It had been hard going, the slope almost vertical in places, the forest floor littered with rocks and vegetation. The mountainside continued about another fifty yards before flattening out.

"The last thing we need is rain," Gavin said, following Winters' eyes. "We've torn up the forest floor enough. With a dose of rainwater we'll be swimming in mud."

"Anyone been to the top yet?" Winters asked.

"I have," Adam Tocek said. "For a quick look around."

"We wanted to make sure there isn't a bone factory or something over the ridge," Alison Townshend said.

"Nothing but forest," Tocek said. "There's a ledge, twenty feet wide or so. Above that the mountain carries on just about straight up."

"Why would our guy, either the dead fellow or whoever brought him here, have been up there? No one would have walked up this slope for a hike, and carrying something heavy like a body? Can't see it. Do you think it might have changed much in fifteen years?"

Everyone shrugged.

"I know someone who'd know," Tocek said.

"Who?"

"Molly. Molly's been climbing these mountains since she could walk, probably before. She led tourists on weeklong trips into the wilderness when she was just a kid. When we were here the other night, she said the park had changed."

"I'll call her. Tell her to come prepared for a good tough hike."

The words were scarcely out of his mouth before the clouds opened and rain began to fall in a torrent. The Mounties had hung tarps from trees to protect their excavations, and everyone bolted for cover.

Winters peered out. The rain was falling so heavily he could scarcely see the massive trees ten feet away. "No hurry. We can do this tomorrow. It'll be too dark before much longer anyway."

Nicole Nolte kicked off her four inch heels the minute she walked through the door.

It had been a good night. A thousand dollar tip. Didn't get that every day. He'd wanted the whole GFE—girl friend experience—expensive meal with excellent wine, starched white linen and candles on the table, a walk through the streets after dinner holding hands. Gooey expressions and soft touches and murmurs of sweet nothings.

To spend the whole night at the apartment.

That wasn't going to happen. She'd mumbled something about her roommate coming home after finishing night shift. As if she'd have a roommate in a one-bedroom apartment. He wasn't interested in reality, and bought into the story happily enough.

There would be no point in taking pictures and rooting through that guy's wallet. He'd love it if all the world knew he was screwing a woman like Nicole.

She wondered if he would be worth cultivating. He was about as ugly as they came, cursed by a bad stutter, but eager to splash money around. As a bonus it took two seconds for him to come, which meant she could get him out the door in record time. They'd had dinner at the ungodly hour of six o'clock, and even with the walk and back to the apartment, she was home by ten. Nice to get an early night for a change.

She dropped her clothes on the bedroom floor and dug into her drawer for the packet of white powder. Spreading out a line on the kitchen table, she called Joey to check in. He didn't answer and she left a message.

What to do about Joey? He wouldn't like the idea of taking on a straight-forward client. There wouldn't be much for him to do if Nicole was just screwing the guy. Joey liked to pretend he was in charge.

Joey or no Joey it was probably not a good idea in any event. She had no intention of whoring for a living. She saw where that road led every time she drove through the Downtown Eastside.

She bent her head over the line of cocaine and jumped when her phone rang. Not the cell she used to communicate with Joey, but the landline in her apartment. No one ever called her on that, and it was getting late.

She looked at the call display. *Restricted Number.*

That can't be good.

She considered not answering. If someone had her number they might have her address too, and come around in person. This was supposed to be a secure building, but all that meant was that political doorknockers and your neighbor who'd forgotten her key couldn't get in.

Anyone who wanted to could always find a way.

"Yes?"

"This is Constable Marian Singh of the Vancouver Police. I'm looking for Ms. Nicky Nowak."

That was a name Nicole hadn't heard for a good long time. No point in pretending it wasn't her. The police, like the taxman, had their sources.

"I'm Ms. Nowak."

"Ms. Nowak, there's nothing to be concerned about. I'm calling on behalf of Sergeant John Winters of the Trafalgar City

Police. Sergeant Winters is attempting to locate you in regards to the matter of the disappearance of your father, Mr. Brian Nowak. If you could call Sergeant Winters in the morning at this number. It would appear your father has been located."

The woman could tell her nothing more. Nicole took down the number, said thank you, dropped into a chair.

They'd found Dad.

The woman didn't say if he was dead or alive, but Nicole doubted it was the latter.

She sure needed a hit now.

Chapter Eleven

It rained all day Thursday. Ray Gavin and his team did what they could to protect their site but the mountainside rapidly turned into a field of mud.

"Might help release more of the bones," Gavin said to Winters. "Save us some work."

"You're such an optimist. More likely it'll bury anything near the surface."

"I'm channeling Alison; she's the optimist. I want to bring in a bulldozer and dump truck and cart the mountainside off to the office where I can work in comfort. Warm and dry."

"No point bringing Molly up there to have a look around today. It's supposed to stop raining overnight and be sunny tomorrow."

"Let me know." Gavin hung up.

Winters looked out the window. Rain slashed against the glass. A woman came down the road, walking into the face of the storm. Her head was bent against the wind and her yellow poncho wrapped itself around her legs. As he watched the wind grabbed her umbrella and flipped it inside out. She threw it onto the ground and stomped on it.

He turned from the window with a laugh.

As promised, Doctor Shirley Lee had consulted with a forensic dentist and, after much huffing and puffing and declaring that he couldn't be sure looking at photographs, and the remains would have to be examined in person, and even then they wouldn't have a positive identification, he grudgingly admitted that the dental records were a reasonably good match to the teeth Gavin had dug up. Thus the case of Brian Nowak was now officially on Winters' desk. A preliminary examination of dental records wasn't proof positive, but close enough for now.

He'd been told the last address anyone had for the daughter, Nicky, was Vancouver. She was long gone from the number her mother had, so he'd put in a call to the Vancouver police to try to track her down.

They'd done so, and the woman had phoned him first thing this morning to say she would be arriving in Trafalgar later in the day.

He looked back at his desk. It was buried in paper. When he'd first opened the old boxes, he'd merely flipped through the contents. Now that it was an official case, he had a lot of reading to do.

He shoved aside a pile of witness statements to clear enough room to access his computer. He logged onto police databases and began a search for reference to Brian Nowak. A couple of claims of sightings, one in Fort Nelson, one in Atlin. About a year ago, a man came into the RCMP detachment in Dawson Creek claiming to be Nowak who'd only just recovered from amnesia. Considering the man had been known to the local police for more than twenty years for his penchant for digging up old newspaper stories and fantasizing that new information had come to him in a vision, the police did nothing more than make a record of his statement. Next month he was back with the breaking news that Princess Diana hadn't really died in that car accident in Paris but was living with him in his off-the-grid cabin and had sent him to town to announce that she had decided to return to the world.

Winters chuckled and turned to the next report.

He found nothing worth following up.

Not a surprise, as it would appear Brian Nowak had never left the mid-Kootenays.

It might all be a waste of police time. Perhaps the man had gone for a hike and gotten lost. Unlikely, without taking his car or any hiking equipment—Winters made a note to see if Keller had thought to check if Nowak had bought anything from an outfitting store in the previous days or weeks—but you never knew what got into people's heads sometimes.

He'd have to interview Mrs. Nowak and her children. Go back to Nowak's employers, his friends, anyone who'd made a statement to Keller about the man.

Open up old wounds, potentially cause a great deal of pain.

Cold cases could be very nasty things.

Nicole Nolte had an errand to run before she could get out of Vancouver. She drove to Hastings and Main and found a parking spot, close but not too close to her destination, easily enough. It was early and most of the druggies and hookers hadn't yet ventured out of the cheap hotels and rooming houses and back alleys to face the day.

She skirted around a sleeping bag-wrapped shape on the ground beneath the barred window of a check-cashing shop. Almost against her will, Nicole glanced down. Wide brown eyes stared up at her. The face was round with remains of baby fat, the skin unlined, the black hair thick.

Nicole hurried away. A policewoman was coming her way, heading for the child vagrant. The cop nodded politely at Nicole, nicely dressed in designer jeans, clean shirt, jewelry, new boots.

Nicole smiled in return and quickened her pace.

They'd found Dad.

After all these years.

She'd clung to her faith in him, long past any hope of his return. Her brother, Kyle, decided soon enough Dad wasn't coming back and wanted to take over his study. Mom jumped every time she heard a sound at the front door, as if Dad would find his way home from the convenience store one day. Nicole remained in her mother's house for three more years, and every evening Mom insisted the light be left on over the front door all night so Dad could find the keyhole in the dark. For all Nicole knew, her mom still kept the light on. Every day Mom cooked enough food for Dad, as though he'd walk through the door at six o'clock and pull his chair up to the dinner table.

For three years, Nicky got the leftovers for lunch. To this day, Nicole wouldn't eat anything not freshly prepared. She wanted her father to be dead, otherwise she would have to face the fact that he had abandoned her, but she still clung to some sort of vague hope that it had all been a misunderstanding. A year ago, she'd seen a man in Royal Park Mall. She'd been on the floor above and had glanced down the escalator stairwell and there he was. Accompanied by a slouching teenage girl, laden with shopping bags. Nicole recognized his walk, the back of his head, the way he held himself. She ran down the up escalator, yelling, shoving startled shoppers aside.

The man turned, regarded her as if she were a psychiatric patient off her meds. He didn't resemble her father in the least. She didn't apologize, just walked away, her head held high, ignoring the teenager's sneering laugh.

A woman stood in the doorway of a pizza shop. The store was closed, the entrance cluttered with fast-food containers and crumpled newspapers and cigarette butts. The woman glanced up as Nicole approached. Her eyes were hollow, her face little more than bones covered by a thin layer of pock-marked skin. She wore a purple tube dress, barely covering the distance between her sagging breasts and non-existent butt. "Got some change?" she asked, in a tone that suggested she knew the answer already. She was missing two teeth and the rest were dark with nicotine and tarter. Her breath smelled like sour milk.

"No."

"Bitch." The woman stuck her middle finger into the air.

Nicole kept walking, crossed against the light to reach her destination. A print shop, clean and well-stocked, smelling of ink and toner. A photocopier clattered and spilled out reams of paper.

"Mr. MacDonald sent me to pick up his order," she said to the clerk.

The young woman smiled. "I'll see if it's ready." She went into the back and came out with a large, bulging envelope. "Here you go. I think it's all there." She put the envelope into a shopping bag.

Nicky thanked her, paid, and left. Outside, she peeked into the envelope. A stack of useless blank paper and a couple of baggies at the bottom each of which contained a few grams of white powder. She didn't usually buy her own drugs—let Joey take those chances. But she wasn't going to Trafalgar without a couple of days' supply.

As she came out of the print shop, a car crawled past. She watched as it stopped in front of the pizza shop. The woman in the purple dress stepped out of the doorway and went up to the car. She leaned over, her flat butt sticking out, said a few words, opened the door, and climbed in. A large blue and black bruise covered most of her inside left thigh. The car pulled away with a burst of speed.

It was a black Lexus, sleek, clean, polished to a blinding shine. A child's safety seat was mounted in the back. The hooker stared into Nicole's eyes as they drove past.

Nicole's whole body shuddered.

Was this what it would come to, in the end?

She went to her car and headed home. To Trafalgar.

Chapter Twelve

Molly Smith woke with a start. Her heart was beating hard and her mind in turmoil, searching for what had panicked it. The sheets were twisted around her legs and the duvet on the floor. It was still night, the yellow glow of street lamps shone against the drapes. Her apartment was above a bakery on Trafalgar's main street, and she could usually tell the time by the level of noise coming from outside. It was very quiet. The scent of the day's baking wafted up from the ovens below, which meant Alphonse had started work.

She kicked off the sheets and padded into the kitchen for a glass of water. She didn't turn on any lights. She'd been raised in a house on the mountainside and spent a lot of time deep in the wilderness. She liked the dark. She was never afraid in the dark. Nothing bad had ever happened to her in the dark.

When she thought about Graham, her late fiancé, he was always surrounded by light. Graham, raised in the land-locked middle of North America, loved the water. Swimming, boating, sitting on the ferry to and from Vancouver Island, merely being near water made Graham happy. She remembered water reflecting off his body as he pulled himself out of Kootenay Lake and flopped onto the beach, sizzling in the heat and light of the sun.

Was it memories of Graham, fading so fast, that made her resistant to returning Adam's love?

If she'd met Adam first, would she be so skittish of commitment?

She took her glass to the table and sat down.

She and Adam had gone to the nearby town of Nelson last night for a concert by her favorite heavy metal band, Savage Blade. The concert had been great, and they'd left pumped and excited and happy. They went to a loud, crowded, cheap bar where they ordered pizza, chicken wings, and beer, laughed and kissed, and licked hot barbeque sauce off each other's fingers, and Adam tried, and failed miserably, to pound out *We are the Hammer* on the scarred wooden table with the handle of his knife.

They'd been walking through the quiet, rain-slicked streets back to the truck. Adam made a joke and Smith laughed and he grabbed her and held her close and kissed her deeply. And then… and then…

His truck was parked outside a jewelry store. As she headed for the passenger door, Adam pulled her into the shop doorway. The baubles on display sparkled in the lights of the windows, a row of gorgeous engagement rings front and center.

"See anything you like?"

She looked up at him, a joke forming on her lips. The words collapsed back into her throat. His dark eyes were serious, his handsome face intent.

She'd wondered why he parked on the main street when plenty of parking was available nearer the concert.

"Molly," he said, his voice very deep.

She turned her head quickly. "They're all beautiful. Dreadfully expensive I bet. Let's go. I'm beat."

She dashed for the truck, and whatever he had meant to say remained unsaid.

When they got back to Trafalgar the town was so quiet the traffic lights were flashing yellow, rather than alternating red and green. He pulled up in front of her apartment, turned off the engine, and started to get out. She put her hand on his arm and said, very quietly, she'd see herself up. She was tired and would be trudging all over the mountain tomorrow. He stayed in his seat, gave her a soft kiss, and watched her climb out of the truck with a long look.

Why was everything so complicated? She loved Adam, in her way, but she feared he loved her more than she loved him. They'd been together for about a year and a half. He'd been hinting it was time she give up her apartment and move out to his acreage in the woods. She loved his place but simply wasn't ready to take their relationship up a notch.

Was he planning to propose?

The thought terrified her.

A wave of hot fragrant bread drifted through the floor from the bakery. When she looked up, the sky was lightening.

She hadn't even decided what to do about her career, never mind a proposal of marriage. If she wanted get ahead in the police, she needed to leave the small, generally peaceful town of Trafalgar. Last year she'd been about to send out applications to big eastern cities when her dad died suddenly. Her brother and his family moved to Scotland, and Molly knew she couldn't leave her mom all alone.

Perhaps now it was time.

She went back to bed to try to get a bit more sleep before she had to head out to Koola Park with John Winters to tramp around the mountain.

"We came up here a lot," Molly Smith said. "The campsite down at the bottom is good for car camping, and those going into the backcountry would use the main parking lot as their jumping-off point. It's been maybe five, six years since I was last here, until the other night, and things have changed."

"In what way?"

"They've moved the jumping-off point for one thing. The campground was getting over-crowded, and when the logging company stopped using their road, the park took it over for the use of backcountry people."

They were heading out of town toward the park. Winters had told Smith she'd be better off in her hiking clothes than risk ruining her uniform. It felt nice to be going to work in sturdy climbing boots, zip-legged pants, polyester shirt, nylon jacket. She'd pulled a baseball cap over her short hair. She wasn't sure if she missed the comforting weight of her equipment belt, or felt freer without it dragging her down.

He was dressed in his usual clothes of casual pants and light jacket over button-down shirt. The only concession to the expedition was the pair of running shoes on his feet. He'd have trouble maneuvering on the steep trails in shoes without much in the way of treads.

She jumped out of the car the moment they arrived at the campsite. The steady driving rain of the past two days had sent the last of the campers scurrying home. Two marked RCMP cars and Ron Gavin's forensic van were the only vehicles parked at the end of the road.

Adam Tocek and Norman sat on the picnic bench in what had been the Paulson's campsite, waiting for them. Norman jumped down and greeted her with an enthusiastic tail wag and lolling tongue. As no one but John Winters was around Adam gave Molly a light touch on the arm and a private smile. Like her, he was out of uniform.

"My memory isn't going to be perfect," she said. "I hope you understand."

"I do," Winters said.

"I'm pretty sure there used to be a trail up that way." She pointed off to the left. "People heading for the backcountry would unload most of their gear here, then leave their car in the lot closer to the entrance."

"There isn't a trail there now," Tocek said, unfolding a map of the park. A black line indicated the road, colored lines marked the trails. Little squares showed shower blocks, the visitor center, the rangers' office. She took the map and studied it. "When the new road went in giving access to the backcountry, they must have let the old trail overgrow. It wasn't suitable, as I remember, for kids or anyone who wasn't used to serious hiking as there are some sharp drop-offs and narrow ledges. I hope it hasn't overgrown too much, John, or I might not be able to find the starting point. It was a rough track even back then."

"Let's start at the top," he said. "What I really need to know if whether fifteen years ago a proper hiking trail was above the spot where we found the bones."

"Does that matter?" she asked, as they headed into the trees, following yellow crime scene tape.

"It'll help to know how the bones came to be here, if we can find out where they came from. If there wasn't a trail whoever brought Nowak must have had some considerable strength. It would have been difficult to drag a body though the forest. It would also reduce the likelihood Nowak walked in under his own free will. If there was a trail, it expands the possible scenario. He might have walked in, under his free will or not, and on the other hand it would have been difficult, but not impossible, to get a body up there."

Gavin and his team were hard at it, scratching through dirt and sifting leaves and forest debris, and scarcely stopped to wave when Winters, Smith, Tocek, and Norman scrambled past them up the steep mountainside.

Winters was breathing heavily by the time they got to the top. Smith knew he was a runner, but he must be pushing fifty and he wasn't used to this sort of terrain. His high-end running shoes had been just about useless on the muddy forest floor, and Tocek had to haul him up in places. Norman bounded on ahead, leaping over rocks, dodging low branches, enjoying the excursion.

It's a wonder, she thought, watching the happy dog, how humans survived long enough to evolve. If they were being chased across this terrain by a bear, it was obvious which species would be able to get away and which would not.

The mountain flattened out, as Tocek had reported. They emerged onto a flat ledge, about twenty yards wide. A wall of solid rock rose on the other side, and from there the mountain headed almost straight up. A few hardy cedars, firs, and pines, most of the pines dead from the beetle infestation, clung to the mountain, their roots digging into almost solid rock in search of purchase and nutrients.

"Oh, yeah," she said letting out a long breath. "I remember this place. It was a perfect spot to stop and take a break before a long hard stretch."

"That wasn't hard?" Winters said.

She laughed. "We didn't climb up that way. It's coming back to me now. The path was fairly easy to this point, and this was a nice place to stop because the trees drop away and the view is great. We're not far from the road, but the trail had to circle around the mountain, so the hike was longer than you might think. An hour or so, maybe, but I'm not too sure about that. You can see all the way to the river and that range of mountains. Might even be able to see your house from here, John, if we had binoculars. It used to be so green, and now look at it." She waved her arm. Mountain range after mountain range, marching north to the Arctic, the tall pines, thousands, tens of thousands of them, green no longer. Brown and purple in death.

"What's the other way," he said, "heading further up?"

"It gets tough not far past this spot. Around that corner, maybe a quarter of a mile, the trail narrows and you have to be very careful of your footing. We had more than a few clients freeze up at that point. Keep going and it's pure wilderness. Another five miles in there's a cabin for over-nighting and a fabulous jewel of a lake. The cabin is still maintained and more trails lead off from there." She grinned at Adam. "Next time we're both off for a couple of days?"

"You got it."

"You think it unlikely Nowak came that way, from the other direction, on his own or not?" Winters said.

"Walking all the way around, when this trail was still in use? That would take most of a day, I'd guess. I wouldn't want to be carrying a body over my shoulder going through the narrow."

"Let's go down, then," Winters said, "and see what there is to see."

Smith led the way. The path was overgrown, impossible to see in places. Branches reached out to grab at their clothes and roots tugged at their feet. Winters slipped in a patch of mud and stumbled. Only a wild grab at a tree limb kept him from falling face first. Norman sniffed at the ground as they walked, but didn't seem to be finding anything interesting.

They walked silently, feet crunching on the forest debris, the occasional scattering of the undergrowth as some small creature scrambled to get out of their way. Smith had brought a GPS and checked it occasionally, although in most places enough scraps of the old trail were visible and she could find her way.

After about an hour they came out onto flat ground. Neatly groomed empty campsites spread out around them. "That's it," she said. "It took us a bit longer than it used to because I got lost a couple of times. The going was tougher but we weren't carrying any equipment so we probably moved about as fast. I'd say it would have taken me forty-five minutes back then with a fit group and our stuff." A drop of rain landed on her hand and she looked up. Dark clouds had moved in. More rain on the way. The forensic officers would not be happy.

"No point in hanging around here," Winters said. "There won't be a trace of anyone passing fifteen years ago."

"Norman didn't seem interested in much up there," Tocek said, "or down here." He looked at Winters, sitting on a log, breathing heavily, rubbing at a scratch on the side of his cheek. "Want me to go for the truck, sir?"

Chapter Thirteen

Lucky Smith rarely drank. She'd open a bottle of wine if she had friends around for dinner, and that was about it. Andy had always liked a beer or two watching TV in the evenings, but she preferred a cup of tea. Her son Samwise bought her a bottle of Drambuie every Christmas and it lasted the entire year. Pastries were more Lucky's downfall than alcohol. She did love chocolate cake and fruit pies.

She'd been more than a little tipsy after lunch with Paul Keller on Wednesday. He'd ordered a bottle of wine and it was such a beautiful day and so pleasant out on the patio they'd lingered over the drinks before ordering food, and somehow a second bottle had arrived. They hadn't left until the first drops of rain hit the table between them and they looked up to realize they were the only patrons remaining and the waitress was tapping her foot on the sidewalk. Lucky tripped over a loose… something and Paul grabbed her arm to steady her. He continued to hold her arm as they walked to the store and when they came in, laughing, Flower looked at them with a considerable degree of surprise.

Lucky went into her office, shut the door, and promptly fell asleep with her head on her desk.

When she woke, it was dark. Flower had closed the store and locked up and left.

Lucky cringed merely thinking about it. Imagine, a drunken lunch with Paul Keller of all people.

She'd expected him to ask what she remembered about Brian Nowak. But he hadn't, and instead they'd talked about things. Life, kids, plans. Nothing much at all, really.

He was back this morning, and when she heard his voice greeting Flower Lucky wanted to hide in the broom closet. Her office door was open, and Flower told him to go right in. Lucky stuck her reading glasses on her nose and grabbed an invoice off the stack in her in-basket and studied it intently.

"Lucky? Hope I haven't caught you at a bad time."

She acted startled and lowered the glasses so she was peering at him over the rims. "Chief Keller," she said. "What brings you here? I am rather snowed under this morning." She indicated the papers on her desk. "Is it important?"

He didn't take the hint and stepped into the office. "Business, I'm afraid." He twisted his hat in his hands.

"Business..." she prompted.

"We have enough of an identification on those bones Molly found in Koola Park to reopen the Brian Nowak case. John Winters will, of course, be handling it, but I thought... well, as I was the investigating detective at the time, I'd give him a hand. I'd like to ask you a few questions."

"Me? I know nothing. I barely knew the fellow."

"But you did know him? And his wife?"

"Their daughter was friends with Moonlight."

"You were at his house the morning he disappeared?"

"Parked outside. I didn't go in, and I didn't see him."

Paul shifted his weight. "I'm sure you'd like a break. How about we discuss this over a cup of coffee?"

He wanted to interview a witness in a coffee shop?

Seemed most irregular. But Lucky was, as always, curious. She took her glasses off and put the invoice down. "I guess I can spare a few minutes."

Big Eddie's Coffee Emporium was almost full. Paul lined up for their drinks while Lucky searched for a table. Espresso machines bubbled and gurgled and emitted clouds of steam. The cooks balanced hot breakfast sandwiches and shouted out names. Jolene served pastries as her body moved to the beat of music coming from the speakers. Eddie stood behind the cash register, ringing up sales and taking money. With no regard to the line-up almost out the door, he stopped for a moment to chat with anyone he knew.

Paul searched the crowd, located Lucky waving at him, balanced a plate of scones, speckled with blueberries, drizzled with white chocolate, a mug of coffee and one of tea, and joined her.

"I enjoyed our lunch the other day, Lucky," he said.

"I did too. It was nice to have an indulgence in the middle of the day."

She knew from Moonlight that police officers liked to sit with their backs to the wall, and just to be ornery she'd taken that seat. Facing the door, she saw the chief's assistant, Barb Kowalski, come in with Constable Dawn Solway. The two women's heads almost spun completely around when they saw who their boss was with. They exchanged a glance, ordered their coffee, and left quickly.

"How's Karen?" Lucky asked.

"Who?"

"Karen. Your wife?"

"Oh, her. Uh, she's fine. Just fine, I guess. Busy with her activities. I don't see her much at all, you know how it gets. She's gone to Calgary." He swallowed a mouthful of coffee too fast and struggled to keep it from choking him.

Lucky nibbled on a piece of scone and wondered what had come over the chief lately.

"Anyway," he said, once he could speak again. "About Brian Nowak."

The coffee shop was full, but with all the noise and bustle there was little chance they'd be overheard. A group of young mothers pushing monster strollers came in with Bev Price, who managed the Trafalgar Women's Support Centre. They snagged the table for six close to Lucky and Paul. Bev came over to say hi.

"You still haven't gotten back to me, Mr. Keller, about having the community officer give a talk to my new mothers on child safety."

"Sorry," he said. "I'll look into it soon as I get back to the office."

"Lucky, give me a call later will you, dear. I have an idea for a new program on nutrition for infants and toddlers and I'd like you to run it."

"You know that's one of my interests," Lucky said. "I'd be happy to."

Bev returned to her group and Lucky turned to Paul with a smile. "Sorry."

"You do know everyone in this town, don't you?"

"No, but sometimes it seems that way. Oh, look, there's Christa." Lucky waved frantically and the young woman, along with most of the other people in line, looked over.

"Hey, Lucky, how are things?" Christa Thompson came over to their table. Christa was practically Lucky's third child, but they'd drifted apart lately.

"Monday night I want you to come for dinner. No excuses, Moonlight and Adam are coming and so are you."

Christa looked as if she were going to make an excuse, but she sighed and said, "sure." Lucky hoped she would come, but doubted it. Christa and Moonlight had been so close once. All that had changed.

When she looked back at Paul Keller he was smiling at her. A smile so full of affection it startled her. "Lucky," he said, "I've always wanted…"

"Brian Nowak. He was not a happy man."

"You knew that?"

"I'm not psychic, and I don't have any special intuition, but sometimes you can tell. We weren't friends, mind. I saw him at kids' sports tournaments, parent-teacher nights at the school, that sort of thing. We'd sit together on the sidelines at the soccer field or chat when dropping off or picking up the girls. I don't recall ever going to dinner at their house, or having them to ours. I didn't know him well, but it seemed to me he had an aura of sadness around him. He worked at a bank, I think."

"Insurance."

"Yes, that's right. He was a pen pusher at an insurance company. I suspect he hated it. Many people grow up without fulfilling their dreams, but they get on with life. We can't all be astronauts or ballet dancers."

"Or chiefs of police."

She laughed. "Was that your childhood ambition?"

"Can't remember a time in my life when I didn't want to be a police officer."

"You're lucky then. Life turned out as you wanted it."

"Careerwise yes, but there are other things that sometimes..."

"Then again, what do I know? Maybe Brian Nowak loved being an insurance salesman. All I'm saying is I remember not being all that surprised when he disappeared. I assumed he'd run off without telling his wife and would go on a bender and be back soon enough with a sore head and hopefully not a social disease. When the days turned into weeks and then months, I figured I'd been wrong. He seemed fond of his children, and I'd thought he was a good father. I don't think he would have willingly abandoned them."

"We felt pretty much the same. The son, Kyle, came into the station the next morning to say his dad hadn't been home the night before, but we didn't pay much attention until a couple of days had passed. Married men go walkabout all the time. But Nowak never returned."

Lucky sipped her tea.

"What was your impression of his marriage?" Keller asked.

"Hard to tell, isn't it, what goes on in a marriage? I knew his wife a bit better than him because she volunteered at the youth center a couple of days a week. That was when we had the kitchen and café and the program to teach some of the at-risk youth to work in a restaurant. It was a good program. When we lost the funding, I was so mad, I..."

"Mrs. Nowak?"

"Sorry. I was about to run off, wasn't I? Marjorie was her name. She was quite stiff-laced, very prim and proper. Colorless, I thought. She dressed in clothes straight out of *The Donna*

Reed Show. Polyester skirts, twin-sets, flat pumps, tiny pearl earrings." Lucky waved her arm. Her colorful, flowing cotton blouse swirled around her and silver bracelets jangled. Even fifteen years ago twin-sets and pearls didn't exactly blend in in Trafalgar. The clothes in the coffee shop overflowed with color and texture. Lucky's own full skirt was made of hemp, and the hem was cut in a zigzag pattern so it came to her knees in some places, halfway down her calves in others. The women wore everything from trendy yoga wear to tie-died T-shirts to loose-fitting camouflage pants. The young men were in shorts and one fellow with dreadlocks almost to his waist wore a sarong slung around bony hips. At the end of summer every color found in nature, and a few that were not, was on display.

"Essentially, Paul, I found her boring. After Brian disappeared, she pretty much withdrew from the world. I tried to involve her more in the goings on at the youth center, but instead she stopped coming all together. I don't think I've seen her now for a year or more. If I thought about her at all, which I haven't, I would have assumed she'd moved away. Moonlight told me she's still here, still living in the same house." Lucky broke off another piece of scone and thought.

"I could be sprouting garbage. Appearances can be deceiving. Gosh, I remember that time new people moved in not far from us. Being neighborly, I went over to introduce myself. They were such nice people, a couple about our age, with grown children, like us. We got together for the occasional beer on the deck and then they invited us, Andy and me, over for the evening. Heavens! I thought that meant dinner, but they opened the door dressed in nothing but a few strips of leather weighted down with chains and zippers and handcuffs. I'd brought an apple pie and Andy had a bottle of wine."

Paul burst out laughing. "What did you do?"

"I shoved the pie into her hands and said we had a prior engagement. Sorry. Andy just about crashed the car into a tree at the end of their driveway in his haste to get away. They seemed like such a… normal… couple. They had two grandchildren."

Paul's eyes sparkled with laughter. "You're blushing, Lucky. I didn't know that was possible."

"Even thinking about that is so embarrassing. They moved about a year later, thank goodness. Anyway, all I'm trying to say is you can speculate until the cows come home but no one on the outside truly knows what people's marriages or family lives are like."

"Isn't that the truth," Paul Keller said, his eyes on her face.

"I've never seen such a load of pure crap."

"Don't talk like that in this house."

"Whatever."

"Doesn't surprise me in the least. You wouldn't know crap when it comes out your ass. And if you don't know what's crap you don't know what's good either."

"Please children, don't fight."

Nicky Nowak glared at her brother. He hadn't changed a bit. Still living in the basement, still throwing paint at the wall and hoping some of it would stick. She'd gone downstairs to his rooms yesterday evening when she first arrived, thinking it would be nice to say hi. Pretend they were a loving family for a few minutes. Instead she'd burst out laughing when he told her he was going to have a major show in Vancouver next year. With that pile of juvenile trash! 'Course he hadn't liked that one bit, and started lecturing her on art, and she'd stomped back upstairs. Visit over.

It was Friday afternoon; they were gathered in the living room awaiting the arrival of the police.

"Aren't you going to change, Mom?" Kyle said.

"Why?"

"Because the police are coming to talk to us about the death of your husband and our father and you're wearing your fucking pajamas, that's why."

"Don't use that word in this house."

"Now I remember why I haven't been back in ten years," Nicky said.

"Get dressed, Mom," Kyle said.

Without a word their mother got up and left the room.

"What, she's a trained dog now, does whatever you say? Does she bark on command?"

"Give it up, Nicky. She gets weirder and weirder. You're not the only one who stays away. I just haven't gone as far."

The house also hadn't changed. It looked exactly as it had the day Nicky left. Furniture a bit tattered, maybe, and she didn't think there'd been that worn patch in the carpet back then, but she might have forgotten. She'd slept in her own room last night, and it had just about freaked her out. She didn't remember the name of her teddy bear any more, but he was there, staring at her through glass eyes from the top of the dresser. And the posters on the walls. Ricky Martin, for god's sake. The Backstreet Boys and Christina Aguilera. The room could have been in a museum.

The basement had changed. It used to be Dad's den. As if he needed a den, but he needed someplace to get away from Mom and calling it the den made it sound important, like he had business to do or something. Now it was Kyle's apartment, with a shower in the bathroom and a compact kitchen. And Kyle's art.

Nicky no longer believed that she could be surprised, but her brother's art was unexpected. It wasn't bad, and she wasn't surprised to hear he was going to have a show; she'd seen worse things in galleries, selling for thousands. The subject matter looked blandly normal but the colors were out-and-out creepy. She saw anger, and a trace of violence, in his art. She didn't think he had it in him.

But, as if they were kids again, she told him his art was junk to try to get a rise out of him.

It had worked.

Some things never change.

They sat in silence. Nicky smoothed down a crease in her jeans. She'd gone for a manicure this morning and the red polish glistened like drops of blood. She picked a magazine off the coffee table, some homemaking thing with a picture of a chocolate cake on the cover. Her jacket fell open and she saw Kyle sneak at peek at her tits. She stretched a bit more than necessary. Give the poor smuck a thrill.

She'd decided to have fun with her mother, and had worn a tight T-shirt, cut very low, cropped just above her belly button. Her jeans were low rise, and her boots had four inch heels. A black jacket, nipped at the waist with elbow length sleeves, completed the outfit.

Hooker clothes, but her sort of hooker clothes, not something to wear cowering in front of a pizza shop in the Downtown Eastside. The jeans and boots were designer, the jacket vintage, and the T-shirt cost two hundred bucks.

Her mother had asked her to button up her jacket, and Nicky replied that she wasn't cold.

"They aren't positive this is Dad, you know," she said.

"Sure enough, it sounds like. They're reopening the investigation."

"What's the point? They went over it and over it at the time. They talked to everyone, people at Dad's work, at church. Even my friend, Moonlight Smith. What happened to her anyway?"

"She's still around."

"Really? Of all the people we knew in school, I figured Moonlight would do something with her life, get the hell out of this town."

"Some people like this town."

"Small town, small people. No wonder Mom had a nervous breakdown. Everyone gossiping about her, pretending to be sympathetic but wanting to know if she'd murdered her husband and buried him under the daffodils. I'm not surprised she's turned into a weirdo."

"She's not a weirdo, Nicky, just reclusive."

"Even you don't believe that. Come on, she was odd before Dad up and disappeared. That pushed her over the edge."

Nicky tugged at a lose thread in her fashionably ripped jeans. Pretty stupid fashion, she thought, but in her job she had to look like she had money and taste. "I don't much care, you know. What happened to Dad. He left us because he was a selfish prick, and if he ended up in an opium den somewhere dying of consumption, tough on him. Women like her, like Mom, who can't look out for themselves, never mind their kids, screw them too. Rely on some man and when he runs out on them, they're left high and dry. Do you remember when the church ladies came around with food? They brought bags of groceries because they knew we didn't have any money. Mom just about died of the shame. But she took the groceries."

Kyle's eyes ran down her body. "And what exactly do you do for a living, Nicky?"

"Me? I screw men before they can screw me." She got to her feet. "I'm going out for a smoke."

The doorbell rang before she could move. "Let the festivities begin."

Mom hurried out of the bedroom. She'd put on a gray A-lined skirt and black blouse with long sleeves and a homemade gray sweater with the knitting coming undone on the right sleeve. She'd put on pantyhose but no shoes. The big toe had the beginning of a run.

Kyle stood up, and he and Nicky went with their mother to the door.

A man and a woman were on the step. The man was in his forties, lean and handsome, with short-cropped hair and a salt-and-pepper mustache. The woman was young, with good skin, sharp cheekbones, gorgeous blue eyes. She was long-legged, and looked fit, although it was hard to tell under the bulletproof vest, unflattering uniform, and equipment laden belt. She took off her hat and tufts of short pale hair, as fine as cornsilk, sprang up.

The cops were here.

Exactly like it had been fifteen years ago. The police at the door, hat in hand, dripping rainwater, apologetic words followed by probing, intrusive questions.

And nothing, nothing at all, worth saying.

Nicky saw the man's eyes on her face. Liking what he saw. Instinctively she cocked her head and gave him a smile. The woman studied her openly, and Nicky felt blue eyes on her breasts and bellybutton.

Did the cop play for the other team? That might be an avenue worth exploring; even today police were sometimes rather closed minded about gays. Although this one was probably too young to have much money.

"Nicky," the female cop said. "You've changed."

Chapter Fourteen

Nicky Nowak had certainly changed. Smith realized she was gaping, and snapped her mouth shut. She wouldn't have recognized Nicky if she'd passed her on the street. As a kid Nicky had been a dynamo on the baseball or soccer field, but otherwise fairly quiet. She had been pretty with thick black hair and olive skin, and young Moonlight had been envious. Smith remembered Nicky as being very short. She glanced down and saw that the woman's unexpected height was due to stiletto heels. In the old days Nicky, like Smith, had been all knees and elbows. Now she was all breasts and skin. Her clothes were certainly not the sort she'd worn back when they were teenagers. She was obviously trying for maximum sex appeal.

And achieving it. Smith glanced at Sergeant Winters, who had paused and swallowed before croaking out a greeting.

Smith wondered if Nicky's breasts were real. She was so thin, it was highly unlikely.

She was not just pretty. She was stunning.

"Nicky," Smith said. "You've changed."

Nicky's expression was unreadable. "Do I know you, officer?"

Smith glanced at Winters. He gave an imperceptible nod.

"I'm Molly Smith. Moonlight Smith."

Nicky stared at her, and then she stepped back and let out a bark of laughter. A big, deep genuine belly laugh. "Oh, my god. Of all things. You're a cop. A goddamned cop. I never would have guessed that in a million years. Yes, I see it now. You haven't changed much, it's just the getup that threw me off. You look good. I'd give you a hug, but don't want you thinking I'm going for the gun. Come on the hell in."

"Nicky," Mrs. Nowak said in a voice much like a squeak, "I don't care for that sort of language in my home."

"I'll try to remember that," Nicky said, with another laugh. Her teeth were straight and white and perfect.

"Mrs. Nowak," Smith said. "It's nice to see you. I'm Moonlight Smith, do you remember me? I used to be friends with Nicky."

"I remember you. You were a nice girl. How are your mother and father?"

"My dad died last year, but Mom's well."

"I'm sorry to hear that." Mrs. Nowak looked much the same, although years older, but something was off. She'd always been small, the sort of woman who kept her hands still and her arms at her sides, of limited expression and conserved movements. Now she was more like a shadow of herself. Her eyes were empty and her face unexpressive. Even when she reprimanded her daughter, her expression didn't alter.

"Please," she said. "Will you have a seat?"

A cloying scent of polish and disinfectant lay over everything.

The son, Kyle, stood to one side and watched. Smith saw him around town sometimes. He pretty much kept to himself. Occasionally, he'd drop into a bar for a beer, particularly if a live band was playing. He didn't seem to have any friends, and always sat alone. He didn't get drunk and didn't cause trouble, and left long before closing. He made a bit of money as a web developer, had several local businesses as his clients. She'd heard he was an artist, but didn't think she'd ever seen any of his work anywhere.

He was a moderately good looking guy, although pale and on the skinny side with a beard that could use a trim. But, like his mother, he had strangely empty eyes.

She remembered the Nowak family as being the same as all the other families she'd known, hers included. The tragedy, the simply *not knowing*, had destroyed them.

Nicky, however, seemed to be doing okay. Smith wondered if she was a model or something. Her hair and make-up and manicure were perfect, and she was beautiful.

They took seats on the uncomfortable furniture. Smith glanced around. It looked as if the place hadn't been updated since she was last in this house.

When they'd arrived in town after the hike in the park, Winters asked her to stop by his office after she changed into her uniform. He told her he'd spoken to Mrs. Nowak and Kyle earlier and needed to go back to not only talk to the daughter, who'd just arrived from Vancouver, but to tell the family they were operating on the assumption, pending further tests, that the remains of Mr. Nowak had been found in Koola Provincial Park.

"It's a somewhat unusual situation in that you, Molly, happen to be the last person, other than Nowak's wife and children, who saw him alive."

"Last, except perhaps for one."

"True. I don't think Nowak took himself to that mountain in order to either go hiking or to die. No one reported giving him a ride, or seeing him walking to the park, and it's a long way. He didn't own any hiking equipment, and Paul's notes say he wasn't known to be interested in wilderness activities. At the time Paul didn't think to ask if he'd bought stuff recently. I told him I was going to start checking into that, although not many stores, if any, are likely to have records of individual sales going back so far. Paul said he'd speak to your mother himself. He'll ask her what she remembers about the family."

"Why would he do that?" she asked.

Winters shrugged and glanced away. "Don't know. Back to the family. As you knew them, I'd like you to come with me. I haven't met the daughter yet. This is going to be very difficult. They might feel better seeing a friendly face."

She'd agreed.

"Dental records are not fully conclusive," Winters told them now. "We have more tests still to do. But at this time it looks like the remains of Mr. Brian Nowak have been found in Koola Provincial Park."

"If you're expecting us to show shock and dismay, Sergeant, Kyle said, "this hardly comes as a surprise. You've been poking around here all week hinting."

"I'm not trying to trick you. I want you to understand clearly what this means. It means that I will be reopening the investigation."

"How'd he die?" Nicky asked. She pulled a tissue out of her jacket pocket and twisted it between manicured fingers.

"That has still to be determined."

"He wasn't exactly Joe Outdoorsman," Nicky said. "Did he get a ride to the park to knock himself off somewhere nice and quiet where it wouldn't make a mess? Mom hates a mess."

Mrs. Nowak sucked in a breath.

"That's a bit harsh, don't you think?" Kyle said. "No one drove him to kill himself."

"Do you think he killed himself?" Winters asked.

Kyle jumped to his feet. "I think I don't fuckin' care. We've been through all this. Over and over and over. Paul Keller tramping through this house in his big boots, prying into everything, peering into every dark corner, looking for lies and secrets."

Kyle waved his arm toward his mother. She had begun to cry, silently. Large tears dripped down her cheeks. She made no move to wipe them away. "Look at her. She's little more than an automaton. Doesn't leave the house, can't bear to face the neighbors. *The woman who lost her husband.* Careless of her, wasn't it. Fifteen years have passed. Fifteen years of gossip and shame and welfare and handouts from snickering church bitches. Can you imagine how humiliating it was having her bank account frozen until they graciously decided she wasn't responsible for her husband's disappearance? The insurance company finally paid up so at least she got off welfare. Some of the neighbors have moved away, and the new people don't even know who we are. You're going to open it all up, and we're supposed to be grateful."

"I'm sorry, Mr. Nowak," Winters said, his voice low and steady. "I don't expect you to be grateful, and I do understand what this means to you and your family, but I have a job to do. What do you think happened to your father?"

Kyle paced, up and down across the small living room. His mother's face was buried in her hands. Nicky watched him. "I *thought* he ran away. Up and left because he was a weasel. Looks like he didn't get far, eh?"

"Why might he have run away, as you put it? Was he having problems in his life? His work perhaps?"

"Christ, I don't know. I was sixteen years old."

"You must have thought about it."

"I have never stopped thinking about it." He let out a long breath. "I guess I always assumed he ran off to be with some woman."

"Leaving you kids behind?"

"I doubt he cared. We didn't matter to him much at all."

"That's not true," Nicky shouted. "He loved us. He was a good dad. He was a heck of a lot better father than *she* was ever a mother." Her long black hair moved around her shoulders and she threw a look, full of long-simmering anger, toward her mother. Mrs. Nowak didn't lift her head.

Smith shifted uncomfortably. The springs on the couch were worn and her equipment belt was dragging her into the depths. This was awful. She glanced at Winters. His face was expressionless.

"Do you remember, Moonlight? Do you remember the time Dad built a swing in the yard and pushed us for hours?"

Smith nodded, although she didn't remember any swing.

"Was there a woman in his life?" Winters asked. "Another woman?"

"There was that one lady, what was her name?" Kyle said. "The one from the church whose husband died a couple of years before. He was always going around to her place to do odd jobs for her."

"Did you tell Sergeant Keller this at the time?"

"Yeah, I did. I thought she was way too friendly with Dad. Funny how when he went to her place he never invited me or Nicky to come along."

"That's ridiculous," Mrs. Nowak snapped. "You were sixteen years old, what did you know?"

"Earth to Mom. Sixteen-year-old boys know more about sex than frumpy church ladies."

"Unlike you and your sordid generation, your father," Mrs. Nowak said, "was not interested in sex."

Kyle burst out laughing, and Nicky looked just plain embarrassed. Mrs. Nowak only looked confused.

"Do you remember the woman's name?" Winters asked.

"Not off-hand. Thing is, you see, she wasn't around when I went to her house to ask if she'd seen Dad. Car gone. House locked up. The police called on her. No one home." Kyle paused and looked into the watching faces. He let a few moments pass, enough time to build the tension, and then he shrugged. "She came back three days later. Had been to Prince Rupert visiting her sister. So she said." The sentence trailed off, full of innuendo. "If he had one special friend, I bet there were more. I always thought so."

"Stop that. You're being ridiculous," Mrs. Nowak said. A vein had started to pulse in her forehead. "I don't know what you think is so funny. Your father was a loving husband and good father. He never looked at another woman in all the years we were married."

"I'm sure that's true." Kyle said, with the trace of a sneer.

"I'd like you to leave, Sergeant Keller," Mrs. Nowak said.

"Winters."

"This is too painful." She got to her feet. Tears carved rivers through the wrinkles and folds in her face. "I'm going to lie down. I can't bear any more."

She walked out of the room. Neither of her children made a move to help her.

"Sounds like a plan," Kyle said. "I'll be downstairs."

Winters and Smith looked at Nicky as the front door slammed behind Kyle Nowak. "Ms. Nowak," Winters said.

"Please," she said, in a deep slow voice. "My name is Nicky."

"Nicky. What do you think happened to your father?"

"Someone killed him. I have not the slightest doubt about that and never have. Someone killed him. He would never have left me here. All alone."

Chapter Fifteen

"That was perfectly dreadful," Smith let out a long sigh when they were in the car.

"Part and parcel of the job. Perhaps I shouldn't have brought you, Molly. You do know these people."

"It's okay," she said. "I knew them, but that was then. Everything's changed. Nicky seems to be doing good, though. I'm glad of that."

Winters gave her a long look.

"What?"

"Nothing. Your impressions?"

"A totally screwed-up mother and son for one thing. Nicky looks like she has her act together. I wonder if she's a model. She might know your wife."

"I doubt that. Are you going to see her again?"

"Sure. Unless you think I shouldn't. Because of the case I mean."

"Go ahead."

As they'd been leaving, Nicky suggested they get together for a drink or dinner. "So this trip won't be a total waste of time," she'd added.

"Your mom needs to have you here," Smith said.

"I doubt that very much. I don't like her and she certainly doesn't like me. I only came because you, Sergeant Winters," she said with a flirtatious wiggle of her fingers, "made it sound like we were going to reach some sort of closure. Instead it's all opening up again, like a raw, open wound. Here's an idea, why don't you join Moonlight and me? I'm sure your wife'll let you out for one night. Not too jealous is she?"

"I wouldn't want to intrude." He'd hustled Smith back to their car.

Smith drove down the steep, winding streets into town. Strands of mist swirled around the mountaintops across the river, and a few drops of rain hit the windshield. She turned on the wipers. "Mom wants me to come around tomorrow and can tomatoes. I guess summer's over."

"I guess it is. Drop me back at the station, Molly. I've got a lot of reading to do. I'll have to find the name of Nowak's lady friend and pay her a call. It's possible, but unlikely, they ran off together and she got cold feet and came back."

"You've probably thought of this already," she said, slowly, testing the waters.

"Go ahead."

"What if Mr. Nowak hasn't been on that mountain for fifteen years. Suppose it's fourteen, or ten. How long does it take for a body to be reduced to bones?"

"Around seven years, I think, depending on conditions."

"Maybe he really did run away, and was coming back, months or years later. Maybe he drove up to the mountain to think things over and got lost or had an accident." She peeked at him out of the corner of her eye. A black cat dashed across the road in front of them, and she barely had time to notice it and swerve to avoid a collision. "Sorry," she mumbled.

"That's a thought," he said. "Not necessarily one I want to hear because it means more angles to investigate. But good thinking nonetheless. I'll call the park and see if they have any record of abandoned cars over, what, a five- to seven-year period."

She felt ridiculously pleased with herself and concentrated intently on the road in front of her. No point in putting the Sergeant into the ditch moments after he'd handed out a rare bit of praise.

They walked into the police station, Winters to get back to his desk, and the mountain of files on the Nowak case, Smith to close out her shift.

Jim Denton stopped them as they came in. "Guy's been calling you, Sarge. About five times already. I told him you'd call back, but I guess he figured I was lying."

"What's he want?"

"Nowak case. Wants to know what's going on."

This morning's *Trafalgar Daily Gazette* had featured a prominent article on the front page under the heading *Nowak Found at Last?* Other than the somewhat sensational headline, the article had been down to earth and quoted the police department without speculation. A picture of the family in happier times was on the third page. Winters did not miss his old nemesis Meredith Morgenstern, who could be guaranteed to not only spice up the story but drop in a lot of insinuations before ending with a hint of police misconduct or ineptitude. Meredith had, at last, been fired from the *Gazette*, but promptly found a job with a Toronto tabloid, where she was no doubt messing with the minds of Toronto's Finest.

"Did he leave a name or state his interest?"

Denton handed over a scrap of paper. It contained a name and phone number. "That's all."

Winters shoved the paper at Smith. "Call this guy will you? If he has information for me, I'll talk to him. If he's wanting to satisfy his curiosity, tell him to read a mystery novel."

She made the call from the constables' office.

The phone was picked up before the end of the first ring. His name was Greg Hunt and he interrupted as soon as Smith said, "Sergeant Winters has asked me…"

"Is he there?"

"Yes, but he's busy at the moment, sir," Smith said. "I'll pass any information on to him that you have."

"Information. I don't have *information*, Constable. Only questions. Is it Brian Nowak you've found?"

"May I ask what your interest is, sir?"

"We were friends. I never believed he'd walk away from his life without a word to anyone. If what they're saying in the papers is true, then it looks like I was right."

She punched the password into the computer, and entered Greg Hunt's name. He lived outside of Trafalgar, on the other side of the river. Not far from her mother's house. It was a nice road, quiet, overlooking the water, some big houses. "We have no cause of death at this time," she said.

He let out a long breath. "Will you keep me informed? I… I want to know, that's all. He was a good man… a good friend."

"Did you speak to the officer in charge at the time of Mr. Nowak's disappearance, sir?" A few more key strokes and she knew he was a Realtor, owned a family business.

"No, I had nothing to tell him. I still don't."

Dawn Solway came into the office and tossed herself into a chair with a sigh. Smith lifted an eyebrow. "You were friends, you said. Did you hear from Mr. Nowak at any time after April 12, 1996?"

"If I had, young lady, I would have told you people."

"Thank you, sir. We'll let you know if there are any developments." She hung up and turned to Solway. "Nosey parker. Thinks the chief's office should have him on speed dial so he can be first with all the gossip."

"Wanna go for a stroll, Molly?"

Of a similar age, the only two women in the Trafalgar City Police, Solway and Smith weren't really friends. They went their own ways and didn't socialize outside of work. But they liked each other and could always be trusted to speak up for the other. "I guess," Smith said, taking a glance out the dirty window. The threat of rain had failed to materialize and the sun was trying to force its way from behind a cloud. "I'm going off now, anyway. What's up?"

"Something on my mind."

"We can't talk here?"

"The walls have ears."

Smith looked around the office. A row of chairs were pulled up in front of computers, pop cans and empty coffee mugs haphazardly scattered about. Filing cabinets lined the walls, and stacks of paper were piled on very available surface. Someone's dress-uniform hat sat in an open drawer. A TV was mounted high on the wall. It showed the front door, where the chief was coming in, a big smile on his face.

"Okay," she said, curiosity building. "Let me tell John what I found out and I'll join you."

"Thanks, Molly," Solway wiggled the mouse to active her computer.

◇◇◇

"You haven't been around to the house for a while," Solway said.

"Just got busy."

"Don't get too busy to train, Molly. It's easy to start forgetting and you never know when you're going to need it."

Last year, fresh from a retraining course, the two women had set up a training schedule. It had frightened Smith to realize how much of what she'd learned at police college had already started slipping away. Solway rented a house in town that had a big basement she'd converted into a home gym. For about four months, they'd worked out together once a week, not just on a fitness regimen, but practicing self-defense techniques and police maneuvers. It had been a while since Smith had been over.

"No excuse, I know. Next week for sure."

"I'll hold you to that." Solway said. "Francesca's coming for a visit."

They were walking down Front Street. Solway was the beat officer this afternoon, and she suggested they walk and talk at the same time.

"Who's Francesca?"

Solway threw her a glance. "I told you about her. My girlfriend."

"Oh, sorry. You didn't tell me her name." Only Smith knew Solway had a girlfriend. She kept her private life completely private, and as far as Smith new there weren't any rumors floating around as to Solway's sexual orientation. Other than those who assumed any woman wearing a uniform and carrying a gun was by definition a lesbian. Solway's girlfriend was in the U.S. Navy, stationed in Seattle. She was a lawyer. Smith wasn't too sure, but didn't gays get kicked out of the U.S. military if they were found out?

"That's nice," she said. Up ahead a boy with a shaved head, multiple piercings, overlarge jeans held up by copious chains, and a tattoo of a snake curling around his neck, dodged traffic to get out of the path of the oncoming police.

"Looks like Ronnie Kilpatrick's back in town and up to no good," Solway said. "Bet if I stuck my hand into his pants pocket, I'd find something interesting."

"And get it bitten off. I wouldn't be surprised if there are rats living in there."

Ronnie Kilpatrick, small-town, small-time troublemaker and drug-dealer, ducked into the used CD shop. "I'll check on him later," Solway said.

"Is there a problem with Francesca visiting?" Smith asked.

"We've decided to get married."

Smith stopped walking. "Wow! That's great. Congratulations. When? Can I be a bridesmaid? I'd give you a hug but I guess that wouldn't appear to be too professional."

Solway didn't look overly enthusiastic, as a woman announcing her engagement should. "It's not so simple for us, you know."

"Are you going to be quitting? Moving to the States?"

"No. Francesca's leaving the Navy. She decided some time ago that she wants to go into private practice. Family law."

"Good afternoon, dear." Jane Reynolds, one of Lucky's dearest friends approached them. She leaned heavily on a cane. "Give my love to your mother. I haven't been around for ages."

"I will," Smith said.

The officers continued walking. "She's going to move here, to Trafalgar, and once all the immigration papers are done and she's passed the bar exams, she'd like to open an office."

"Sounds perfect. Why are you looking so glum about it?"

"I like to keep my head down. Keep a low profile."

"Yeah," Smith said with a laugh. "That's why you have a job in which you walk around town armed to the teeth."

"Geeze, Molly, don't you get it?" Solway snapped. She stopped walking and turned to face Smith. "You and Adam, there are rumors, you know, you're thinking of getting hitched."

Smith shifted. "He might be thinking. I'm not."

"Theoretically speaking then. What do you suppose will happen when you announce the happy news? You'll come to work sporting a nice ring, and Barb and the clerks will make a big fuss, and your mom'll throw a party and get weepy, and you'll start sending out invitations. The guys'll take Adam to a strip club and try to get him drunk."

"Yeah," Smith said, seeing where this was going. "That's about the size of it. For us."

"For Francesca and me?"

"Probably not, eh?"

Solway continued walking. "I'm thinking of quitting, Molly, leaving Trafalgar. I don't think I can take the dirt."

"Come on, Dawn. Don't you think you're overreacting? This is Trafalgar, maybe the most liberal town in all of B.C. Geez, look at that guy up ahead. He's wearing a dress. Well, I guess it's a sarong, but no one's pointing fingers and laughing."

"I admit, this is a great town. And if I were anyone else, I'd have no problem marrying the woman I love and settling down here. We're thinking we might like to go for *in vitro* one day, and I know that would be accepted. But the police?"

Smith chose her words carefully. "I think you're judging them prematurely. Most of them are a great bunch of guys and are as much a part of Trafalgar as anyone else."

"Most of them. What about the likes of Dave Evans? He even has trouble with you, and you're the straightest woman on earth."

"Which proves my point. Evans needs to get in digs at me because he doesn't like women. Period. At least women he can't screw. But when push comes to shove, I've never felt that he didn't have my back. Isn't that all that matters?"

"I don't know, Molly."

"Whatever you decide, I'm here for you. But I think if you do quit, you'll be feeding into the hands of those who want to keep the police a straight male club. You did okay on your last performance review, didn't you?"

"Better than okay."

"I'd like to meet Francesca. And when you're ready to announce your engagement, you can be sure I'll make a big fuss."

"Thanks, Molly. I'm not totally convinced, but I'll think about it. Excuse me, sir, but are you not aware dogs are prohibited in this area."

He was standing at the corner, waiting for the light to change. A long-haired black dog on a leash sat patiently at his feet. "What the hell does that mean?" the man said, so quickly and aggressively Smith knew he was perfectly aware he was disobeying the by-law. Solway pointed to the painting on the pavement. A dog inside the universal symbol of a red circle with a line though it. Smith hummed "here comes the bride" under her breath and walked away.

Chapter Sixteen

Eliza had brought a book and sat beside the cash register, reading. Summer tourists were gone and winter ones yet to arrive, and traffic through the gallery was slow. This month she featured a handful of artists from the nearby town of Nelson, including Carol Reynolds, who painted street scenes of typical Kootenay homes and backgrounds, beautifully and realistically detailed. Reynolds' paintings were popular and several had little red stickers on them indicating they'd been sold.

Eliza had been reluctant to take on any shifts in the store, retail was hardly her thing, but she found she liked sitting in the pale well-lit space surrounded by art and enjoyed engaging in conversation with potential customers who wanted to talk about the work.

She looked up as the bell over the door tinkled to announce an arrival. "Kyle, this is a surprise." She slipped a bookmark between the pages and put the book down. "What brings you here?"

"Thought I'd check the place out." He glanced around. The gallery was long and narrow with wooden floors painted off-white and light cream walls. Carefully placed lighting illuminated the paintings, and a round glass vase full of deep red roses sat on the counter beside the cash register. Classical music, Beethoven at the moment, played softly in the background.

"I'm happy to see you," Eliza said, "but I did say if I decide to show your art it will be at my location in Vancouver, not here."

"Yeah," he studied a painting. Not by Reynolds, it was a watercolor of Kootenay Lake, the ferry in the distance and a sailboat in the foreground. "Paint-by-numbers," he said with a sneer.

"Few people are going to want your art hanging on their living room wall," Eliza said, defensive toward the picture, which she'd been ambivalent about in the first place. "Your art we will be positioning for collectors and galleries."

"*If* you decide to show me."

"Indeed."

"Tell you the truth, I'm only here because I had to get out of the house and figured I'd walk into town. The police, meaning your husband, were at my mother's."

"I don't discuss my husband's business."

"Chill, Mrs. Winters. I'm not asking you to. It wasn't a pleasant scene, that's all I mean. You know about my dad?"

"I read the *Gazette* this morning."

"It wasn't easy growing up with that hanging over my head, I can tell you. I was sixteen when he left, and Mom told me I had to be the man of the house."

"What do you think happened to your father?" It wasn't any of Eliza's business, but Kyle had brought the subject up and he did seem to want to talk. And she wasn't exactly swamped with customers needing attention.

"He ran off with some broad. Far as I'm concerned, there's no doubt about it. How he ended up in the woods is the question. Maybe she realized he didn't have any money and bumped him off."

"Do you know who this woman was?"

He shrugged and picked up a small bronze sculpture off a display table. A boy, fishing rod over his shoulder, dog at his feet. Tourist stuff, but perfectly executed down to the folds in the boy's pants and the notches in the dog's collar. Kyle studied the piece for a long time. Itzhak Perlman continued to play Beethoven's Violin Concerto.

"Not a clue. My dad was a player, a real man-whore. You'd think in a town this size people would have been talking, but he was good at hiding it. There were a couple of women at church he was having it off with. Church ladies would have been good prospects. They wouldn't blab to their friends, would they? They'd have had more to lose than he did if word got out. There are always some people who figure it's okay for a man to screw around. Particularly if he's married to a human statue like my mother. Mom, of course, was too stupid to know what was going on under her nose."

"You don't like your mother very much."

"I don't like her or not like her. She's my mother. Losing Dad, the way it happened, was hard on her, I'll admit that. The sneers of her friends as they handed out charity, being on welfare, police hanging around, asking questions, probing. That interfering priest, so solicitous while slyly suggesting that she should have been a better wife. She dropped all her friends, all her activities, stopped going to Mass. These days she barely leaves the house. Only the garden gets her outside. In the winter she doesn't even make it that far. I was supposed to be the man of the house. Take care of her. What else could I do but stay and move into the basement? My sister had the good sense to leave town soon as she turned sixteen."

Eliza stood silently, listening. She could think of nothing to say. From what she'd seen of Kyle's own living conditions, she didn't think he was in much a better situation than his mother. Had he stayed to help her? Or did he stay because he also was afraid to leave the house? Notably he had a job that allowed him to remain in his room, huddled over his computer most of the time.

"Do you blame your father?" she asked.

"Every single day. He always was a selfish bastard. He wouldn't let Mom have a job, even a part time job. Said it would be disruptive to the family schedule. He had to have his meals smack-dab on time, had to have his private hour in his den every night. He was a lousy father too, but Mom and Nicky have this saintly image of him. He had not the slightest interest in me or anything I was doing. He took Nicky to soccer games so he could flirt with the mothers. He'd drop Nicky, pick up one of the moms and they'd disappear for an hour and a half, getting back as the game finished. I told the police all this at the time, but they didn't go anywhere with it.

"We were never allowed into his den, you know. I figured he went there to look at porn and jack off. After he disappeared, the police went through it, and then Mom locked the door. About a year later, she let people from the second-hand store come and clear out his stuff. I bet they got an eyeful when they opened the desk drawers."

Eliza stole a longing look at her book. She sensed that Kyle had held this in all these years. Now he'd started talking, he simply couldn't stop. Like other reticent people she'd met, he didn't seem to know when too much became way too much.

"I'd been planning to go to art college. My dream for a long time. While other boys grew up wanting to play in the NHL or be in a rock band, I always knew I wanted to make art. Then the dream ended. No college for me, no money, a whiny neurotic dependent mother. Do I blame Mom?" Eliza was the only other person in the room, but Kyle was not talking to her. To himself mostly, but also to the bronze boy in his hand. "It was Dad who ran away, but I guess part of me does blame Mom. She thought being a good wife meant cooking a roast for dinner on Sunday, making neatly-cut sandwiches for him to carry to work in a paper bag, and dressing the kids well to go to church. Better if she'd let him fuck her, but she didn't like to mess the sheets."

He took a long look at the boy and his dog, heading off to the fishing hole. Then he put them down, very gently.

He waved his hand in the air, taking in the room and everything in it. "You're selling a fantasy here, Mrs. Winters. Pretty pictures, pretty statues, of a world that doesn't exist. What do you think goes on behind the doors of those neat houses? Nothing good. My art, it tells the truth. That's why people don't like it."

The Hudson House Hotel was the best in Trafalgar, British Columbia. It had gone through many manifestations in its life, from working man's hostel to backpacker's lodge, ending up a luxury hotel. The bar was designed to resemble a gentleman's club at the turn of the twentieth century. Wood paneling, red accents, leather elegance. A large painting hung behind the bar. A ruddy-faced, heavily whiskered man being choked by his stiffly-starched shirt collar glared down at the patrons. This was supposedly Hamilton Hudson himself, who'd found gold in the Klondike in 1897 and lost it all because for some unknown reason he'd been convinced there were diamonds to be found in the mountains outside of Trafalgar. Town gossips maintained that the only diamonds Hudson was after were those he could put around the neck of the wife of a certain Vancouver politician. Hudson died, alone and penniless, in 1905, probably from complications of syphilis.

No one knew why the hotel had been named after him.

Molly Smith saw herself reflected in the glass protecting Mr. Hudson's visage. She'd gone to some trouble to look nice tonight, and had dressed in black slacks with a black and white blouse under a red leather jacket, cropped at the waist. Her necklace was a simple silver chain and her earrings were long strands of finely-worked silver Adam had given her for her last birthday. She wondered if she should get a haircut. She'd decided to grow it out—it was ridiculous to have a short croppy hair style when she had to wear a hat most of the day. But now it was at that awful growing-out stage when it was impossible to get it to do anything half-decent.

She made a face at Hamilton Hudson.

"Molly?" the bartender said. "You okay?" His name was Ryan, and she'd known him since grade school.

"I was thinking of old Hamilton up there. I wonder what he'd think of this town now."

"I can guess what he'd think of seeing the likes of you leaning on the bar."

"You mean a woman?"

"I mean not a *professional* woman."

"Probably that the end of the world was nigh."

"You still want to wait?" he asked. Smith had told him she wouldn't order until her friend arrived. She nodded and sipped at her glass of ice water.

At eight o'clock on a Friday night the hotel bar was packed. A group of men surrounded her, dressed in dirt-encrusted overalls with orange reflector stripes and steel-toed boots. A highway maintenance crew.

They drank pints of beer and laughed very loudly. One of the men had turned to her with a smile, all ready to offer to buy her a drink, but his colleague had given him a quick elbow in the ribs and a shake of the head and the offer had turned to a simple nod. *Her reputation,* as the saying went, *had preceded her*. The after-work crowd jostled and laughed and drank, and staff dodged patrons and each other while bearing trays piled high with food and drink. Smith had laid her bag on a stool next to her, reserving it for Nicky, but she was beginning to think she'd have to give the seat up. Nicky was almost half an hour late.

"If it was anyone other than you, Molly, I'd tell you to order or leave," Ryan said, with a grin to show he wasn't serious. "But I'd be afraid next time we had a punch-up in here the police would be slow to react."

"Most amusing. I'll give her another five and then I'm outa here."

At that moment Ryan's eyes opened wide, and Smith heard one of the highway workers suck in a breath. All around her, conversation died.

She swung on her stool to see Nicky picking her way through the crowd. She looked amazing, simply dressed in a short white skirt sprinkled with pink flowers. The skirt, light and summer-flirty, swirled around her legs as she walked. The matching pink T-shirt was cinched with a wide green belt, and a large necklace of green stones plunged into her cleavage. Her thin strappy high-heeled sandals showed perfect tiny feet and blood-red nails. Long black hair swung around her shoulders, so shiny it reflected light. Every man in the room watched as Nicky glided across the floor. Smith had invited Adam to join them later. *That,* she thought, *might have been a mistake.*

The construction workers' faces split into huge smiles the moment they realized Nicky was heading their way.

"I am so sorry I'm late," she said, giving Smith a peck on the cheek. Her perfume was musky and fragrant. "Is this chair for me?" She smiled at the men. Their heads nodded like a row of Pez dispensers. Nicky slid onto the stool, wiggling her bottom to make herself comfortable. Her breasts, clearly outlined under the shirt, moved. The men swallowed.

"Buy you a drink?" one of them asked. He was young and good-looking with nice eyes and a lock of brown hair falling over his forehead. His shirt was streaked with dirt but his hands and fingernails were clean.

"Another evening perhaps," Nicky's voice was more of a breath. "My poor friend here must have been waiting for positively ages."

She swung her stool around and smiled at Smith. "Thanks for waiting." Nicky changed in matter of seconds; her smile was smaller but friendlier and less brittle. Her body seemed to almost pull into itself and she became smaller. The center of the room no longer, just a pretty woman sitting on a bar stool on a busy Friday night. The men went back to their drinks and grumbling about their job.

"Not a problem," Smith said. "I'm going to have a glass of Pinot Grigio."

"That sounds perfect. Me too," Nicky told Ryan.

"You got it."

"Tell me you were playing dress-up at my mom's," Nicky said. "You are not a cop."

"Yup."

"The terror of drunks and miscreants everywhere." The bartender placed cocktail napkins on the bar, and served glasses of pale yellow wine. He gave Nicky a grin and went to serve a group of new arrivals.

"That is so cool," Nicky said.

"You know what I've been doing. What about you?"

Nicky's shoulders shifted and she sipped at her drink. Her lipstick was a deep red, the exact color of the nails on her fingers and toes. "I live in Vancouver. I own a small interior decorating business."

"That sounds interesting."

"It pays the bills." Nicky drank more wine. "Not married. No boyfriend at the moment."

"Speaking of boyfriends, I've invited mine, Adam, to come by later. I hope you don't mind."

"Oh, no. I'd love to meet him."

They chatted about people they'd known in school: who had moved away and who had stayed, who was married for the second time, and who wasn't married but had three kids already. Nicky drank two glasses of wine for every one of Smith's, but Smith reminded herself that her friend's alcohol consumption was none of her business. As long as she wasn't driving.

Smith asked about the interior decorating business, how she'd gotten started in that, but Nicky's answers were vague and Smith suspected she didn't want to talk about it.

Which was fine, as Smith didn't want to talk about her job either.

It was nearing ten o'clock, the highway workers had long left after a couple of attempts to barge into the women's conversation, which Nicky had politely, but firmly, rebuffed. The crowd was thinning out, and Nicky had consumed about six glasses of wine. She could really hold her drink, Smith thought. She was on her third and feeling a warm buzz in her head. Nicky finally bought up the subject that had been hanging over them all evening. "Do you know any more about my dad than what you told us officially, Moonlight?"

"Nicky, can you call me Molly, please."

"Whatever. Tell me what you know."

"We're not holding anything back, if that's what you're asking. The early dental identification looks like a match, but it's not positive yet. They'll be doing a detailed examination early next week."

"The chances of some other guy with almost the same dental work as my dad having died about the right time and place are pretty slim, eh?"

"I'd say so."

"Your sergeant, what's his name?"

"John Winters."

"Is he hot or what? Nice clothes too. Married?"

"Most definitely."

"You're not trying to get a little action on the side there, Moon, I mean Molly? I'd be tempted if it were me." Nicky gave her a lewd wink.

"No," Smith said. "Absolutely not. Not only am I not interested in older men, but if I were I'd never even consider putting my career on the line. Anyway, if you get a look at his wife, you'll know why he's not the type to stray."

"They're all the type." Nicky swallowed the last of her wine, and held her glass toward the bartender. "Some just don't have the guts."

Smith shook her head. "Mrs. Winters is a retired model. Really. Not only beautiful, but rich too."

Nicky's right eyebrow rose. "The wife has the money in the family, eh? Do tell."

"Nothing to tell. Maybe we should go for something to eat. Adam's running late, but he can call if he wants to find us."

The bartender placed a fresh glass in front of Nicky.

"Once I've finished this," she said. "Another?"

"I've had enough."

"Come on. Don't make me drink alone. Don't be so prissy. Let your hair down sometimes, Molly."

"I don't have much hair to let down. Okay, one more. I'm not working tomorrow."

"That was my mother's problem, you know."

"What was?"

"Prissy. Little Miss Perfect. The house is still as neat as a pin, as she used to say, although she looks like hell."

"She's had a tough time."

"Nothing she didn't deserve."

"Gee, Nicky, isn't that a bit tough? After your dad left she still had to raise you and Kyle and that can't have been easy."

"My dad didn't *leave*, Moonlight. He was murdered."

"That hasn't been proven."

"It doesn't have to be proven. I know. He never would have left me behind. Never." Nicky's eyes blazed and her chin quivered. She lowered her voice. "Never. I wouldn't have been surprised if he ran out on *her* though."

"Your parents didn't have a good marriage?"

"They had an awful marriage. He couldn't do anything right. She picked at him all the time. Nag, nag, nag. Everyone thought we were the perfect family. Yeah, perfectly boring."

"Take it from me who's seen some things, Nicky, boring isn't a bad place to be when you're a kid."

"I'm not talking about me. I'll admit I had an okay childhood. Nice house, friends at school, at church. I had sports and clubs and stuff. Until Dad died, and then it all went to hell mighty fast. But for him, trapped in that marriage? It must have been a nightmare. I'm surprised they had kids. They sure as hell weren't doing anything that would make babies."

"Come on, Nicky, no kid wants to think their parents are having sex."

"But they didn't, Moonlight. For as long as I could remember, they had separate bedrooms and there was certainly no tiptoeing around the house at night. Not that Dad would have been able to breech her defenses in any case. Those nightgowns she wore said back off as well as any shotgun kept by the bed."

"I bet lots of long-time married people aren't doing it anymore."

Nicky laughed suddenly. It wasn't a nice laugh, sharp and bitter. "You have no idea how right you are, kiddo. But it was more than just the sex. She crushed him. She crushed his sprit.

He was a very unhappy man. Even as a kid I knew that. He sat at the breakfast table reading the newspaper in the morning, and at the dinner table at night, never talking while she blathered on spitefully about this person and that person. She told us gossip was a sin, but somehow that didn't stop her running off at the mouth all the time. I think the only times my dad was ever happy was when it was just him and me. He'd take me to soccer or baseball games and always stayed to cheer me on. She never came to any of my games. The house needed to be cleaned."

"Lots of sad people in the world."

"I always thought my dad had more depth than he was allowed to show." Nicky swirled the liquid in her glass. "If he'd left her, I wouldn't have been surprised, as I said. But he wouldn't have just walked out. As unhappy as he was, he knew he had responsibilities. He would have provided for her, and for us. Guaranteed."

"Surprised you're still here." Adam planted a kiss on Smith's cheek, and slipped his arm around her. He had spent the day at a friend's place, helping to put up a new fence, and was casually dressed in jeans, a brown sweater, and work boots.

He glanced at Nicky, and Smith saw a smile cross his face. "This is Nicky Nowak. We were great friends in school. Nicky this is Adam. My boyfriend." She put her arm around his back.

Adam reached out a hand and Nicky took it. Her delicate fingers almost disappeared in his big paw. She fixed her expressive brown eyes on his face. "Nice to meet you, Adam. I hope you're joining us."

"We're going for dinner," Smith said. "I guess you've eaten, eh?"

"Maureen made cornbread and a big pot of chili so I figured I had to stay. I'll have a beer while you eat."

"Wonderful," Nicky said.

Smith slid off her barstool. "I have to go to the washroom. I'll be right back."

"So," she heard Nicky purr, "what line of work are you in, Adam?"

Chapter Seventeen

The Nowak case wasn't exactly urgent, and nothing else of major interest was on his desk, so John Winters allowed himself to enjoy a few days off.

Eliza had gone into town to work at her gallery, and he decided to pop in and invite her to lunch. She looked up when the chime over the door announced his arrival, and he was pleased to see a smile touch her lips.

Pleased. He realized with a jolt that he was more than pleased, he was thrilled. She was the center of his life, and he'd been terrified she would leave him because of his own crass stupidity and bungling. But this morning's smile was the old, familiar one that she'd given him for the twenty-six years of their marriage. His heart turned over in his chest. "Hi," he said, "how about lunch?"

"Do you have something in your throat?"

"No." He coughed. "No. Lunch?"

"Bit early, isn't it?"

"I'm hungry. And I missed you."

She laughed. She had a beautiful laugh. "I've only been gone for two hours, John. We've been separated for a lot longer than that over the years." Which was certainly true. Her modeling career had taken her all over the world, sometimes for extended periods. Her mother spent the winters in Florida, and Eliza usually went down to visit and help out for a couple of weeks. Maybe he was just getting old. He liked that the gallery business kept her in Trafalgar, Vancouver at the furthest. He had an image of them as an old couple, sitting on the front porch in matching rocking chairs with blankets across their knees, and it made him smile.

"What are you looking so pleased about?"

"Nothing. Lunch?"

She slid off her stool. "I am supposed to be running a business here. But as it's my own business and we're not busy, I guess I can take a break. Just a quick one, mind."

It was raining heavily, no doubt part of the reason there weren't any customers, and Eliza grabbed her umbrella from behind the counter. She popped it open as they left the gallery, and they walked the half-block to George's. Late for breakfast, early for lunch, the usually crowded restaurant was empty and they got a nice table by the window. A plastic daffodil was stuck into a bud vase.

Winters ordered off the breakfast menu and Eliza requested a spinach salad. "Any particular reason you've come into town?" she said, handing the menu to the heavily-tattooed young waiter with a smile.

"Just wanted to see you." Her hand was on the table, the nails trimmed short, the polish light pink. He reached out and touched it. "And tell you I love you."

She said nothing, but folded her fingers into his.

They separated to let the waiter pour coffee.

"I've decided to offer a private show to Kyle Nowak. Next year in Vancouver." Eliza's green eyes narrowed. "Is your investigation going to interfere with that?"

"I don't see why." He looked around the empty room, and dropped his voice. "I'll take the case seriously and do everything I can to find out what happened to his father, but fifteen years have passed. People move away, they forget, overlooked evidence is destroyed or lost. If he was murdered, and I have no evidence to that effect, the person responsible has had a lot of time to cover his tracks. So, unless something new comes to light, not much is likely to happen."

"Will the… uh, remains, be able to tell you anything?"

"Possible. They're at a lab now. Certainly if they find a bullet imbedded in the skull or a knife slice along a rib that'll be meaningful, but bones have a way of keeping their secrets. In this case, they haven't found much of the skull or ribs anyway. Animals and time can carry them a long way."

"Regardless of what happened all those years ago, the consequences were tragic. Kyle's an insecure, bitter young man. The family had no money and he wasn't able to go to art college, which had been his ambition. He felt he had to stay in Trafalgar to look after his mother."

"You're not giving him a show because you feel sorry for him are you?"

"My galleries are a business. I intend to make them profitable in the long run. I do not take charity cases."

He felt as though his hand had been slapped out of the cookie jar. Eliza balanced the two sides of her life well. At home, to her family and friends and community, she was a generous, loving woman, but when it came to work and money she was all business. It was good part of why she'd survived in the sewer that was the modeling world. Not only survived but thrived.

"He hates the memory of his father, still carries all that hate around. It's got to be destroying him. The tragedy of his father and the feelings he holds toward the man are likely the reason Kyle creates great art. I suspect if their lives had continued as normal he'd be painting the sort of pretty little mountain scenes he's so contemptuous of now."

"He hates his father? Why?"

The waiter appeared at the table, and Winters cut himself off. Too easy, sometimes, to get talking about a case and forget that people could be listening. "Hold that thought," he said to his wife, "I'd like to hear more, but not right now." He dug into his pile of huevos rancheros and asked her if she'd given any thought to a winter vacation this year.

They were finishing their meal and Winters was refusing a coffee refill when two familiar people walked by the window, sharing an umbrella. Lucky Smith and Paul Keller. Lucky threw her head back and laughed and Keller grinned at her. They stopped at the restaurant door, and Lucky shook raindrops off while Paul furled the umbrella.

They saw Winters and Eliza immediately. Winters wondered if a flash of guilt passed over his boss' face. Keller's eyes darted around the room, perhaps looking for a table tucked away somewhere, but Lucky lifted her hand in greeting, said something to Paul, and they came over.

"John, Eliza. Nice to see you. Do you folks know Lucky Smith?"

Winters got to his feet. "I know Lucky well," he said. "Lucky, I'd like you to meet my wife, Eliza."

"The famous Lucky Smith," Eliza said. "I'm pleased to meet you at last."

Lucky laughed. She was short and dumpy with a mop of uncontrollable red hair, now mostly gray, and she emitted energy like a light bulb. "Good heavens, is that what I am?" She turned her smile to Paul Keller. "You might not want to be seen with me, Paul."

Keller returned the smile.

Eliza slid her chair back and got to her feet. "I'm sorry," she said, "but I have to be getting back to my shop. I've lingered over lunch far too long as it is. We're almost neighbors now, Lucky. I'm sure you know I've opened an art gallery where Mildred's Fashions used to be. Let's have lunch one day and you can give me some business tips."

"I'd like that."

John and Eliza left as Paul and Lucky were being shown to a table in the back.

"From what you've told me about Lucky Smith," Eliza said, opening her umbrella, "I wouldn't have imagined her and Paul as friends."

They began to walk. "No."

"That's a no that says a great deal."

"Paul told me Karen's gone to Calgary for a friend's daughter's wedding. He couldn't get away, he said, because of work, so she went alone. I can't think of anything so pressing he couldn't take a long weekend."

"John." Eliza sounded quite shocked. "Don't tell me you're reduced to spreading gossip."

"Just thinking out loud."

She shook her umbrella, folded it, and then unlocked the door and flipped the closed sign.

"If you have a minute," he said, "can you tell me what you meant earlier about Kyle hating his father? The guy disappeared, almost certainly against his will."

"Why must it have been against his will?"

"People can disappear, get new identities, start new lives. But they have to know what they're doing. We're ruled by numbers and everything is electronic. Transfer more than ten thousand dollars into a bank account and that triggers a money laundering flag. Can't get a job without a social insurance number, at least not a legal job. Can't go to the hospital or see a doctor without a health card. Can't even drive to the States without a passport or catch a local flight without photo ID any more. Most people, respectable law-abiding people, would have no idea where to go to get false ID. Not the sort of thing kids use to sneak into a bar, but good enough to fool government officials. It can be done, living under the radar completely, but not a guy like Nowak."

"Why not?"

"Because from everything I've read in Paul's notes the guy had no secret life. He wasn't in the witness protection program, he had never been a CSIS agent, never been in the military or police, he wasn't related to anyone in the mob. He was a middle-class Canadian guy who'd lived in Trafalgar for twenty years and worked at an insurance company. He wouldn't have lasted more than a week before doing something to trigger a record. Run out of cash and need to use an ATM, slap down a credit card thinking it would be okay just this once.

"Fifteen years ago it would have been easier to get across the border, but he would have had to have some sort of ID, driver's license most likely."

"Perhaps someone helped him get those things."

He shrugged. "Sure, anything's possible. Say you had to disappear, Eliza. Who would you go to? Who would you trust enough to lay your life in their hands?"

He could see her mind racing. "I have absolutely no idea," she said at last.

"And you, more than most people, have international contacts. Nowak could have left town without planning to be gone for long, or planned to disappear but never got far enough to need ID. But he didn't take his car, and no one came forward to say they'd given him a lift. I don't buy it."

She let out a breath. "Kyle was sixteen years old, don't forget. He's unlikely to have gone through the thought processes you have. He thinks his father abandoned the family, probably ran off with another woman. Apparently Mr. Nowak was quite the lady's man."

"How do you know that?"

"Kyle told me. His parents' marriage wasn't a good one, and his father was always having affairs with women in their social group. Mothers of his daughter's teammates, women from church. That sort of thing."

Kyle had mentioned something about his father being friendly with a woman from their church. Keller had spoken to her at the time, but she claimed to know nothing about Nowak's disappearance.

Was Kyle on the right track, but had the wrong woman?

Surely if a woman had run off at the same time Nowak disappeared that would have been mighty obvious. She could have been from out of town, but that didn't answer the question as to how he left and where he went and why he ended up with his bones scattered across a mountainside.

"You have your cop face back on," Eliza said.

"I have a cop face?"

"You certainly do. I can always tell when my husband leaves me and a police officer takes over. Makes me think of those horror movies where the mild-mannered innocent is possessed by the devil or some such creature."

"I shudder to know that you think I'm mild-mannered."

She leaned over and ran the tip of her tongue playfully across his lips. He started to respond, but she pulled back. "Only mild-mannered some of the time. Are you going into work?"

"No. This case has waited fifteen years, it can wait until Monday. I was going to go for a run, but not if it keeps raining. I might just relax with a good book."

Chapter Eighteen

First thing Monday morning, Winters checked the files for the name of the woman Keller had interviewed regarding Nowak's disappearance. Irene Sexton. Still living in the same home she'd been in fifteen years ago. Winters headed for the van.

Mrs. Sexton was in her sixties, pink-cheeked and robust, with slate-gray hair cropped short and piercing blue eyes.

"I was wondering when you'd call," she said before he'd introduced himself. "I read in the paper that Brian's body's been found." She drew a quick cross on her chest. "Poor man. I assume you're here in pursuit of common gossip that he and I were having a sordid affair and I ran off with him but changed my mind and came back to devote my life to good works as penitence. Oh, well, come in and let's get this over with."

She stepped back and held the door open. She lived in an older house nestled into the foot of the mountain. Tall and thin, stairs everywhere. Neat and clean and functional.

A substantially overweight beagle yawned at the newcomer from the living room couch. Mrs. Sexton shooed it down. It sniffed at Winters' pant leg, without much interest, before waddling into the kitchen. Presumably in search of something to eat.

"I have the kettle on. Won't be a minute. Take a seat," Mrs. Sexton said.

Winters eyed the dog-hair-encrusted couch warily, and then chose a chair that didn't seem to be one of the animal's favorite places to snooze.

The woman was back in moments, carrying a tray with tea pot, china cups and saucers, matching milk and sugar bowls, and a plate of cupcakes. The little cakes were decorated beautifully, pink icing piled high, topped with a candy rose petal.

"Church lunch tomorrow," Mrs. Sexton explained, pouring tea.

He took a cake and bit into it. The inside was as white as a cloud and tasted almost as light. The icing wasn't as sweet as it looked. He devoured the cupcake quickly.

Mrs. Sexton smiled at him. "Have another."

He took one. "I'm sorry to have to bring all this up again. Yes, I am here because there were rumors at the time you knew Mr. Nowak well."

"There were no rumors, Sergeant. Just that boy of his causing trouble. My husband died in 1994. Cancer. This is an old house and in the last two years of Ralph's life he wasn't able to maintain the house and we couldn't afford a contractor. After his death, Father O'Malley organized some of the men from church to come around to do what needed to be done, Brian among them. Brian continued to give me a hand when I needed it. Odd jobs mostly, leaky faucet, fence falling over. I paid him by sending baking home with him. That was the total extent of our relationship. I went to visit my sister in Prince Rupert the morning he disappeared. Didn't know anything about it until I got home three days later and found that the police were searching for me. That," she added firmly, "was most embarrassing."

He ate the second cupcake slowly. "Did you have any suspicions as to what happened?"

"Not a one. Some people said he ran off, but I never believed that. He was a good family man. I didn't like his wife, truth be told, she was as cold as a wet fish, and his son was a nasty piece of work. Most teenage boys are, I've found. But his daughter was a lovely girl, and he adored her. He wouldn't have abandoned them. He was a good Catholic family man," she repeated.

"Why do you think his son, Kyle, told people he was having an affair with you?"

"I'd forgotten his name. Yes, Kyle. Who knows what boys that age get up to? Perhaps he was projecting his own frustrated sexual desires onto his father. Living vicariously, so to speak."

She must have seen something in Winters' face, and she laughed. "I don't mean Kyle had a mad passion for me. I'm only saying that I understand boys of that age can be obsessed with sex. Yet not mature enough to understand that everyone else in the world doesn't think the same way they do."

Winters chose his words carefully. "Let's say hypothetically the boy was onto something. Had the wrong woman, perhaps. Were there rumors of Nowak having affairs?"

She shook her head. "I don't repeat gossip, Sergeant, but I can say I never heard any such rumor. The boy made it up out of whole cloth. Father O'Malley was the priest here then, still is. He knew the family as well as a priest does. Perhaps you can talk to him. He won't break the confessional, of course, but I'm sure he can put an end to this foolish line of enquiry." She stood up. "I have more than enough cupcakes for the luncheon. I'll prepare you a box to take home. I've seen your lovely wife around town, and can't imagine she's much of a cook."

Winters knew when he was dismissed.

A wave of heat washed over her as Lucky Smith opened the oven door. She peeked in. The lasagna was browning nicely. She'd made her specialty, what she modestly thought of as her world-famous five-hour lasagna. So called because that was the amount of time it took to make.

Andy had loved it.

She closed the door with a sigh. She'd made a lemon cake, another of Andy's favorites. Perhaps that was a mistake. Andy wouldn't be sitting down to dinner.

Sylvester jumped to his feet and ran to the door with a bark. Seconds later Lucky heard a truck coming up the long driveway. Moonlight and Adam. She smiled. She liked Adam, and he obviously adored Moonlight. Lucky was happy that after

Graham's death Moonlight had been able to move on and find love again.

Even if it was with a police officer.

She opened the door and Sylvester dashed out, overwhelmed with excitement. Adam and Moonlight got out of the truck and it pleased Lucky to see a third person climb out of the back seat. Christa. Next came Norman, Adam's police dog. Norman was a working animal, not a pet, but he tolerated the exuberant Sylvester.

Lucky suspected that Sylvester hero-worshiped the other dog.

Everyone trooped into the kitchen, tripping over dogs.

"Smells fantastic," Adam said, giving Lucky a light kiss on the cheek.

"I brought you something." Christa handed her a bunch of pink carnations.

"Thank you, dear."

"It's been too long."

"Yes, it has."

Moonlight gave her mom a hug before going to the fridge to get a beer for Adam and wine for the women. She twisted the cap off the bottle. Lucky had laid glasses on the table, and Moonlight began to pour. "One for you, Mom?"

"Please, dear."

"Why are there five places set?" Moonlight put the bottle down and looked at her mother. The girl's eyes were full of water.

Lucky swallowed. "I didn't forget your father won't be joining us. Although sometimes I do."

Moonlight wrapped her mother in a tight hug. Adam and Christa shifted their feet. Norman helped himself to the contents of Sylvester's water bowl.

"Who's coming?" Moonlight said, pulling away from the hug.

Sylvester barked and Lucky said, "That must be him now."

She went to the door. Paul Keller had been in Big Eddie's when she'd invited Christa to tonight's dinner. Somehow on Saturday, when they were having lunch in town, he'd invited himself.

She didn't mind. She always loved having a houseful at meal times and missed no longer having anyone to cook for.

"Mom," Moonlight said from behind her. "You have not invited my boss for dinner, have you?"

"His wife's out of town and I thought he'd enjoy a good meal."

"How do you know his wife's out of town?"

"Paul, welcome," Lucky said. "I'm so glad you could make it."

He was carrying an enormous bouquet of peach roses and had a bottle of wine tucked under one arm and a big smile on his face.

"Wine or beer?" Lucky asked, accepting the flowers.

"A beer would be good."

"Moonlight?"

"What?"

"Can you get another beer?"

"Beer?"

"Paul would like a beer."

"Oh, right."

"Dinner will be about half an hour. It's too wet to sit outside, I'm afraid. Let's go into the living room for a visit. Now, Paul, I hope you remember I told you there will be no police talk here tonight."

"I'd like to know what's happening with Brian Nowak," Christa said. "I remember when that happened. You were friends with Nicky, weren't you, Molly?"

"I was. She lives in Vancouver now, came back when she heard he'd been found. I had a drink with her the other night." Moonlight stole a glance at Adam. "She's turned out to be beautiful."

"Really?" Adam said, "I hadn't noticed."

"Owns an interior decorating company."

Adam snorted.

"What's that mean?"

"Nothing. Good beer, this." He hurried into the living room.

"So much for no police talk," Lucky said with a sigh.

She followed her guests.

Chapter Nineteen

Steve Brooks, Brian Nowak's former boss, told John Winters now that he was retired, he and his wife spent every winter in Hawaii. They left on a Tuesday, the day after Thanksgiving. No life like it, ha ha. Retirement: best job I've ever had. He laughed heartily at his own joke and pulled out photographs of the condo on Maui.

Winters refrained from rolling his eyes, admired the pictures, agreed that he too was looking forward to retirement and yes, Hawaii was a nice place, tried to refuse tea, but finally managed to get the conversation on track by explaining he was short on time.

Mrs. Brooks served tea while the two men settled into patio chairs on the deck.

"I remember it as if it happened yesterday," Brooks said. "Hard to forget. Brian didn't come to work that Monday morning. He was always punctual, so when he was late, Patty, that was my receptionist, works at the Royal Bank now if you want to talk to her, checked his diary. He had no appointments indicated. We didn't think much about it, figured he'd forgotten to tell Patty he had a call to make before coming into the office, although he was good at keeping her notified of his schedule. Around ten or so his wife called. Looking for him." Brooks shook his head. "What do you say to a woman who assumes her husband's at work?"

"What did you say?"

"That he wasn't there, of course."

"How did she take that?"

"She apologized for disturbing me, said there must have been a misunderstanding. She was about to hang up, so I asked her when she'd seen Brian last. Sunday after church she said. She repeated that she must have made a mistake. Sorry to bother me. She hung up."

"What did you think?"

"That it was mighty strange, that's what I thought. Patty and I talked it over. You see, Brian wasn't the type to spend the night away from home. He wasn't much of a drinker, not into following sports, didn't go to bars. If he had any vices he kept them secret."

"Do you think he had any? Vices?"

"No. He was an ordinary guy who worked for me for five years."

"Would you say Mr. Nowak was a happy man?"

"How do you define happy?" Mrs. Brooks said.

A hard question to answer.

"Tell you the truth, Sergeant, Brian was a lousy salesman. Aside from the matter of his disappearing the way he did, I wasn't all that disappointed to see him leave. I was thinking of letting him go. You ask if he was happy. Sure, I guess he was. Can't say any different. We got together with his wife and him now and again. Office parties, that sort of thing, nothing personal. The wife, don't remember her name, seemed nice enough."

Mrs. Brooks nodded. "Marjorie was her name. I liked her. I tried to befriend her after Brian… left. I made a casserole, took some groceries around, invited her out to lunch, my treat. She took the food and groceries, refused lunch, and didn't invite me to come back. I haven't seen her for quite some time."

"Did you speculate about what happened to Brian Nowak?"

Mrs. Brooks shook her head and her husband said, "I figured it was obvious."

"It was?"

"Guy must have come across a crime being committed. Saw something, or someone, he shouldn't have. So he was grabbed, taken out of town, killed and dumped. I always figured he was in the woods somewhere, didn't I say that, Elena?"

"Yes, dear. You did."

"Turns out I was right."

The thought, Winters knew, had occurred to Keller as well. What Nowak might have seen in the couple of blocks between his house and the convenience store had never been discovered.

"You don't think he simply ran off?"

"Who knows what people do, sergeant? Or why. But nope, I don't. He was a normal guy, solid citizen. That's why I hadn't gotten around to firing him. I couldn't bring myself to tell him he was out of a job. I always was too soft for my own good, wasn't I, Elena?"

"Yes, dear."

◇◇◇

Brian Nowak had one brother, Kevin, living in Toronto. Winters phoned him, but the man said he hadn't heard from his brother in fifteen years. Like everyone else Winters spoke to, Kevin Nowak claimed that Brian had no noticeable vices, no secret past. No reason to walk out his front door and disappear.

Winters was beginning to wonder if Steve Brooks had been right. Had person or persons unknown grabbed Brian Nowak on his way to buy cigarettes, dumped him in the woods, and left Trafalgar?

Had Nowak seen something he wasn't supposed to?

If so, whoever was responsible had fifteen years to cover their tracks.

Nowak had been gone for a couple of days before the case became a police priority and Keller searched the Nowak home. He'd found nothing of interest. The man's clothes were neatly hung in the bedroom closet, his shaving things on the bathroom shelf. His driver's license and credit cards were missing but it was assumed he would have taken his wallet when he went to the store. They'd found well-thumbed copies of *Playboy* and *Hustler* magazines in the desk in his den, but nothing illegal. No kiddie or violent porn. The family didn't have a computer, but in 1996 that wasn't unusual. A search of his bank account uncovered nothing out of the ordinary.

Other than the ten thousand dollars that had passed in, and out again, in a matter of weeks.

Keller had wondered if the man had a gambling problem, but Nowak didn't travel much, if at all, beyond the occasional Christmas visit with the family to his brother. He wasn't spending weekends in Vegas or Atlantic City.

Winters put his feet up on his desk and stared out the windows. By all accounts Brian Nowak was a pretty ordinary guy.

The only unordinary thing about him was his death.

Chapter Twenty

Molly Smith shifted the substantial weight of her belt. "Would you like to come for a ride, Mrs. Galloway?"

"That would be lovely. Where shall we go?"

"How about home?"

Smith reached out her hand and helped the elderly lady to her feet. She lived with her daughter and son-in-law, who had four children under five including infant twins, and couldn't always give the old lady the attention she needed. She was well known to the Trafalgar City Police.

Mrs. Galloway blinked. Her eyes were enormous under thick glasses, watery and confused. "Do I know you, dear?"

"Yes, ma'am. I'm Constable Smith."

"Now I remember. You're such a nice young man."

"Right. My car's over here."

"Perhaps I should wait for the bus."

"I'd be happy to give you a ride."

It was one o'clock in the morning. It had rained earlier and the wet streets reflected the blinking yellow of the traffic lights. A car passed slowly, the only one she'd seen in the last five minutes. White faces peered out, hoping to see some action. The dark bulk of the mountains loomed over the town, the flashing red light on the top warning airplanes away.

Mrs. Galloway's daughter had gotten up for a crying baby and saw her mother's bedroom door open. The bed empty, the front door unlocked.

The old lady, dressed as if going to work or shopping, had walked two kilometers into town and was sitting at the bus stop, patiently waiting for a bus to pull up and take her who-knows-where.

This couldn't go on. It was the second time in three months the police had been called to find the poor thing. The last time she'd been sitting on a bench outside Big Eddie's, waiting for them to open. Which would have been in about six hours.

Mrs. Galloway was lucky it was the police who found her, not someone looking to make trouble. She was as innocent and docile as a toddler.

Smith helped her into the passenger seat of the patrol car.

"How's your wife?" Mrs. Galloway asked politely as they pulled into the deserted street.

"Fine," Smith said. She had no idea who Mrs. Galloway thought she was. Probably back in a world where all people in dark blue uniforms were men. She was eighty-nine years old. Her mind was mush, but her body was in as good shape as a woman in her sixties.

Which would I rather lose first, Smith thought, *my mind or my body?*

She shivered.

Mrs. Galloway began to chat about someone named Alice who was getting married and Smith drove her home through the empty rain-slicked streets.

She delivered the woman, now chatting about a trip to Toronto next month, to her home where a young woman, baby balanced on her hip, stood in the open door, framed in yellow light.

"Oh, Mom," she said. "I don't know what I'm going to do."

"You shouldn't be up this late," Mrs. Galloway said. "Children need regular hours."

"Thank you, constable."

"My pleasure. You know you have to speak to someone about this, don't you? Next time she might head into the woods." Smith thought of Norman scratching at long-missing bones.

"We've been putting off making a decision, but I guess we can't do that much longer. Thank you again."

"Good night."

The woman drew her mother inside and closed the door.

Smith went back to her car.

It was cool, a sign of winter on the way. A breeze stirred the leaves in the walnut trees lining the road, and the scent of wet grass was heavy on the wind.

Up the mountain a coyote howled.

She drove back to town. Up and down the quiet, dark streets. Her eyes constantly moved but her mind wandered.

It had been awkward, to say the least, last night at her mom's. The chief constable coming for dinner. Sitting in Dad's place. Mom laughing at his stupid jokes.

Smith had virtually shoved Adam and Christa out the door as soon as they finished dessert. Keller followed, somewhat reluctantly.

"Everyone's talking about them, you know," Christa said from the back seat.

"Talking about who?" Smith asked, although she would rather not know.

"Your mom and Chief Keller."

Adam laughed and Smith glared at him. "Nonsense."

"I'm telling you, Molly. I was in the bagel line at Big Eddie's this morning, and that woman who works at George's on the weekends was behind me, and she told her friend that Lucky Smith had come in for lunch with Paul Keller on Saturday. And then Jolene looks up from making bagel sandwiches and said they were in here one day too. Together. Laughing and having a grand old time."

"You're talking rubbish."

"Molly," Tocek said, "Christa's only telling you what she heard."

"Yeah. They're two of the most prominent people in town. Everyone knows the chief and almost everyone knows your mom. They're like chalk and cheese. Can't imagine an odder couple."

"They are not a couple."

"I meant couple of people, not a romantic couple." Christa let out a bark of laughter. "Oh, god. Maybe that is what I meant. Did you see those flowers he brought, and the way he smiled all night?"

"He's married," Smith said, remembering that her mom never did tell her how she knew the chief's wife was out of town. "She invited him around for dinner because his wife's away."

"I wondered where she was," Christa said.

Town came into view. A thin line of lights clinging to the riverbanks and crawling up the lower levels of the mountain. The big black bridge over the Upper Kootenay River clattered as the truck drove over it.

"Do you think you should tell Lucky people are talking about her?" Tocek asked.

"There's nothing to tell. You know Mom, she likes people. She thinks she has to look after them. If Mrs. Keller is away, then Mom probably thought the chief needed feeding, that's all."

Adam pulled up in front of the old house where Christa occupied the top floor. Street lights shone though the leaves of the walnut trees lining the sidewalks, bathing them in a soft yellow glow.

"I bet that's it. Thanks for the ride, Adam." Christa leaned forward and touched Smith's shoulder. "It's been too long, Molly. My fault."

Smith laid her hand on her friend's. "See you soon, eh?"

Christa gave Norman a slap on the hip in farewell, opened the door, and began to get out. "He must really need feeding. Coffee, lunch, now dinner." She laughed heartily and slammed the door.

"What are you smiling at?" Smith said to Tocek.

"Nothing."

"Make sure you don't," she'd said.

Smith had long suspected the chief had a crush on her mother. Was he moving in now Lucky's husband was gone? The chief was married, for heaven's sake. His wife was all over the community: hospital board, Rotary, the arts' council, volunteer at the museum, the BIA.

"Five-one?"

"Five-one here."

"Noise complaint. 90 Elm Street. Loud music and people shouting."

"Ten-four," she said, all thoughts of her mother gone.

Elm was a quiet street of nice houses and clean sidewalks. They didn't often get complaints there. She turned downhill and drove through the dark streets. She didn't need the house number, she could hear the noise before she even turned the corner.

A group of young people were on the lawn outside one of the bigger, newer homes. There were about ten of them, dancing on the grass. Music blared from the open windows. As Smith pulled up, a young woman shoved her glass into another woman's hand, broke away from the crowd, and ran toward the car. A long summer dress clung to her thin body and her feet were bare. Smith told dispatch she'd arrived and got out of the vehicle.

"I'm sorry, officer," the woman said before Smith could open her mouth. "Are we being too noisy?" Shiny blond hair swung around her shoulders and her embarrassed smile showed perfect teeth.

"Yes," Smith replied. She studied the woman's face. Her pupils were normal sized, her face clear, although her make up was a bit smudged. The scent of pot hung over her. "It's two o'clock. Are you having a party?"

"Yup. It's my birthday."

Smith doubted the young woman was the owner of this house. "Are your parents inside?"

"They've gone to a hotel for the evening, so I could have my party."

Big mistake that, Smith thought. The music ended abruptly. The rest of the crowd had stopped dancing and were standing watching, feet shifting. She saw a couple of faces she recognized, but just from around town: these people kept themselves out of trouble.

Smith asked the young woman for her name and she gave it, full of profuse apologies. "It's getting a bit hot in the house, you see. So much cooler outside after the rain."

"Nevertheless you'll have to take it back inside," Smith said.

"Okay. Sorry, Officer. We'll be quiet."

"Make sure you are."

"Uh, you won't tell my parents, will you?"

"No. Not unless I have to come back here tonight."

"Thanks."

"Good night."

The woman ran across the lawn, waving her arms, shooing her friends back inside.

The radio on Smith's shoulder squawked.

"Five-one?"

"Five-one. Finished at Elm Street. They promise no further trouble."

"Can you take a call at 324 Redwood Street? Neighbors report they hear shouts and a woman screaming."

"Ten-four."

She jumped back into the car and punched buttons to bring up the lights and sirens, did a U-turn in the middle of the road and headed back up the hill.

Redwood Street was quite a contrast to Elm. Older houses, many falling into disrepair. Most rented out or divided into apartments. Weed-choked gardens, broken fences, old furniture piled on front porches to rot in the rain and snow.

Half-way down the block a man stepped forward and lifted a hand to flag her down.

She pulled up and sat in the car for a moment. A couple of blocks further down this street she'd killed a man. She didn't think about it much. Not any more. She took a breath, radioed that she'd arrived, and got out of the car.

"It's gone quiet," the man said, pointing to a dilapidated house behind him. "but a couple of minutes ago a woman was screaming and a man yelling."

"Do you know the people who live here?"

"No. I'm Gerry Mann," he waved his hand to his left. "My wife and I live next door. These people moved in a week or so ago. The house is a rental and it has a high turnover."

"Thanks. I'll check on it." An old car, more rust than metal, squatted in the gravel and weed driveway.

She touched her radio and read out the license plate, adding, "Can you send me some backup, Ingrid?"

"Four-two has an ETA of about five minutes."

She started up the driveway. The front door opened and a man came out. He was big, with a bald head, broad shoulders, and slim hips, dressed in jeans and a dirty white T-shirt tucked into a wide belt. He shut the door behind him and walked toward her, hands stuffed into his pockets. "What seems to be the problem here, constable?" He looked into her face, and then his eyes darted away.

"We've had a report of a disturbance. Can you take your hands out of your pockets please?"

"Why?"

"Because I'm asking you to."

One at a time, he lifted his hands. "We were watching a movie, the girlfriend and me. A horror movie. She loves horror but it really scares her, you know. So she screamed at the scary bits." He grinned at her. No warmth was in his smile and his eyes were dark. He shot a look at the watching neighbor. It was not friendly. "I'll tell her to keep it down next time."

He took a step toward Smith. She could smell beer and rancid sweat.

"Stay where you are, please," she said.

He stopped walking and planted his legs firmly in the path. His eyes moved, looking at everything but her. The short hairs at the back of her neck tingled, and she placed her hand on the baton on her belt. "What's your name?"

"Jim."

"Jim what?"

"Jim Ferguson."

"Is that your car, Mr. Ferguson?"

"Yup."

The radio crackled. The vehicle was owned by James Ferguson. No outstanding warrants, but one conviction and jail time for assault causing bodily harm.

"I'd like a word with your girlfriend."

"She's gone to bed."

"Nevertheless, I would like a word with her. Will you please ask her to come outside and talk to me, otherwise I'll have to go in and check on her."

"Okay, okay. Not a problem." His arms were at his sides but his fists were clenched. His shoulders were tight and a vein bulged in his neck.

Where the hell is that backup?

He moved without making a sound.

Chapter Twenty-one

His hands hit Smith's chest, hard, and she tumbled backwards. Instinctively, she dropped her arms and rolled on her butt to break her fall. Her lower back hit the ground but she kept her head up and her feet planted on the ground. Then he was down, dropping to his knees, looming over her. He lifted a fist, his black eyes were clouded with rage and spittle rained down on her face.

This is not training. This is not Dawn Solway taking me through the moves. No plush mats, no laughter.

No second tries.

She lifted her right leg and pushed against his chest, holding him back, knowing the leg would soon give way. She hooked it around his hip. He fell toward her. She stretched out her other leg and, with a shout to give her strength, brought them both in. Her bottom leg chopped his knee out from under him and the upper leg knocked him to one side.

She heard a siren in the distance and someone yelling. She leapt to her feet, blood pounding in her head. He was on his back. "Fucking bitch," he roared. He shook his head and started to move.

She couldn't let him get up. He had muscle and power.

All she had was speed, agility, and training.

She dropped down, placed her right knee in his sternum and held the other leg wide for balance. Pressing all her weight into her right knee, she grabbed his arm and pulled it toward her.

Her other arm gripped the back of his head and jerked it in. Unable to breathe, in considerable pain, the fight abandoned him. She felt the moment he surrendered.

She released his head, grabbed his hand and got her feet, rolling him onto his stomach as she moved.

By the time Dave Evans reached her Jim Ferguson was face down in the grass, hands cuffed behind his back.

"Nice," Evans said, somewhat grudgingly.

"That was fabulous." The neighbor clapped his hands.

"Call an ambulance," Smith said. Her heart was pounding, and now that it was all over she was terrified. Her knees felt like rubber. Her voice quavered. "Get buddy into a car. I have to check the house."

"I'll take the house."

"No. I have to do it." If she went back to the car, she was afraid she'd crawl in and never leave.

"Don't go inside without me," Evans said. "I'll be right back. He jerked Jim Ferguson to his feet. The fight had been knocked out of the man, and he let himself be led away, head down, face red.

Evans stuffed him into the back of the car and joined Smith on the steps.

They stood on either side of the door, and Smith reached for the knob. She turned it shouting, "Police."

The door swung open. Smith went in first. Evans followed.

The room was a mess of mismatched furniture and cardboard boxes. It smelled of burned food and spilled beer. The cheap coffee table was covered with brown bottles, overflowing ashtrays, an empty pizza box. Smith kicked a bottle out of the way and it rolled under the couch. A woman sat against the far wall, legs outstretched. She cradled one arm to her chest. Her left eye was open, the right swollen shut. Blood leaked from her smashed nose and a vicious cut on the side of her forehead. Her face was a mess of blood, snot, and sweat. Smith dropped to her knees beside the woman, as Evans repeated the call for an ambulance.

"Hi," the woman said through broken teeth and bloody, swollen lips. "Hurts."

"Help's coming. Don't try to move."

"Jim?"

"He's in custody."

"New boyfriend. Mistake, eh?"

"Welcome to the party," Evans said. Smith got to her feet and let the paramedics do their job.

Chapter Twenty-two

"I'm thinking of staying on for a while."

"You can't do that. You've got appointments. Leung tomorrow. Should be the last time, we've got enough to make our move."

"Call them and tell them I'm sick. Maybe not, they'll think I've got AIDS or something yucky. Tell them I had to rush to my dying mother's bedside. That's a good one, play the pity card and they might leave a big tip next time."

"Nicole, you're not running out on me are you? I thought you hated your mother and that town."

"I'm going to say a few more days, Joey. They're pretty sure it's my dad they've found and I want to be here when they tell us for sure. But, because I don't want my stay here to be a total waste of time, I have a plan."

She eyed herself in the bedroom mirror. Tiny red sticker hearts were stuck to the glass. If she had to hang around her mother's house, where the TV blared all afternoon and evening, she'd go insane.

"What kind of plan?"

"There's a guy here. Nice-looking, a prominent, respectable citizen. His wife's loaded. I did some checking on the Internet and she's a model, moves in the big leagues, at least what passes for big leagues in Canada. Owns two art galleries, which means she's got to be concerned about her image."

"What's he do?"

"He's a cop."

"Are you nuts? We don't mess with the cops."

"Hear me out." She ran her fingers through her hair. "Small-town cop, small-town gossip. Rich wife. He won't wanna sully his image, or get the wife pissed off at him."

"No. For one thing, maybe she keeps him on a short leash. You don't know if he has access to the sort of money that'll make it worth our while. Plus, you're not set up there. What you gonna do, fuck him in your mother's house?"

Nicole looked around her bedroom. Now that would be fun. While Ricky Martin on the wall watched. She'd moan loud enough for her mother to hear in the room across the hall.

This house could use some action.

"You need cameras, remember," Joey went on. "Out of sight. Remotely operated. Your mother isn't likely to let me into your bedroom to install the equipment."

"If I'm not in there, she won't care. Say you're fixing a window or something."

"This is a bad idea. It's not going to happen."

"Can't I have some fun for once? It's not often I get to do it with a guy I can stand to touch."

"I'm warning you, Nicole. I won't have any part of it, and if you go freelance and you're busted, that'll be the end of our relationship."

"Oh, pooh." She stuck her tongue out at her reflection in the mirror.

"I'll see you tomorrow then."

"No. Like I said, I'm staying at least another week." Wouldn't hurt to make sure Joey remembered this was a partnership. Sometimes he started acting as though he were the boss.

Never forget which one of them was doing the *real* work.

Chapter Twenty-three

Winters paid a call on the priest at Sacred Heart. Father O'Malley was in his office, surrounded by piles of papers. The man was dressed in a blue track suit and well-worn running shoes, but the office might have come out of a chapter in Dickens. Heavy red wallpaper tearing along the edges, scarred and battered desk, overflowing bookcase, faded armchair covered with cigarette burns. No computer, no fax, no printer. A black telephone with a heavy receiver and a rotary dial squatted on the desk, the only nod to modernity, albeit 1950s-era modernity, in the room.

The priest stood up and came around the desk to shake hands. He gestured toward his clothes. "Pardon the attire. I've come from the tennis court and haven't had time to change."

"I appreciate you seeing me, Father." Winters said.

"You've caught me just in time. I'm moving out next month. Retirement. I've been at this parish for almost thirty years. I'm sure my superiors have left me alone because they think this is a provincial backwater, but I've been glad of it."

"You were here when Brian Nowak disappeared?"

"Yes. I hear he's been found. What's left of him, they say."

"Positive identification hasn't been made yet, but it's close enough to reopen the investigation."

"Marjorie hasn't wanted to see me for many years," the priest said. "Nevertheless, I'll go around and offer what help I can."

Winters asked the old priest what he remembered about the Nowak family and learned nothing new. Brian Nowak was an upstanding member of the community, a good family man, good Catholic. His daughter, Nicky, was a lovely young woman, polite and respectful, a good athlete, if memory served. The boy, what was his name? Something with a y in it. Ryan. No Kyle. Kyle was a handful. Rude, sullen, rarely attended Mass, never confession. But no worse than many other boys of that age.

Winters asked about women. Any hint of affairs with women in the congregation?

"Most definitely not. The idea is preposterous. Brian was faithful to his wife and a good father to his children."

"After Nowak's disappearance, I gather times were difficult for the family."

The priest shook his head. "Hard. I did what I could, Sergeant Winters, but I'm sorry to say I failed. I called in regularly to check if they needed anything. I organized men from the congregation to help with yard work or maintenance that needed doing. The parish women took meals, groceries sometimes because we knew Marjorie had been left without financial support. She had family, a couple of siblings I believe, but they didn't seem to be able to help her."

"Perhaps she didn't want to ask."

"I suspect that has something to do with it. She didn't want my help, our help, either. I tried to explain to her about the purpose of the church community. How we all come together when one of our members needs us, and I knew that she and Brian would have done the same if others needed help. It's not charity. She didn't see it that way. A couple of months after Brian's disappearance, several of the ladies made plans to attend a weekend church retreat. They invited Marjorie to accompany them, arranged for someone to look after her children, offered to pay her expenses. Her son, Kyle, shut the door in their faces.

"Marjorie's anger was a terrible thing to see. Anger at God for taking her husband, resentment of everyone else. She was viciously rude to people who only tried to help, angry at me for interfering. I should have tried harder. The boy was difficult even before his father disappeared, but the girl needed our help.

Marjorie stopped coming to Mass and removed Nicky from all of her church activities. I heard she'd quit school sports teams and wasn't allowed to take a summer job assisting at a children's camp she'd been offered. I'm ashamed to say, Sergeant, I let it go. Marjorie became more and more reclusive, and she forced her children to be reclusive with her. She was angry at God, and I could understand that. I prayed she would someday find it in her heart to forgive God and return to church. Nicky quit school as soon as she turned sixteen and left town." He shook his head. "Another lost soul."

Winters left after wishing Father O'Malley well in his retirement. He got the feeling the old man wasn't looking forward to it.

He hadn't learned anything, hadn't really expected to.

Everyone insisted that Brian Nowak was a "good family man". They said the words almost by rote, as if they were expected to do so.

Or was John Winters just too cynical? Maybe it was time for him to follow Father O'Malley out to pasture.

Detective Ray Lopez, the only other member of the General Investigative Section, was at his desk when Winters came in. Winters glanced over Lopez's shoulder at his computer screen.

"Hard at work?" he asked.

Lopez pointed proudly to the picture displayed. "Cup winners." It was a girls' soccer team. Shiny ponytails, big smiles, scuffed knees, filthy shoes. Winters recognized Lopez's youngest daughter Becky front and center.

"Congratulations."

Lopez's chest puffed up, just a little. "Once I've finished reliving my moment of glory as father of the winning-goal scorer, I'll get back to work. We finally gave in and let Becky have a puppy. I'm thinking that might not have been my best idea."

He moved the mouse and the picture went away. "Guess who's back in town?" A smile touched the corners of Lopez's mouth.

"I probably don't want to know, but you'll tell me anyway."

"Ronnie Kilpatrick."

"Why are you looking so pleased at that? Guy's a bottom feeder. I knew he'd be getting out soon, but foolishly hoped he'd find someplace else to go."

Lopez pointed to the computer. "He let all his buddies on Facebook know he's back. He's at his mom's house and interested in doing, quote, business."

Winters laughed. "You're one of his Facebook friends?"

"If they weren't morons we wouldn't catch half of them."

"True enough."

Still chuckling, Winters headed into town to get something for lunch. He usually had the officer who took the run to Germantown Deli to get lunch for the prisoners in the cells pick him up a sandwich, but today he was in the mood for something hot and spicy. The day was warm, but the deciduous trees on the mountains were a brilliant yellow, heralding winter soon to come. He went to Trafalgar Thai to pick up a yellow curry. When he got back, carrying a plastic bag emitting clouds of mouth-watering steam, a man stepped out from the doorway of the library next to the police station.

"Sergeant Winters?"

"Can I help you?"

"Forgive me for laying in wait like this. My name's Greg Hunt. I've been wanting to talk to you about Brian Nowak, but everyone keeps putting me off. Did the policewoman I spoke to even tell you what I had to say?"

Winters shifted his lunch bag. "She did. You're wanting to know the progress of the case. The media will be informed in due course."

"I'm not with the media. I'm a citizen. Just an ordinary citizen. Brian was my friend. I think I have the right to know what's going on."

"Do you have some new information for me?"

"No."

"Then you don't have any rights to information about this investigation." Hunt was about Winters' age, a bit older perhaps, in his early fifties. He was short and slightly built with thick eyeglasses magnifying rapidly blinking pale blue eyes. He twisted his hands together as he talked. He was well dressed in casual pants and a beige shirt, open at the neck. Winters knew who he was: owner of a local real estate company. He didn't remember seeing the man's name in Keller's reports.

"Did you speak to Sergeant Keller at the time of the initial investigation?"

"I had nothing to tell him," Hunt sighed. "I have nothing to tell you. I want to know what happened to Brian, that's all. He was here one day, gone the next. It was… most upsetting, for the community, for everyone. And now they're saying he's been found."

"You were friends. Did you and your wife go to the same church, did you live near them?"

"I'm in real estate. Brian was in insurance. A natural enough reason to be acquainted."

Winters' lunch was getting cold. "Did Mr. Nowak say anything to you about leaving town?"

"He wasn't, at least as far as I know, planning on going anywhere without…"

"Without?"

"Telling anyone."

"When did you see him last?"

Hunt sighed. He took off his glasses to rub his eyes. "A few days before. We had a beer after work. I'm sorry to have bothered you, Sergeant Winters. I hope I haven't spoiled your lunch."

He walked away, heading downhill toward town, a small sad figure. Winters suspected that Greg Hunt didn't have many friends.

He took his now-cold lunch back to his desk and ate while leafing through Paul Keller's notes. The phone rang as he scooped up the last mouthful of thick yellow sauce.

It was the Provincial Parks office. They'd checked into all cases of cars abandoned in their jurisdiction, and nothing had been reported in Koola Park for the years in question.

Winters thanked them and hung up. His hand was still on the phone when it rang again.

"We're packing it in," Ray Gavin said without words of introduction. "I figure we've found all we're going to find."

"How much do you have?"

"Nothing more than the last time we spoke. A goodly part of the skeleton, but not the entire thing. Missing most of the skull, all of one leg, a lot of ribs. No signs of violence or trauma, other than what you'd expect being out in the woods for fifteen years. The odontologist has finished his work and says he's as positive as he can be that the teeth are those of Brian Nowak. We suspected that anyway, right?"

"Thanks, Ron. I'll let Mrs. Nowak know we'll be releasing the body." He made a note to contact Father O'Malley as well. Unlikely Mrs. Nowak would be able to handle the arrangements herself.

"Let me know how it goes."

Winters tossed the food packaging into the garbage. He'd give this case another day, and then wrap it up. With no new evidence, other than the sizeable matter of the body, he wasn't making any inroads onto Paul's original investigation. The same people saying much the same things they had fifteen years ago.

He flipped through the box of reports. Nothing on Greg Hunt. It seemed Keller hadn't spoken to him. Which was meaningless as the man had nothing to say.

As for the idea that Nowak was some local lothario, Winters could find no evidence. Women reported him as being nothing but polite. Although they wouldn't necessarily up and confess if they were having an illicit relationship. The priest thought the idea preposterous, but he might be the last person to really know what was going on amongst his flock if no one brought it to confession.

Nevertheless there didn't seem to be a hint of impropriety, at least not where women were concerned.

Some mysteries remained mysteries.

Tough on the family, though.

Chapter Twenty-four

Not knowing what the situation would be regarding her father, Nicole had brought a lot of clothes with her. She was ready for every occasion.

The priest was paying a visit. Father O'Malley, the same guy who'd been priest when she was a kid. She remembered him as a creepy old man, basking in the fawning adoration of devout women such as her mother. Trying to pretend he understood—or even cared—about young people and their world. Always organizing tennis and baseball games as if he were one of the kids.

Nothing had changed. Now he was older and if anything even creepier.

Her mom had been a not-bad baker when they were growing up. She could be counted on to do a nice cake for birthday parties, decorate cupcakes for church bake sales, bring an edible pie to a pot-luck. For Father O'Malley's visit today she opened a bag of chocolate chip cookies that must have been in the back of the cupboard since the house had been built.

Nicky would feel sorry for her mother if the bitch hadn't brought it all on herself. She had as much backbone as the quivering mass of red jelly she'd made for tonight's dessert.

Father O'Malley mumbled routine platitudes, while Mom wrung her hands and dabbed at her eyes and drank up his attention. Kyle had not bothered to show.

The police had called to tell Mom the body would be released within a couple of days, and Father O'Malley dropped by to offer his help with the arrangements.

The body. A bag of bones more likely.

All the air rushed out of her lungs and she felt a lump rise in her throat. She pushed it back and gave Father O'Malley one of her most seductive smiles.

Sometimes she pretended to herself that it was possible her dad had had a fall, hit his head, got amnesia, been picked up at the side of the road by a well-meaning passer-by, taken to someplace like the Yukon or Mexico where news of the search for him wouldn't reach.

But really, deep down where she kept the thoughts that could only fight their way to the surface when she was alone and drinking hard, she knew if he'd wanted to come back, he would have.

He'd deserted his family, run away. With a woman probably. Perhaps he'd started another family; maybe she had a half-sister somewhere.

A little girl he loved more than he loved Nicky.

It would have been so much better if he'd died. But the police kept saying there was no evidence he'd been killed or had an accident.

All these years, she'd thought she'd be nothing but relieved when he was found. Relieved that the uncertainly was at last over. She should have been pleased to find out he hadn't run out on her. That he hadn't had another family, another daughter.

But now she understood that she'd have preferred it if he'd started a new life. Rather than lie alone on the mountainside while rain and snow fell and wind blew and the seasons and years passed and his body rotted away leaving only a scattering of bones for animals to fight over.

Tears pricked behind her eyes, as she sat in her mother's living room knowing she no longer had even an impossible dream to cling to.

Dad was dead, and they were discussing plans for his funeral.

She'd deliberately worn a tight, low-cut T-shirt and short denim skirt for the priest's visit. When he first arrived, and Mom was bustling about with tea things, Nicole had leaned back and crossed and uncrossed her legs and dangled her high-heeled sandal from the tip of her toes. The old man didn't react as she'd hoped, either by getting a hard on or glaring at her as though summoning lightning to strike her down.

Maybe he preferred boys. Didn't they all?

Or maybe he just believed in his vows of chastity.

She felt a niggle of what might have been shame. The man was here to talk about her father's funeral. She sat up straight, pulled a cushion onto her lap, and paid attention to the discussion about the service.

◇◇◇

Lucky Smith tucked her hair into its habitual bun at the back of her head. She studied herself in the mirror.

She looked like a grandmother.

She was a grandmother, but no need to look like one.

She took the hair out of its pins and rearranged it, tying the front pieces back and letting the rest fall.

Now she looked like a grandmother trying not to look like a grandmother.

She let it stay that way.

Paul Keller had called shortly after lunch, to ask if he could stop by later with more questions about Brian Nowak. Lucky sensed he was enjoying getting the chance to play detective again. His wife wasn't back from her trip to Calgary, so somehow Lucky found herself suggesting he come around for dinner again.

Life-long feminist that she was, Lucky still couldn't stop thinking a man on his own needed a woman to cook for him.

She patted a bit of blush on her cheeks and went downstairs, Sylvester padding along behind. She'd taken a container of beef stew out of the freezer and put it in the oven to reheat. She was standing over the sink, scrubbing potatoes from her own garden when the dog ran to the door with a bark and Lucky looked out to see Paul's SUV coming up the drive.

She tossed the potatoes in a pot of water set to boil before opening the door. Sylvester ran out to offer his greetings.

"Really, Paul, you don't have to bring flowers every time you visit."

"I like buying flowers." The bouquet of soft pink roses was so large he was almost hidden behind it.

"I doubt you bring flowers to all your witnesses." She accepted the gift with a laugh. "Help yourself to a beer while I find a vase for these." The bouquet he'd brought on Monday was still fresh and lovely on the sideboard. "Let's get business out of the way first and then we can enjoy our dinner."

"Good idea." He opened the fridge and found the open bottle of Chardonnay, left from Monday's dinner. "Wine?"

"Why ever not? Have you learned something new about Brian? Is that why you wanted to see to me?"

"I never need an excuse to see you, Lucky," he said. His voice broke and she tossed him a startled glance. *What an odd thing to say.*

He cleared his throat. "The dental identification has been completed and the forensic dentist is prepared to say the remains belong to Brian Nowak. We'll be releasing the body as soon as Mrs. Nowak has made arrangements. John Winters and I went over the case this afternoon. He's coming up with nothing new, except that there have been suggestions Nowak was a lady's man."

"Really? That's a surprise." He held out a wine glass and she accepted.

"Why a surprise?"

"Is that what you wanted to ask me? I didn't know him well, as I've said. He was Moonlight's friend's father. We didn't mix socially."

"I guess what I'm asking, Lucky, is if he ever hit on you."

"Hit on me? What an idea."

"It's not all that far fetched, you know. You're an," he colored slightly, "attractive woman."

The room shifted. Lucky took a big swallow of wine. Paul was looking at her. His color was high, his eyes full of emotion.

She realized, at last, that he was not really here to discuss an old case.

"Paul." She cleared her throat. The potato water on the stove boiled over and hot water splashed and sizzled. She ran to turn the heat down. When she looked back at Paul Keller, he was standing by the window, looking out over the garden.

"Dinner won't be long," she said. "Why don't we take our drinks to the deck. Enjoy the last days of summer while we still can."

He smiled at her. "That would be nice."

"Back to your original question," she said once they were outside. She pulled a box of matches out of her skirt pocket and lit three candles in hurricane lamps while Paul settled into a seat. She took a lounge chair, stretched out her feet and folded her skirt around her legs. She kicked off her sandals. "Brian Nowak never hit on me, as you put it. And, as far as I know, not on anyone else either. I heard rumors after he left that he'd run away with a woman. I can't remember her name off hand, but didn't she show up a few days later, knowing nothing about it?"

"That's right."

"Then the story went around that he had a lover in Vancouver he wanted to be with. I think he was supposed to have had a second bigamous family or something. You know how people make up stories in the absence of facts."

"I know."

The long northern twilight lingered around the deck. The property was rimmed by tall pines which had so far avoided the attention of the mountain pine beetle. Lucky's vegetable garden was well tended, but the lush lawn that had been Andy's pride and joy showed signs of neglect. In the long shadows they couldn't see the creek that ran through the property, but they could hear it splashing over rocks, hurrying toward the river. Undergrowth rustled as Sylvester followed a scent. There were no lights other than the spill from the kitchen windows and flickering candles. In pots along the railing, white geraniums glowed in the dusk.

"What do you think happened to him, Paul?" Lucky said.

He took a sip of beer. "I haven't a clue. Even at the time I simply didn't know. We may never know."

"The family has a body now. They can come to some sort of closure."

They were quiet for a long time, enjoying the peace of the woods settling down for the night and each other's company. The moon was a large white ball high in the sky.

"I'd better go and check on dinner," Lucky said. She was resting in a lounge chair, feet stretched out in front of her. She struggled to swing one leg over the side and push herself to her feet. Keller had taken a straight-back chair, and stood to help her.

She took his hand and he pulled her up. He was taller than her, most people were, but not as tall as Andy. He looked down, and she looked up and neither of them said anything. He lifted a hand and touched her cheek. She knew she should move it away and step back.

But she didn't.

Chapter Twenty-five

Molly Smith wanted to talk to her mom. If Christa was right and the whole town was talking about Lucky and Paul Keller, Lucky needed to know. Smith had finished work at three in the morning and set her alarm to get her up at six so she could get to the house before her mom left for the store. This was not something they could discuss over the phone or when likely to be interrupted by customers.

The sun was rising over the mountains when she drove across the bridge and headed north. The house was located at the end of a long dirt road, up against the mountain, and a branch of the Upper Kootenay River meandered through the property. It had, she thought with a burst of sentiment, been a great place to grow up.

A car was parked beside the kitchen door.

Lucky had sold her old Pontiac Firefly when Andy died and kept Andy's Toyota for herself. This car was an SUV. A new thing, huge and black and ugly, the sort of gas-guzzling, environment-destroying vehicle Lucky detested.

Instinctively Smith checked the license plate. She recognized the number.

This was Paul Keller's vehicle.

The chief constable's car was parked in her mother's driveway at six-thirty in the morning.

There were no lights on in the house.

Smith threw her car into reverse and almost took out a dead tree backing up as fast as she could.

John Winters would pay one last call on the Nowak family before returning the case to the City Hall basement. Perhaps nothing was to be found, no case to solve. Perhaps the man had simply decided to go for a walk in the woods and hitched a ride with someone passing though. Perhaps he did intend to have a hike before returning home for Sunday dinner with his family. Once alone in the wilderness, anything could have happened: an incapacitating fall, a heart attack, getting lost and dying of exposure. It had been early April when Nowak disappeared. Cold nights in the mountains, good possibility of snow.

He'd phoned Mrs. Nowak to say he was coming and had asked that her son and daughter be present.

Both of the Nowak children looked as though they weren't accustomed to being roused from their beds at ten in the morning.

The boy, Kyle, scowled from the depths of the living room couch. He hadn't, it would appear by smell as well as sight, had a shower for a couple of days. He wore a white T-shirt spattered with paint and faded jeans with tattered hems. His feet were bare, his toenails yellow and overgrown.

The girl, Nicky, had wrapped a red silk dressing gown around herself. She'd not bothered with make-up and had stuffed her hair into a simple ponytail. She sat in a chair opposite her brother with her legs tucked under her and looked not much older than she must have when her father disappeared. Was this her real face, Winters thought. Clean and innocent and fresh and pretty?

Or was the other face the true one? Expensive clothes, well groomed, made-up. Charm and sex appeal. Then she was beyond pretty, she was dazzling.

Underneath that façade, Winters suspected, lay a hard, brittle woman.

She had no police record but Winters would bet money she was a prostitute. Or had been so at one time. She sized men up as if she were inspecting beef in the supermarket, and only if she found them acceptable did the smile switch on and the flirting begin. Unlikely she worked the streets: she dressed well and cared for herself and showed no outward signs of the drug abuse that got most hookers through their days and nights.

He didn't know if he should be flattered that she was still trying to charm him.

"Forgive me, Sergeant," she said in a low voice. "But I had a late night and Mom didn't give me much advance warning you were coming. I'm afraid you find me as I am. Warts and all." Her smile was all innocence while she waited for him to tell her she looked beautiful as she was.

Instead he thanked them for seeing him and took a seat.

Mrs. Nowak, dressed in a faded housedress and once-fluffy slippers, bustled about with tea things and packaged cookies. When she'd placed the tray on the coffee table, she went to the dining nook and turned a chair around so it faced the living room. They were sitting in a square. Kyle on the couch, Nicky and Winters in armchairs, Mrs. Nowak in her own chair.

Every one of them alone.

It was a sunny day, but the curtains were still drawn and the house, as well as the family, was wrapped in gloom.

Winters asked them to go over, one more time, the events of Sunday, April 12, fifteen years ago.

"Why don't I make a recording, and play it every time you come around?" Kyle snapped. "Then you don't have to keep wasting our time."

"You think the investigation into your father's death is a waste of time?"

"Don't put words in my mouth. I'm getting sick and tired of telling the damn story is all."

"I can understand that, but bear with me. Your father didn't go to church with the family that morning, correct?"

"Yeah. He bowed out. I guess he was just ahead of the rest of us. We don't go any more either."

"Did he usually go to church with you?"

"Every week," Mrs. Nowak said. "Every Sunday."

"Why did he not accompany you that day?"

Mrs. Nowak spoke to her lap. "He said he wasn't feeling well."

"Did you believe him?"

"Of course I believed him. Trust is the foundation of marriage."

"When he disappeared, did you wonder then about him missing church?"

She lifted her head. Her eyes were red and full of grief long-held. She sniffled and dug in her pocket for a tissue. "I wondered then about everything I had ever believed and everyone I had ever held dear in this life."

Nicky looked at her mother. Kyle shuffled his feet. Neither of the children made a move to console her.

Had this family been so unloving, so distant, before tragedy ruined their lives? Molly said the Nowaks had seemed like a normal family, but what thirteen-year-old paid attention to group dynamics not involving teenagers? She had painted Nicky as a good athlete and student. It was unlikely she would have turned into an iron-shelled, hard woman pretending to be soft and adorable if her father had remained in her life.

"Kyle, why were you so sure your father was having affairs with women from the church? Everyone I've spoken to, including Father O'Malley, says there's no truth to that."

"Father O'Malley," Kyle snorted, "is a pervert."

"Do you have reason to believe that?"

Kyle shrugged. "Aren't they all buggering little boys?"

His mother gasped.

"No," Winters said, "they aren't. But if you have reason to believe so, I will investigate your claims. Did Father O'Malley ever interfere with you, or attempt to do so?"

"Nah. I never let him get near enough. Okay, I don't know anything about that. I just mean that when it came to matters of men and women the good Father was clueless."

"I never heard a single whisper about Father O'Malley's behavior," Nicky said. "You can put that idea to rest. Kyle's just trying to stir the pot. Like always."

Kyle didn't reply.

"Father O'Malley's always been a perfect gentleman around me," Nicky added with a secret smile at Winters. "Even now that I'm all grown up."

No doubt he was expected to make a comment about how well she had grown up.

"Newsflash, Nicky," Kyle said. "Fags don't flirt with women."

"We're getting off topic here," Winters said. "Did your husband smoke a lot, Mrs. Nowak?"

"I didn't approve. I didn't allow him to smoke in the house, but his den was his private space so he would go there for a cigarette or out onto the deck if the weather was nice."

"He went through about a quarter-pack a day, I'd guess," Nicky said. "He always smelled of tobacco. I can't stand the smell of it. It makes me think of Dad, every time." Her whole body shuddered. "Sometimes, it's more than I can bear."

"He went out to buy cigarettes but never got to the store on the corner?"

"That's right."

The corner variety store was gone. Torn down and replaced with a duplex when the owner retired. He was dead now, but his statement to Paul Keller lived on, saying he had been working alone in the store that Sunday afternoon and had not seen Brian Nowak, whom he knew well.

"Any chance he might have gone someplace else to buy his cigarettes?"

"Where else would he go?" Nicky said, "Without taking the car? I suppose he could have walked into town, but even if he had, no one saw him."

"Mrs. Nowak," Winters said, "I know how hard this is for you, but I'm sure you understand why I have to ask. Your husband withdrew ten thousand dollars from his investment account shortly before he left home. You said at the time you had no idea what he intended to do with the money or what happened to it. Is that correct?"

The woman shot a glance at her son. Then her eyes fell back to her lap.

"My mother knows nothing about that money," Kyle said. "She didn't then and she doesn't now."

"I could have used ten thousand dollars," Mrs. Nowak said. "He left us with nothing. Nothing."

"It's not as if he planned on being killed, Mom," Nicky said. "You've got to stop blaming him."

Kyle stood up. "I'm sick of this. Nothing but the same crap over and over and over for fifteen years. Do you think if we remembered something we wouldn't have told you? I'm going downstairs. I have work to do. I've been offered a gallery showing in Vancouver, you know. Time for you to leave, Winters, my mom doesn't want to talk to you anymore. Can't you see how hard this is on her?"

Winters glanced at the woman. He could see. She was like a dog, a small starving dog who'd been beaten too many times. She huddled into herself, wrapped in a tattered sweater, red, chapped fingers tearing at the damp tissue. She was little more than bones held together by a thin layer of skin. Her face was gray, her cheeks had fallen in on themselves, her blue eyes were so washed out they were the color of the sky on a cloudy day.

"People remember your husband," Winters said, getting to his feet. He wanted to leave having said something comforting. "Very fondly. People like Lucky Smith, Father O'Malley, Greg Hunt."

"Who?" she asked. Kyle stared at Winters.

"Greg Hunt. The realtor?"

"Don't remember him," she said.

"He was your husband's friend."

She said nothing.

"Good bye, Sergeant," Kyle said. He opened the door and made shooing gestures.

"Wait," Nicky said. "What happens now?"

"The RCMP is ready to release Mr. Nowak's body."

"We know that. We've made the arrangements. The funeral will be on Monday at Sacred Heart. I meant what happens about finding the person who murdered my father."

"Unless further evidence comes to light, I'll be winding down the investigation," Winters told her. "We have no reason to believe your father died as a result of foul play."

"Of course it was *foul play*," Nicky shouted. She jumped to her feet. "And you know it."

"Goodbye, Sergeant," Kyle repeated.

Chapter Twenty-six

"I thought I told you not to come."

"So ye did. But I figured I would anyway."

The park was high over the city and offered a spectacular view down into the blue and green bowl of mountains, town, and river.

"Set up a telescope here, and a chap could watch everyone. See who's sneaking into whose house soon as the husband leaves for work." Joey Stewart made a circle out of his fingers and held his hands to his right eye as he pretended to survey the town.

"You were right: going after the cop was a bad idea. I'm going to stay until my father's funeral on Monday, leave first thing Tuesday morning. That has nothing to do with you. Go home and wait for me."

"I'm not good at waiting, you should know that."

"Sure you are. You wait outside a mark's house for hours until it's time to snap pictures of the wife and kids."

"Yeah, but that brings a payoff. I don't sit and wait for you to call, Nicole. Get that idea out of your pretty head."

"Fuck off, Joey." She stood up and unconsciously brushed the dust from the park bench off her cream pants.

Joey Stewart, her *business* partner, had shown up that afternoon. Not stupid enough to ring the doorbell, he'd parked down the street and sat in his car waiting. When she'd come out in pursuit of a decent cup of coffee he followed her into town. She hadn't even known he was there. By the time she'd parked her own car outside Big Eddie's and was waiting to cross the road, he pulled up beside her, rolled down the window and said, "Get in."

Not wanting to either go into Eddie's with him or make a scene, she had.

"Sit down," he said now.

She sat.

"The way I see it," he said, in a tight voice that emphasized his Scottish accent, "is that your wee holiday's costing me money. I put Leung off for one week but won't be doing that again. You said you were coming here for a couple of days. Well, time's up. We've had some new calls, and I've made appointments for early next week. You can come back with me—today—or, if you want to stay on in this pleasant wee town, get to work."

For the first time since she'd met him, Nicole felt a frisson of fear. He was an ugly little bastard, about as tough as they came, but she'd always figured she was tougher. She refused to let him intimidate her, or boss her around, and they'd made a lot of money together over the years. She'd never stopped to think how he might take it if she decided to leave the partnership.

"You are not my boss." She pushed the fear aside and let contempt take its place. She looked into his face. "Don't you forget it." She'd taken drama classes in school, thinking she'd become an actress one day. That dream, like all the others, disappeared along with her father. She never had appeared on stage, but her job was acting all right. "I told you, I'll be home on Tuesday."

"We're partners, Nicole. We run a business. Our product just happens to be your body. And as you have it with you, use it."

"I'm not turning tricks here, in my hometown. Forget that. Everyone knows me."

He reached out one hand and grabbed her chin. She tried to pull away but his grip was tight. His fingers dug into her skin and pressed on the bone. "Like I said, your body is our business. Me, I can always find another cunt to put to work. Might not even have to put up with one who doesn't know the proper use for her mouth. You, Nicole, cannot find another body." He twisted his hand so her neck turned. "Get my meaning?"

She lashed out, aiming her long red fingernails at his face. He pulled back and she merely brushed the stubble on his chin. He let go abruptly and laughed. "Consider that a partner's meeting. No need to take the minutes."

A white Jack Russell darted out from a clump of bushes. Its short hair was standing on end and its teeth exposed. A low growl came from its throat. A young girl ran up the path, waving a leash. "Scissors, come here. Stop that. Bad dog." She was tall and thin and pretty with long brown hair, dressed in running shoes, shorts and a T-shirt that did nothing to conceal the burgeoning curves of her body. She grabbed the dog's collar and fastened the leash. "Sorry about that. He's usually quite good."

Scissors growled.

"That's okay," Joey said, giving the girl a big smile. "I like dogs."

"It's usually quiet this time of day so I figured I could let Scissors off the leash. I'm sorry."

"Not a problem. I'm Joey." He held out his hand. "Just visiting. Nice town you've got here."

"Becky. Becky Lopez." She shifted the leash to her left hand, and shook Joey's. "Pleased to meet you, Joey." She glanced at Nicole, who ignored her. "You're from England, right?" Becky said. "I'd love to go to England one day."

"Great place for a holiday."

"See you around maybe." She tugged at the leash.

"That would be great. Bye now."

"Bye." She walked away, pulling a reluctant dog behind her. They disappeared down the path to the parking lot.

"Pretty girl," Joey said.

"That dog has a hell of a lot more intelligence about people than the girl does. It knew you were a miserable bastard from a mile away." Joey had been talking to Becky, but aiming his words at Nicole. She didn't much care. There were plenty of girls in the world; the cities were full of them. Runaways, druggies, kids looking for adventure. Joey might like to think he was the brains of their operation, but without Nicole he'd be lucky to manage a string of twenty-dollars-a-blow-job street hookers.

"I'm thinking of starting a line in kiddie traffic," he said. "Perverts like that innocent, fresh-faced look. Think Becky'd be interested? The mud on her knees was a nice touch."

"What you do with your hobbies is none of my business. You get busted for using underage girls, I won't bother to visit you in jail."

"Until that happens, I want you back at work."

"I came to you with an idea. You didn't like it."

"Not the cop, no."

"I'm not hooking in this town, Joey. Forget it. We need a little thing called anonymity. If that word's too big for you, look it up in the dictionary. This town, everyone knows everyone. And this week I'm the star of the show. I can't tell you how many old ladies have come up to me on the street to tell me they're happy to see me again." And, they always added, so sad about your father, but you and your family must be glad to have his body back.

"Did you bring much of the white stuff with you, Nicole? You're staying longer than you'd expected. Not running out, I hope."

She tried to keep her face impassive, but he knew he'd struck home. She was almost out of cocaine, and didn't know where in Trafalgar she could get more. They practically sold marijuana out in the open at the Happy Tobaccy, but anything harder than pot was a different story.

She dug in her purse and pulled out a cigarette. Her hand shook as she lit it.

Joey smiled.

If she was going to get through the days leading up to her father's funeral, and the funeral itself, she had to be able to have a hit when she needed one.

"Thought so," he said, "I'll see what I can do for you. We'll drop the escort service line, go for the temporary girlfriend thing. See, Nicole, I'm thinking we can do better in this town than back in the city. Not only will the marks be wanting to keep the pictures away from their wives, but everyone else in town too. Does the local paper have a gossip column?"

"Damned if I know." Despite herself, she was thinking it might not be a bad idea. They had, a couple of times in Vancouver, picked on a man who refused to give in to Joey's blackmail. Publish and be damned, one fellow had said. Joey sent the photos to his wife's office. They'd never heard what happened after that, but hurriedly found a new apartment and re-opened the escort agency under a different name and phone number.

What would it hurt? Hang around a couple of bars, pick up men.

"Okay," she said. "But I don't want you approaching them until I've gone. In case something backfires. My father's funeral is on Monday and I intend to be there, with my head held high. Get it?"

"Sure."

"We don't have a place to use, where we can set up properly. I assume you brought the mobile equipment."

"Sure did."

Joey liked gadgets. He had a nice collection of tiny cameras. The sort that would fit into the stone of a necklace or fasten to the mirror in a car. The pictures wouldn't be all that good, but one or two pics of a man spread-eagled on a hotel bed stark naked, his prick like a flag pole, or the back of her head buried in his lap in the front seat of a car would go a long way toward loosening his wallet.

"Besides." She ran the idea over in her mind, liking it more and more. She took a long drag on her cigarette. "Time to shake up this stuck-up town. If they want to gossip about the Nowaks, I'll give them something to *really* talk about."

"Do you know a guy name of Greg Hunt?" Winters asked when he walked into the office.

Ray Lopez glanced up from his computer. "There's a Greg Hunt who owns Alpine Meadows Realtors."

"That's the one." Winters dropped into his chair. "Know anything about him?"

"Why are you asking?"

"He's interested in the Brian Nowak case. Phoned to speak to me, and I got Molly to talk to him. Not happy with being passed onto a subordinate, he waylaid me outside the building yesterday. He says he was a friend of Nowak's, but his wife didn't seem to remember the name."

"Hunt's local. His father owned the company before him, maybe his grandfather before that. And that's about all I know. He's on the boards of some community organizations. All part of the job. I don't remember him ever coming to our attention, but that doesn't mean he didn't before I got here."

"Do a little checking, will you? When someone shows interest in a case he's not directly involved in, I'm interested. What are you working on?"

"Incident at a convenience store in Vancouver yesterday afternoon. Guy pulled a knife on the clerk and asked for money, but ran off when a customer came in. None too bright, he'd parked right outside, and the customer got the plates. The perp has family in Trafalgar, and we've been asked to keep an eye out."

"Finish what you have on the go first, and then check into Hunt. This case has waited fifteen years, we're in no hurry."

Molly Smith came on duty at three in the afternoon. She had planned on going back to bed and getting some more sleep after visiting her mother, but with all that was happening her head was spinning and she knew she would not be able to fall asleep. Instead she'd gone for a long run through the trails that circled the side of the mountain overlooking the town of Trafalgar. She'd seen no one but a couple of mountain bikers and a feral cat and had run until her legs were on fire and her shirt soaked through.

Had Chief Constable Paul Keller spent the night with her mother?

It didn't bear thinking about.

Should she confront Lucky or not? Smith changed her mind about twenty times over the course of the run. By the time she arrived at work, she was coming around to the say-nothing side of her internal debate.

She'd bought a ham and cheese on baguette sandwich (half-price as the bakery was about to close) from Alphonse and took it to the lunch room to put in the fridge. Someone had stuck a fundraising flyer from the Women's Shelter on the notice board, and she stopped to read it. Several local musicians were playing at the benefit and it might be a fun night.

Barb Kowalski and the law clerk were fixing tea and chatting in the lunch room.

"He forgot about the meeting with the mayor," Barb was saying. "Fortunately, I got back from the doctor's, and there he was sitting at his desk staring into space, so he wasn't too terribly late."

"My friend Susan is friends with Karen Keller, and she says Karen's left."

"I thought she went to a wedding in Calgary?"

"That's the story, but Karen quit her job and took a lot more stuff with her to her sister's than anyone would need for a visit."

Smith stood at the door listening. Jim Denton at the dispatch desk gave her an odd look, which she pretended not to see. Her skin began to crawl as she listened to the women's low voices.

Barb Kowalski was the chief's secretary. She was unfailingly loyal to her boss and tight-lipped about police business, but when it came to personal gossip Barb was the go-to girl.

"He was a mess this morning," Barb said. "You know how well-pressed he keeps his uniform. Today, I think he was actually wearing the same shirt he had on yesterday. He missed a spot when shaving and cut himself somewhere else. Looked like he'd used a dull razor."

"Proves my point," the clerk said. "Some men can't manage to even dress themselves when their wives are away."

"She's been gone for a while and this was the first time he looked so rumpled."

"Ran out of clean shirts probably."

"Whatever. I hope it doesn't cause problems around here." Barb dropped her voice even further. "There's some talk that the chief and a recent widow who shall remain nameless are..."

"Hi," Smith said in a bright cheerful voice as she walked into the kitchen. The bylaw officer had come in search of a can of pop and Smith could no longer stand eavesdropping. "Whatcha talking about?"

Barb's eyes slid away from Smith's face. "Nothing. Nothing at all. Gotta get back to work. Say hi to your mom from me, Molly. I mean, if you want to." She almost ran from the room. The law clerk followed at an equal pace.

"Did that seem odd to you?" the by-law officer said.

Smith didn't reply. She had changed her mind once again.

She definitely needed to talk to Lucky.

"Greg Hunt," Detective Ray Lopez said, "has form, as they say in the police movies."

"Do tell." Winters leaned back in his chair to give his back a good stretch.

"Misappropriation of funds. More commonly called theft."

"Go on."

"Hunt was born in Trafalgar and went to school here. Then to UBC for a degree in economics and to Toronto for a job with a big investment company. He worked there for several years before being abruptly fired. He was charged with two counts of theft. Some tricky stuff involving his client's money passing through his own account before actually being invested."

"How much money was involved?"

"Not a lot. Between both charges, twenty thousand."

"What'd he get?"

"Fine and probation as it was his first offence. Needless to say his career in high finance was over."

Winters snorted. "I would have thought it was only beginning."

"If he'd tried to steal twenty million it probably would have. Anyway, he came back to Trafalgar later that year and began selling real estate for his father. His dad retired in 2001, and Greg took over. The father died last year."

"When did this happen?"

"Court case was summer 1985."

"Anything since?"

"He seems to be squeaky clean. I remember the dad, Gregory Hunt, Sr. He was mayor before I moved here but still had his fingers in a lot of pies including the police board. He ran for MLA once but lost by a large margin. He was seen as way too right-wing. He tried again but didn't even get the nomination."

"The son?"

"Keeps a low profile. Low for a real estate agent, that is. He's not into the community or political stuff in the way his father was. His mother's still alive and active but I don't think she ever did much with the business."

"Personal life?"

"Not married. Lives in a nice house on the other side of the river. Apparently alone. Never a whiff of trouble that I've heard. He and the company have a good reputation."

"Thanks for doing that."

"Mean anything to you?"

"I don't know. It's possible Hunt learned the error of his ways and has kept to the straight and narrow ever since. But Brian Nowak's family was out ten thousand bucks when he disappeared and I'd give a lot to know what happened to that money."

Chapter Twenty-seven

"You can ask a lawyer to look over the contract, you know," Eliza said.

Kyle Nowak shrugged. "I trust you."

"You shouldn't."

"I trust you more than I trust lawyers. They were eager enough to help Mom sort out Dad's affairs until they found out we didn't have any money. Left her high and dry quick enough."

"Perhaps you just had a bad experience."

He shrugged, not much caring, and signed the document. Eliza scrawled her own signature at the bottom of the page. She put down her pen and held out her hand. Kyle looked at it and for a moment she thought he might refuse to shake. Then he took it. His handshake was damp and floppy.

"Congratulations," she said. "You have an art gallery showing next year in Vancouver. I will do everything in my power to make the exhibit a success."

He mumbled his thanks.

"You have a lot of work ahead of you."

"Not a problem."

Eliza would have appreciated a bit more enthusiasm. Kyle didn't seem to care much about the chance he'd been given.

She got to her feet and gathered up her own copy of the contract. "I know it seems like a long way ahead but a year has a way of passing quickly. I'd like to keep in touch, make sure your work is going as well as we both expect."

"Keep an eye on me, you mean."

"Keep in touch, like I said."

"If you want."

She sat back down. "You do realize this is a business venture, Kyle? For both of us. I'm investing money in you because I believe in you and your art. If you don't want to take it seriously, please let me know, and we can tear up the contract and I'll find someone else."

He focused his eyes on hers. He was a cold, emotionless man, but this time she saw a flash of determination. "I want to do it. I want people to see my art."

"Glad to hear it."

The bell over the door to the street tinkled to announce a visitor.

"Larry," Eliza said, getting to her feet once again. "How nice to see you. Don't tell me you've finally made up your mind?"

"I'm afraid to say, my darling, that the answer is no. I popped in for another peek."

Eliza presented her cheek for a kiss and he obliged. Larry Reinhardt owned the men's clothing store on the next block and had his heart set on a Reynolds painting. Problem was he couldn't decide which one.

"Pooh," he said with a sniff. "You've sold the rainy day picture. I was tending toward that one."

"I keep telling you, Larry, there will be nothing left by the time you make up your mind."

"It's a difficult decision, dear heart. You can't rush a boy." He wiggled his fingers and fluttered his eyelashes at her and she laughed. Larry was in his late fifties, still handsome. He had been a model in his teens, and then worked for years as a wardrobe consultant in Hollywood. He dressed conservatively in white shirt, subdued tie, and charcoal slacks, and lived a quiet life with his partner and their cats. Only with Eliza, because they both came from the modeling world, did he enjoy playing up the flagrant gay persona.

"Larry, I'd like you to meet my newest protégé. Larry Reinhardt. Kyle Nowak. Kyle's going to have a show in Vancouver next year."

"That's great," Larry said, extending his hand. "Congratulations."

The hand stretched out between the two men. Kyle looked at it, and then he turned to Eliza. "As you said, I've got a lot of work to do. Better be getting to it. If you need anything you know where I am."

He walked out of the gallery. Larry's hand dropped to his side.

"I am so sorry," Eliza said. "That was unpardonably rude."

"Not the first time a man's refused to shake my hand. I try not to take it personally. I'll cut him some slack because I recognize the name. I assume he's related to the guy whose body was found the other day?"

"The son. I didn't know him when he was a boy, maybe he was bizarre back then, but from what I've heard about him and his family, the shock of the father's disappearance and the aftermath of never knowing did a number on their heads. If he's going to have a show, with potential buyers to be charming to, he's going to have to shape up."

"What's his art like?"

"Kyle's? It's exactly like him. Angry at everyone and everything."

"Unlikely I'll buy, then. There's too much ugliness in the world, Eliza. I don't want to bring any of it into my life. Do you think the one with the yellow roof would clash with the walls in the living room?"

Molly Smith walked into Mid-Kootenay Adventure Vacations. Flower was helping a customer try on hiking boots and Lucky was arranging books on the shelf. She looked up at the sound of the door opening and started to give her daughter a smile. But the smile died as she saw the look on Moonlight's face.

"What is it? Has something happened?"

"Mom, we have to talk."

"What about?"

Moonlight glanced at the customer and Flower, both of whom had stopped whatever they were doing to stare.

"In private." Moonlight marched to the back to the room.

Lucky threw a quick glance toward the photo of Andy behind the counter before following Moonlight.

The girl slammed the office door behind her mother.

"Are you aware that everyone in town is talking about you?"

"About me?" Lucky said, hoping she wasn't understanding what had Moonlight in such a fuss.

"About you. And the chief constable."

"Oh. That."

"Yes, that."

"It's nothing, dear. We've been talking about the Brian Nowak situation over the occasional cup of coffee."

"For god's sake, Mom, what are you thinking? We can hope I'm the only one who saw his car parked outside your house this morning."

"You did?"

"Yes. I. did."

Lucky sank into her office chair. "Perhaps that was a mistake."

"You think?"

"Whether it was a mistake or not, it isn't any of your business."

"Of course it's my business. You're my mother. He's my boss."

Lucky studied her daughter. Moonlight had pale skin, matching the blue eyes and blond hair she'd inherited from her father. Red patches were breaking out across her face as if she were about to give in to one of the tantrums that had been a feature of her early childhood. Lucky found herself smiling.

"This isn't funny, Mom."

"In some ways, it is. I appreciate your concern, but if I choose to see Paul I will do so. I am, to my regret, not married."

"But the chief is."

"You'll have to speak to him about that."

"Mom."

"Good-bye, dear. I'm sure the citizens of Trafalgar would rather you spend your day keeping our streets safe than gossiping with your mother."

"Gossiping? I hardly…"

"Good-bye, dear." Lucky said.

Moonlight looked as if she were about to argue. She took a deep breath, and then turned on her heel and left the room. She slammed the door on her way out.

Lucky groaned and put her head into her hands.

She had slept with Paul Keller.

Not that it hadn't been nice. It had. He was a good lover, soft and gentle and fully aware that Lucky would be thinking of her late, much-loved husband. Paul smelled, heavily, of tobacco, but that didn't bother her. Probably because Andy had given up smoking many years ago, and thus Paul's smoking habit did not bring memories of Andy to mind.

She hadn't taken Paul to the big bedroom at the front of the house, to the bed she'd shared with Andy all those years, but to Samwise's old room, now the guest room.

He told her his wife had left him. The marriage had been over in all but living arrangements for some time, and last week Karen moved out. Gone to Calgary where she had family and friends. She told him she would not be back, other than to get her things.

He had been persuasive; Lucky had been lonely and needy.

Lucky Smith didn't care one whit for gossip. She would do what she always had and go her own way regardless of the opinions of others. Even Moonlight.

But she would not see Paul Keller again.

For dinner they had roast beef. It might have been from the same cow she'd eaten the last time she'd been in this house. Tough, stringy, cooked as though it would later serve as a door stop. Served with lumpy mashed potatoes and canned green peas.

This time of year farmers' markets and backyard gardens were overflowing with tomatoes fat and red with sunshine, vibrant greens, orange carrots, purple beets. Everything fresh and delicious and cheap. Yet her mother still served potatoes from Prince Edward Island and peas trucked thousands of miles to canning factories in the Midwest.

Fifteen years ago no one had heard the word locavore, and Nicky's mother hadn't moved forward one single day since her husband disappeared. Nicky remembered her mother as being a good cook, but she realized now that their meals were large and regular, but not necessarily good and certainly not imaginative.

She put her knife and fork on the plate.

"You've hardly eaten a thing." Nicky wondered if the next words out of her mother's mouth would be "you have to sit right there until you've eaten every bite."

Kyle shoveled a mass of potatoes and peas onto his fork.

"Sorry, Mom, I'm not hungry," Nicky said. "I guess it's the stress and everything."

"But I've gone to so much trouble."

"I appreciate you doing that." She had gone to some trouble Nicky knew, but didn't much care. Kyle never ate with their mother and judging by the contents of the cupboards she dined regularly on Campbell's cream of mushroom soup and Hamburger Helper.

Nicky pushed her chair back.

"There's dessert," Mom said with a plaintive whine that set Nicky's back teeth on edge.

She'd seen dessert sitting on the kitchen table. A formless blob of red Jell-O. Leftovers from last night.

"Save some for me to have later. I'm going out."

She went to her room and quickly changed. She was, in fact, starving, but most of all she needed a hit. Being out of coke, as Joey had yet to deliver, she'd have to make do with a drink. No wine was served with dinner in their mother's house. Even when Dad was alive, he would have a beer in his den or while watching TV, but wouldn't bring it to the family table.

No doubt Nicole could find some guy to buy her a couple of drinks, maybe even dinner.

She pulled a dress out of the closet. It was sleek and elegant, expensive, sexy as hell. Time to rock this miserable town.

The bar at the Hudson House Hotel, where she'd gone with Moonlight the other night, would be the best bet.

It seemed like a good place to ply her trade, so to speak. Despite her earlier conversation with Joey, she was beginning to have her doubts that this was a good idea. At home, they picked their clients carefully and pulled them slowly into their web. The escort service front allowed them to filter out anyone who might be single and looking for an easy date or who, worst of all, didn't have money. Here she'd be as likely to pick up a travelling salesman who considered a casual screw to be a perk of the job as a respectable businessman desperate to avoid scandal.

Nicky Nowak did not take pleasure in sex. She'd never once had an experience she'd genuinely enjoyed. When she left home at sixteen for the streets of Vancouver, she'd serviced one smelly old man after another. Fumbling at his zipper, farting and breathing beer fumes all over her. Accompanied by the occasional punch or slap and more often than not a stream of insults.

She hadn't spent long on the streets before realizing the life wasn't for her. Maybe some of her parent's churchy ways had had an influence on her after all, and she'd avoided the hard drugs pimps used to control their women.

She got caught in a sudden, unexpected rainstorm one day, and sought refuge in a shelter for street kids.

They found her a cheap apartment and a job at a fast food restaurant. It didn't pay much, but at least no one tried to beat her up. She worked long hours, saved enough money to pay for half-decent clothes and hair and makeup, and started looking good again. Soon as she turned nineteen, she quit tossing burgers, changed her name, and got a job as a stripper in a better-quality "gentlemen's club." "Private clients" brought in more money. She started using a bit of cocaine. Then a bit more, until it was costing more than she'd intended.

Five years ago Joey Stewart came into the club. He sat in the back, nursing a beer, watching her dance, every night for two weeks. Then he approached her during her break. She'd already decided he wasn't worth bothering with. He dressed poorly and was badly groomed; his parents obviously never spent much on dental work or acne medication.

He didn't want her private services, or even to try to "save her" as some of them claimed was their intention.

Joey presented her with a business offer.

He knew of a man, a prominent politician, who had a thing for tiny white women and visited prostitutes regularly. He wasn't into children, and Nicole didn't have a child-like body in any case, but with the right camera angles they should be able to get some pictures that looked like he was having sex with an underage girl.

Joey offered her five thousand dollars.

She dressed in hooker clothes and stood on the street corner. She hadn't been there for more than five minutes before the man she'd been told to look for drove up. She took him to her room—which Joey had provided.

At first she felt a bit sorry for the politician, but that ended when he chomped down on her nipple and wouldn't let go. When it was over, he slapped fifty bucks on the dresser and left without saying thank you or good-bye.

A week later she saw his picture on the front page of the paper. He'd resigned in order to devote more time to his family. She never heard of him again.

Only later did Joey tell her it was never about blackmail. Someone wanted the politician's head on a platter and hired Joey to help him get it.

Joey suggested they try it again. She told him she didn't want a set fee; she wanted half the profits.

Over the last five years they'd made a lot of money. She rented an apartment in an expensive building overlooking False Creek, had great clothes, jewelry, a new car. She ate in good restaurants and vacationed in the Caribbean. She still liked her coke, but was fortunate enough to be able to keep the habit under control.

She'd never thought about the future, and saved not a cent of her money. No one knew better than Nicky Nowak there was no point in making plans for your life.

After the talk in the park yesterday, she wondered if it was time to break off with Joey. For the first time he'd threatened her. It had frightened her. Badly.

What else could she do? Her résumé wouldn't exactly get her another job that would give her the standard of living to which she was accustomed.

She pushed the thoughts aside and went into the bar. She decided not to set out to deliberately pick up a sucker, but instead to let the evening fall where it may.

She made it a point of pride never to buy her own drinks or dinner. She made an exception the other night for Moonlight, who, even if Nicky had wanted her to, probably couldn't afford much on a cop's salary.

Imagine, Moonlight Legolas Smith, hippie child of hippie parents, a cop.

The room was packed and Nicole made her way through the crowd to the bar. Joey sat in a wingback chair in a dark corner, hunched over a bottle of beer. They did not acknowledge one another.

Men shifted as she approached and a stool suddenly became free. She slid onto it. A group of men surrounded her. She gave them each a smile. There were four of them, reasonably young, fit-looking, clean clothes, short hair, no beards.

She recognized one and her smile widened. "Hello," she said. "Remember me? I'm Nicky."

He shifted in his size twelve boots. "Of course, I remember you."

Of course.

"Buy a girl a drink?" she said, touching the tip of her tongue to the side of her lip and shifting her rump on the stool.

"What you having?" Adam Tocek asked.

◇◇◇

The world would be a better place, Molly Smith thought sometimes, without alcohol. Then again, she'd probably be out of a job.

She frowned at the young man and placed her hands on her hips and watched him pour the contents of a can of beer into the gutter. He had the grace to look embarrassed at being caught, not necessarily drinking on the street, so she told him she'd let him go if he got rid of it.

He tossed the empty can into the street.

"Pick that up and put it in the garbage," she said.

"Sorry, ma'am," he mumbled, scrambling after it.

"Don't let me catch you again."

"You won't." He deposited the can in a trash container and waited patiently for the light to change before crossing the street.

She walked on.

She'd visit every bar in town, one after the other, and then start all over again. Letting the bouncers know she was around, checking out potential trouble spots, looking for drugs being sold or consumed, letting dispatch know the number of people out.

Boring, routine. Usually. Initially she'd been pleased with herself for handling the man who'd knocked her down the other night. It was only later, in the women's washroom back in the station, when her hands began to shake and her knees felt weak and she had to hold onto the sink to keep herself from falling. She'd had a very close call.

The next morning she called Dawn Solway and arranged to get together to train on the weekend.

The Potato Famine featured a heavy metal band tonight and motorcycles were beginning to gather in the parking lot. Dave Evans was in the car and they'd been told to concentrate their attention there at closing time.

It was still early, but Smith decided to pop into the Famine and let the nervous new bouncer know they'd be close by. The night air was soft and warm and a large bright moon hung in the sky to the east.

She turned the corner into Tenth Street, intending to walk through the bar at the Hudson House on her way to the Potato Famine. Adam's truck was parked near the hotel entrance. He'd told her he was getting together tonight with some of the guys to buy a round for Alan Dobson, a Mountie who'd been promoted and transferred to Ottawa.

No doubt, she thought with a smile, a round would turn into several.

The side door leading to the bar opened in a burst of yellow light and laughter. Two people came out. She was tiny and curvy and he was large and solid. Even in high heels the woman barely reached the center of the man's chest. She laughed and her heel caught on something and she tripped. His arm shot out to grab her. She took it to steady herself and did not let go.

Smith stopped in her tracks. The couple didn't see her standing in the deep shadow of a shop doorway.

The man clicked his key and the locks sprang open. They separated to get into the truck. The woman's bare legs flashed as she stretched to reach the seat and she laughed again. The engine turned over and the truck drove away.

Molly Smith stepped out of the doorway. Her heart pounded and tears rushed into her eyes.

Ryan, the bartender, came outside pulling a pack of cigarettes out of his pocket. He bent to light one and started when he saw the dark, silent shape in front of him.

"What the… Oh, it's you, Molly. Scared me there."

"Everything okay inside?" she asked. Her voice broke and she coughed as though to clear her throat.

"Nice and peaceful. Helps having a bunch of Mounties leaning up against the bar. Adam just left. You must have missed him. The other guys are still inside though."

"Call us if you need anything." She ducked her head down so the brim of her hat hid her face and walked past him.

Hopefully the bikers would be making trouble at the Potato Famine and she could smash heads in. It was either that or go home and cry.

Chapter Twenty-eight

The call from the bartender at the Potato Famine came shortly before two.

I didn't really want to bash heads in, Smith thought as she broke into a jog.

She'd been having a glass of water while chatting to Mike, the bouncer at the Bishop and Nun, where the crowd was thin and everyone behaving themselves. She downed her water, shouted bye to Mike over her shoulder, and ran out the back door. In the alley, the light was poor and a jumble of wooden poles and thick wires stretched overhead. The canopy of a dead jungle. At the last second she saw a pile of dog dirt, a big pile, lying in her path and jumped to one side with a muttered curse.

Ingrid, the night dispatcher, was calling for Dave Evans, in the car, to go to the Potato Famine. He replied that he was on his way, but would be several minutes.

Smith crossed the street at a trot. Away from the bars, the streets were empty. Lights shone from a scattering of homes up the mountainside and from the thin line of civilization on the far side of the river.

She rounded the corner and the Potato Famine came in sight. It was a cheap bar, serving cheap drinks and food with plenty of grease, and attracted those whose idea of a night out was as much looking for a fight as talking to friends.

A crowd had gathered in front. Flashing blue and red lights from beer advertisements in the windows reflected off bald heads, long beards, leather jackets, short tight skirts, and a drugstore's supply of make-up.

"Kill the faggot," a man shouted.

Smith glanced up the street, hoping to see the patrol car heading toward her.

"Police," she shouted. "Break it up." She radioed to say she'd arrived and needed backup. Fast.

Onlookers shifted aside and she could see the center of attention: four men. Two were grappling with each other, pulling clothes, wild swings, enraged eyes. One man was on the ground, curled into a ball, his arms protecting his head and his legs curled up to defend his groin. A man stood over him, big, ugly, bulging muscles and out of control rage. *Steroids,* she thought. He pulled his leg back to plant it in the man's ribs.

"Police," Smith shouted again. Her heart pounded. She was, under the blue uniform, equipment belt, gun, just a woman. She made a conscious effort to calm her breathing, and reminded herself that she was not just a woman. She was the law, and she was trained to do this.

The big man hesitated. He looked over his shoulder and saw the crowd parting as the policewoman came forward.

"Don't do it," she said. He stepped back and lifted his hands in surrender. The other man rolled onto his back with a groan.

The two men on their feet continued to circle each other. The bigger one, heavily muscled with a shaved head and a tattooed snake curled around his right bicep, feigned a jab. His opponent was smaller, lean and fit, with dyed blond hair well cut, expensive jeans and leather boots. His eyes flicked toward Smith, but he kept his hands up and his gaze focused. He acted like a trained fighter whereas the bigger one looked like he got by on muscle and aggression.

Smith dared to toss a glance into the crowd, looking for someone out to make trouble. A sea of faces watched her. Some frightened, some concerned, most amused.

The big man was closest to her, and she spoke to him, careful to keep herself out of striking range. "Step back, sir. This fight is over." Her hand rested on the pepper spray on her belt.

"Come on, lady, let him give the faggots what they deserve," a not-at-all-helpful citizen advised.

"Fuckin' cops," the big man said. He kept his eyes focused on his opponent, but his shoulders relaxed, his fingers uncurled and he stepped back. "We're just havin' us some fun."

"Great fun." She looked at the other guy. "Back off," she ordered. Warily, he did so. He chanced a look to one side, at the man on the ground.

"Help your friend up," Smith said.

The man on the ground accepted the offered hand and was pulled to his feet. He was small and finely boned, with long thin fingers and neat nails. His beige pants were streaked with dirt, but he didn't seem to be harmed. "Thanks," he said to Smith.

Excitement over, onlookers began drifting back into the bar. The man who'd been shouting abuse stood beneath a streetlamp, watching. She couldn't see his face: he wore a ball cap and the strong light threw his features into shadow. His hands were resting on his hips, and he had his weight balanced casually on one leg. She sensed he wasn't any sort of a threat, but all it took was one loose word, some inadvertent gesture, to turn an observing crowd into a fighting swarm.

Where the hell was Evans?

"Is this over?" she asked the big man.

"Yeah." He spat into the gutter. "It's over."

She looked at the two men. The one who'd been down dusted himself off. His friend's eyes were on her. "Is this over?" she repeated.

"Yes, ma'am."

"Good," she said. No one was hurt, no one seemed inclined to want to take matters further. Only a couple of people were still watching hoping, no doubt, for further excitement.

"Get out of here then. All of you. Go home. I don't want you going back inside."

"That's a violation of our rights," the blond one said. "We can visit a public place if we so desire."

"Geeze, Buddy. I've just saved your ass, don't give me any lip. If you want to go down to the police station and argue about your rights to a judge tomorrow morning that can be arranged."

"I doubt you saved any ass, ma'am," he said, very politely. "I'm more than capable of taking care of myself."

He was young, in his early twenties. Well dressed, carefully groomed. She guessed he was a law student. *Spare us.* "Your friend there didn't seem all that capable when I arrived."

"Him? Never seen him before in my life." He looked at his opponent. "No hard feelings, eh? I'm off, but if I run into you again I'll buy you a beer."

"Deal."

Men.

She reached for the radio at her shoulder. Ready to tell dispatch it was all clear. No need for Evans after all.

She had taken her awareness away from the fourth man. The one ready to put the boot to a person lying defenseless on the ground.

Big mistake.

He was behind her, slightly off to the left. The sudden movement of his arm, swinging around his back, caught her attention. Realizing he'd come close to her, she began to turn.

He pulled a knife out of the waistband of his pants. With an audible click the blade sprang free. It wasn't a big knife, almost swallowed by the man's fleshy fist, but big enough. Sharp enough.

"Look out," someone shouted. "He's got a knife." Everyone scrambled to get out of the way.

She pivoted on her heels, came around to face him. He charged, blade held high. Light from the lamp on the far side of the street glistened on steel. She stepped to one side, out of his path. Her right hand struck his arm, shoving him aside. He stumbled and she stepped back, moving her body out of his reach. Without conscious thought, she had Glock in her hand and she shouted, "Drop it, now."

At last she heard the sound of a siren, coming toward them, getting closer.

The man stared at her. His eyes were glassy and unfocused. He was on something. Cursing herself for failing to notice, she held her arms steady, the weapon clenched in both hands. "I said drop it."

He looked at the knife. He looked at Molly Smith. She knew she could stand here all day, waiting. If he came toward her, or moved toward the onlookers, she'd have no compunction about shooting him. She kept her breath steady and controlled.

Blue and red lights washed the street. The police car came to a stop half on the sidewalk. Evans was out, moving, talking into his radio. He saw Smith, holding her weapon, the man with the knife facing her, the shifting nervous crowd of spectators. He pulled his own firearm, and shouted, "Police. Drop the knife." Far in the distance came the sound of another siren.

The knife clattered to the ground. "Get down, get down," Evans yelled. The man dropped. Evans holstered his gun and was on him. Only when he had the cuffs on, did Smith put the Glock away.

The man lay face down, arms bent behind him, Evans's knee planted in his back. Evans looked at her. They exchanged a glance, and she felt the tension flow out of her body.

It had all happened so fast, she hadn't even had time to be frightened.

Evans hauled the man to his feet. He hadn't said a single word. He was on some heavy stuff.

"Show's over," Smith told the watching crowd, grown as news of a potential knife fight or gun battle spread through the Potato Famine. "Get lost." She turned to the biker with the snake tattoo. "Your friend's under arrest. You can visit him tomorrow."

He shrugged. "No friend of mine. He sat beside me at the bar. We had a couple drinks, complained about this damned boring town. The music was shit." He tossed his head toward the smallest of the group, the one who'd been on the ground when Smith first arrived. "That guy got up to go to the can, knocked his arm and spilled his beer. Wouldn't apologize, so he," with a nod to the man being stuffed in the back of the car, "figured he had to teach him some manners. Hell, can't let a good fight go to waste. Didn't know he'd pull a knife on a cop. Sorry about that."

"Get the hell out of here," Smith said. "I see your face again tonight, I'm taking you in."

"I like a lady with spirit. I'm at the Falls campground. Drop around after work."

"Get lost."

He walked away, chuckling. His new best friend followed.

Dave Evans waited for her beside the car. Only one person was left. The man who'd been egging the fighters on. He was thin, pale, dressed all in black.

"Show's over," Smith snarled at him. "Go home."

"Shoulda let them draw some blood," he said.

The door to the bar flew open. A man ran out. He looked around, eyes wide and panicked. His fly was half undone. A woman peered over his shoulder. She was a brassy blonde, dressed in a short skirt about two sizes too small. Her lipstick was smudged and the buttons on her fluffy blouse done up incorrectly.

"Where the hell have you been?" Smith shouted. "I coulda used some help here."

"Sorry, officer." It was the Potato Famine bouncer. "Rodney's sick tonight and I was on my break."

"You take a break half an hour before closing time?" He'd been on the job about two weeks. She'd make sure tonight was his last.

She got into the car, and Evans drove away.

The man in the back snored all the way to the station.

Chapter Twenty-nine

John Winters tapped on the open office door. "Got a minute?"

Paul Keller looked up from the pile of papers on his desk. "Happily. The city council is meeting next week to discuss cutting the police budget. They always discuss cutting the police budget, and I always point out that they get what they pay for, and so they reluctantly agree to fund us for another year. It's like the dances in those stupid movies Karen likes. Historical costume dramas, where everyone knows the exact steps. I've often wondered why they even bother. The dancers as well as the city councilors. Sometimes I wish I was back out on the streets, I can tell you, John."

Keller looked well this morning, Winters thought, which made a change. The chief had been run down lately. New lines had appeared on his face, the bags under his eyes were deeper and darker, and his color wasn't good. But this morning he had a sparkle in his eyes and his cheeks were pink. Although a coffee stain marred the right sleeve of his white uniform shirt.

"How is Karen?"

Keller shot him a glance. *Trouble on the home front,* Winters thought. *That would explain the stain.*

Keller glanced at the open door. They could hear Barb on the phone. Out in the hall someone laughed.

"Shut the door, will you, John."

Winters stood and did as asked. When he got back, Keller said, "She's left me."

"Sorry to hear that."

"It's been coming for a long time. Now the kids are gone, I'm surprised she didn't leave earlier. We've simply been going through the motions the past years. She's found herself a lawyer and the house is going up for sale next week."

"That's tough. If you want to go out for a beer one night, to get out of the house, let me know."

Keller didn't appear to hear him. "There is, I guess everyone will find out soon enough, another woman. Here I am, going on fifty and I'm in love."

Lucky Smith.

Keller gave Winters a grin. "I'm guessing you didn't come in to ask me about my love life. What's up?"

"Greg Hunt. Owns Alpine Meadows Realtors."

"What about him?"

"His name's come up in connection with Brian Nowak."

"Really? That's news to me."

"Which is what I wanted to ask you. I don't see any mention of Hunt in your notes on Nowak's disappearance."

"Don't think he figured in any way. We canvassed the neighbors, of course. Talked to people Nowak worked with and socialized with. Put a notice in the *Gazette* and other papers in the Kootenays asking anyone with information to come forward. Never heard from Hunt."

"You know he has a record for theft?"

"Now that you remind me, yes. I'd forgotten about that. I see him around town sometimes, Rotary and stuff. He was on probation when he moved back here. He seems to have kept his nose clean ever since. Have you found something to the contrary?"

"No. Perfectly respectable businessman. Prominent member of the community. He came to me on his own, said he was interested in the reopening of the Nowak case because they'd been friends. Wanted to know what I'd found."

"That's it?"

"That's it. Just enough to niggle my interest. Makes me wonder if Hunt knows something about the missing ten thousand. He had been some sort of an investment manager before getting caught with his hand in the cookie jar."

"You think Hunt killed Nowak for ten thousand dollars?"

"I've seen men killed for a heck of a lot less, but that's not what I'm thinking. If Greg Hunt were the sort to try to cheat a man out of ten thousand and killed him to cover it up, he'd have been in trouble since. Leopard doesn't change his spots. Hunt appears to have led a quiet life since coming back to Trafalgar. Runs the family business, which is doing well, maintains his mother's garden, goes to Vancouver every couple of months on business. Where he is unknown to the police. Takes vacation twice a year."

"But something's caught your attention?"

"Cop's instinct? He seemed more interested in a fifteen-year-old case than he should be." Winters got to his feet. "It's probably nothing. Maybe he spends too much time watching *CSI* or *Law and Order* and thinks he can help us do our job."

"Another one of *those*."

"Thanks for listening. And uh… well, if you need to… uh."

"Maybe when Karen's lawyer has started the formal process I'll invite you and Eliza out to dinner to meet my lady friend." Keller grinned and his eyes sparkled. "I'm sure you'll like her."

I already do.

Lucky Smith carried the laundry basket upstairs. Rain drops pattered against the roof and she could hear the trees moving in the wind. It was so quiet.

Too quiet.

The house was always quiet these days. She put the basket on the neatly made bed. The bed where she had slept with Andy nights beyond counting. Where they had conceived two children.

She wandered out onto the landing. She gripped the banister and closed her eyes, listening.

She could almost hear the house coming back to life. Echoes of the children, the family. Sam teasing Moonlight. She always believed everything he said and then would be furious when she found out he'd been making it up. Moonlight's temper tantrums. No one could have a tantrum like that girl. She would scream to the point of vomiting. Good thing they lived deep in the woods, out of hearing of the neighbors, or people would be reporting them for child abuse. Downstairs Andy would have the television on too loud and would be cheering on one sports team or another. He loved the Seattle Mariners and the Vancouver Canucks. Hated the Toronto Blue Jays and Maple Leafs. Children coming and going, Moonlight and Samwise's friends visiting, laughing, wrestling, arguing, slamming doors, playing their music, the time one of the kids hit a home run—through the living room window.

She felt tears gathering behind her eyelids. Toenails clicked on the hardwood floor and she opened her eyes. Sylvester, the big sloppy golden retriever, was coming up the stairs. He gave her a long look and barked once, and she realized he hadn't been outside yet this morning.

She went downstairs, the dog running ahead, and opened the kitchen door.

Sylvester stuck his nose out, got it wet, and hesitated.

She touched his rear with the toe of her slipper. "Out you go, old boy."

He caught sight of a movement in the woods and dashed across the lawn, barking. Lucky followed, kicking off her slippers. The rain poured down. She lifted her face to the water and raised her arms. She swung around, enjoying the feel of the soft rain on her face, the wet lawn beneath her bare feet. Sylvester came back and ran in circles around her, howling.

She laughed. *It's been too long since I've danced in the rain. The dog will think I've gone mad.*

She twirled and danced and laughed. And if Sylvester had been capable of laughing he would have laughed as well.

Eventually she stopped, and leaned up against the side of the house, breathing heavily. Life, she reminded herself, is too short and too sad to spend it wrapped in memories of the past.

She scooped a wicker basket off the outdoor work table and danced barefoot down the lawn to her vegetable garden. As the rain continued to fall, Lucky Smith picked squash and peas and spinach and popped the last of the cherry tomatoes into her mouth.

Chapter Thirty

"Let's see the pictures."

"Don't have any."

"Why the hell not?"

"'Cause I didn't take any, that's why."

"Nicole, are you messing me around? Not thinking of going freelance are you? That would be a foolish move."

"Don't threaten me, Joey." Nicole leaned across the table and stared into his black eyes. She'd stuffed the two small twisted pieces of paper he'd given her into her purse. She made sure to have the drugs before giving him the bad news. They were sitting on the patio at Big Eddie's, an awning sheltering them from the downpour. It was ten o'clock in the morning, and people were streaming into the coffee shop. Business people mostly, grabbing a coffee and muffin to take back to the office. Other than a handsome gray standard poodle, left outside while its owner chatted with friends inside, the patio was empty.

"Not a threat," Joey said. "A promise."

She lit a cigarette, leaned back in her chair, and gave a light laugh. A sparrow settled on the table next to them, nibbling at crumbs. "For a moment there I thought you were serious. We've got a good deal going here, right? Neither of us is going to do anything to mess it up."

The vein in his neck stopped throbbing. He unclenched his fists and picked up his coffee mug. "Right you are, Nicole."

She knew he had a temper and suspected he could be violent when he thought himself provoked. But, knowing which side his bread was buttered on, he'd never shown any trace of violence toward her.

Until now.

She was getting frightened.

"I don't have pictures to show you because I didn't have the chance to take any. He wasn't interested."

"You expect me to believe that?"

"Joey, I am not out to cheat you. Get it? That's not the first time nothing's happened. I've had dates who left me at the front door with a chaste kiss on the cheek."

"You were all over that big guy. If I hadn't known it was you I'd almost have expected you to climb up on the bar and spread your legs right there."

"Don't be disgusting."

"You left with him. His friends were drooling as they watched you go."

"I failed, okay, Joey. I failed. He wasn't interested."

And wasn't that the truth. Give her some credit, she did consider herself to be a professional. She knew how to signal that she was available for sex without, as Joey so crudely put it, spreading her legs.

She'd turned the charm on Adam Tocek. She'd flirted and teased, while at the same time chatting to his friends and basking in their attention, all the time letting them know Adam was the one she found attractive. Fastest way to a man's wallet is through his ego. They'd bought her drink after drink, but only one of the men was drinking heavily. It had been his promotion party, apparently.

Finally, when a new arrival joined them, and the other men turned to talk to him, she wiggled off her stool and gave Adam a big smile. "Oh, dear," she said. "I feel a bit wobbly. I'd just as soon not walk back home alone." She reached out a hand and rested it on his chest, as if needing support. "Can you give a tipsy girl a ride?"

"I'll call you a cab," he said.

"Won't take a minute. I'm staying at my mother's. It's not far." Mention of the mother was a nice touch, she thought. She fingered her necklace. A large blue stone hung at the end of the gold chain. Heavier than it looked, it contained a miniature camera. Another camera was in her purse, in a special pocket with a tiny hole cut into it.

Adam glanced at his friends, as if seeking support. The newcomer made a joke and they laughed. The drunken one stared at her. Nicole took Adam's arm, pressing her breast against his chest. "They're having their fun," she breathed. "Let's us have ours."

He tossed a couple of bills on the counter and led the way through the bar.

She wasn't sure why she'd separated Adam Tocek from the herd. He was young and just a cop, unlikely he had much money. Not married, so not a good prospect for blackmail. Maybe only because he was cute, and it would be nice to screw a good looking guy for a change.

He was Molly Smith's boyfriend.

Perhaps that was the reason. Molly'd had everything easy in life. Great parents, good family, university education, a job with power and prestige. Handsome boyfriend who seemed to adore her. Pretty soon she'd have the two point five kids and the house in a nice area.

She had a future.

Well, tough luck for Molly. This one time Nicky Nowak would have some of what Molly had.

Except she hadn't.

Adam Tocek drove her straight to her mother's house. She didn't fail to notice he didn't need to ask the address. No doubt every cop within a hundred miles knew where Brian Nowak had lived. She suggested they go someplace for a drink first. He said he couldn't drink any more because he was driving. She suggested they go to his place.

He didn't even answer that one.

He pulled up in front of the house and made no move to get out. "Night, Nicky," he said.

She purred and leaned close. She ran one fingernail down his cheek. "Sure you don't want to go someplace nice and quiet, Adam? It's so early." For one quick moment, she thought she had him. His face softened and his eyes glazed over. She cupped her other hand behind his neck and started to pull his mouth toward hers.

He jerked back and grabbed her hand. "Good night, Nicky. I'll tell Molly you said hi."

She got out of the truck without another word and marched up the steps, face burning, heels rapping furiously on the cement. She'd heard his truck roar off into the night.

"Think he's an arse bandit?" Joey asked her.

"If that's a rude way of asking if he's gay, he is not. As flattering as it is to know that you think a man has to be gay not to screw me, I've been told some men have morals."

Joey laughed. "Don't you believe it. Try again tonight. The more I see of this town, the more I'm convinced there's gold here."

A white bundle of excited fur ran onto the patio. The poodle snoozing in the shade of a maple tree opened one eye. The little dog barked in its face, but the poodle simply went back to sleep. The rain had stopped.

A gaggle of young girls ran up the steps. "Scissors, come here," one of them called. She grabbed the dog and scooped him into her arms. She turned and saw the two people at the table.

"Oh, hi. Remember me? I bet you remember Scissors. I'm Becky."

"Sure I remember you, Becky." Joey got to his feet with a smile. "Are these your friends? Hi, girls."

There were four of them. Three white, one Asian. All had clear skin, shiny white teeth, thin muscular legs, and budding breasts. Becky introduced her friends. Nicole dropped her cigarette to the floor and ground it out underneath her heel. She lit another.

"Why don't you join us? We can pull up some chairs. Can we get you girls a drink?" Joey asked. "Our treat?"

The girls looked at each other. Then Becky said, "Sure," and they echoed her. Becky dropped Scissors, and looped one end around a tree and snapped the leash on the dog.

"One of you can help me carry," Joey said. "What are you having?"

They ordered drinks that were more like milkshakes than coffee and Joey and Becky went inside.

The three remaining girls smiled at Nicole awkwardly and then started chatting among themselves. She glanced inside and saw Joey rest his arm on Becky's shoulder.

Nicole knew nothing about Joey's personal life. She wanted to know nothing. She wasn't even sure if his last name was Stewart. Until this week, he hadn't known her real name. It was possible he had another business on the side, but he'd always been available when needed.

She wondered if he were looking for a new opportunity. Running kiddie hookers or taking pictures for child porn was risky, and the law cracked down hard.

Which made it highly lucrative.

She'd had enough of Joey. The bag of cocaine was burning a hole in her purse. She pushed her chair back and stood up. She walked away without saying good bye to the girls. Scissors barked.

◇◇◇

Molly Smith stared at the phone in her hand. Adam. Probably wondering where she was. They were supposed to be going to the youth center to hear the son of one of the RCMP civilian clerks playing with his new band.

She'd dressed for a night out in jeans and a loose blue blouse shot with gold threads and gold sandals with killer heels. Adam loved stiletto heels, and if she weren't going to be waking far, she liked to please him.

Nicky Nowak had been wearing sky-high heels last night. When she got into Adam's truck. Adam also liked long legs. Nicky was very short, but somehow in the flowing skirts and sexy shoes she favored she managed to look as if her legs were endless. *Perhaps,* Smith thought, *Nicky acted as if her legs were long and sexy, ergo they were.*

She and Adam had never said they had an exclusive relationship. She didn't think that was something that had to be said.

She'd thought Adam was going to ask her to marry him.

Had she been wrong about that?

Had he taken her coolness to mean he could screw around anytime he wanted?

Or had he been screwing around all the time, and just happened to be seen this once?

Giving a woman a lift didn't mean he slept with her.

Did it?

The phone rang again, and this time she flipped it open.

"I'll be there in a couple of minutes. Are you ready?"

"Almost," she said.

She didn't know what, if anything, to say to him.

She certainly didn't want him to think she was spying on him. She hadn't been spying, only walking down the street as it was her job to do.

But she had seen him. With another woman.

Tonight he was going out with her.

Not Nicole.

She decided she had to believe in him. She'd let it go, unless something happened to make her think otherwise.

Three minutes later the doorbell to the street rang. She plastered a smile on her face and ran downstairs. She opened the door and turned and walked up the stairs without looking over her shoulder. By the time she got to the top, Norman was ahead of her. She gave him a pat and let him into the apartment.

Adam kicked the door closed behind him and leaned down to give her a kiss. "You smell nice."

"Thanks."

"Is something the matter?"

"No. What makes you think that?"

"You seem a bit off. The band's probably going to be pretty bad. Noise and enthusiasm but not much talent. We don't have to stay long if you don't want to. Show our faces and sit through one set should be enough. Marie's hoping to get a big crowd out to make the boys happy."

"I'm sure they'll be fine." She picked up her bag.

"New shoes?"

"Like them?"

"Like you in them." He pulled her close. "Think we can be late?"

"No." She pushed him away.

The band was much as Adam had predicted. Plenty of enthusiasm, little musical talent. But the boys were loving their moment in the limelight, and the crowd applauded each song with gusto.

Smith sipped at her Coke and felt herself relax. Adam squeezed her hand under the table. She squeezed back.

They went to the Bishop and Nun after the show with a group of officers and partners. They pulled tables together and dragged over chairs and were a loud, laughing bunch as they devoured burgers and wings and pitchers of beer and told war stories. Tocek was spending the night at Smith's apartment, so he was able to enjoy his beer.

He was telling about Norman finding Nowak's bones, with much embellishment and not a little exaggeration, to some of the people who hadn't heard the details, when the door opened and Dawn Solway came in. A woman followed her.

"Hi," Solway said, "Mind if we join you?"

Everyone moved as more chairs were dragged over.

"This is my, my girl… my friend, Francesca," Solway said. Her cheeks were red, her shoulders set, and her voice sharp.

Francesca was older than Smith expected, quite a bit older than Solway. Of average height, about twenty pounds overweight, with olive skin and short, brittle gray and black hair. She wore loose jeans, a red shirt, floppy black sweater, and peered at the room through rimless glasses. She shook hands and said hello, but her smile was tense.

Smith got to her feet and held out her hand. "Hi, I'm Molly. Pleased to meet you. Adam, shove over." She waved toward the bar, trying to attract the waiter's attention.

"First time in Trafalgar, Francesca?" Tocek asked.

"Yes. It's very nice."

The waiter waved in acknowledgment, and Smith resumed her seat. So this was Dawn Solway's mad passion. Oh well, no accounting for taste.

The police officers and their friends had greeted Francesca with warmth and then immediately resumed their own conversation. Solway's shoulders relaxed, and Smith gave her a wink. The waiter took orders for more drinks.

Alan Dobson staggered over to their table. He rested his hands on the back of Molly and Adam's chairs and leaned in between them.

"Thought we'd lost you last night, my boy," he said with a leer. His eyes were red and he blinked to focus.

Tocek shot him a dark look. Dobson laughed again. "Could of knocked me over with a feather when you came back so soon."

"Shut the hell up, will you," Adam said.

"What happened?" Smith asked. She'd almost forgotten about Nicky and last night. Dobson would have been there—it was his promotion they'd been celebrating.

Dobson leaned into her face, breathing beer and undercooked hamburger. "Now that I'm leaving, Molly, I can tell you that you're way too sexy to be a cop."

Adam's chair scraped the scarred wooden floor as he got to his feet. "Get lost, Dobson. You've had enough."

The people around them stopped talking. A couple of men pushed their chairs back, ready to intervene. Solway and Francesca exchanged glances.

"Hey," Dobson said, raising his hands in submission. "What'd I say? She's cute, okay. Must be darn good in the sack to keep a man's hand out of that short one's pants. God, she wanted you."

Ron Gavin grabbed Dobson's arm. "Come on, Alan. I'll take you home."

Dobson pulled away. "Nah. I'll have another beer." He staggered off toward the bar.

Gavin gave Smith and Tocek a shrug. "His wife's in Ottawa house-hunting. With the baby. Guess it's the first time since the kid was born Alan's had a chance to let loose. He's overcompensating."

"Any more overcompensating," Tocek growled, "and he'll be spending the night in the drunk tank."

"I'll keep an eye on him," Gavin said. He followed Dobson to the bar.

"Want to tell me what that was about," Smith said once everyone had sat down and conservation began flowing again.

"No."

"But you will anyway." She kept her voice low. "I assume he means when you left the Hudson last night with Nicky Nowak."

Adam looked at her. "You know about that?"

"Saw you. I was walking past on the beat. About to come in and say hi." She felt tears prickle behind her eyes.

"God, Molly. I dropped her at her mother's house. Nothing happened."

"So Dobson said." She looked into his soft brown eyes and whispered. "I love you, Adam."

He pushed his chair back. "Let's get the hell out of here."

They walked the few blocks to her apartment holding hands. She'd said the words. For the first time. It felt good.

"About Nicky," he said, as they turned the corner into the alley that led to her apartment over the bakery.

"Never mind Nicky."

"I know she's your friend, Molly."

"Used to be my friend. When we were in grade school. I was hoping we could be friends again, but I guess not."

"You know she's a hooker, right?"

"What?" Smith stopped walking.

"She's a hooker."

"You're kidding."

"I am not."

"Did she ask you for money?"

"Didn't have to. A guy can tell, Molly. I wondered about her when I met her that first night, when you were there. There's just something… a way that a guy can tell when a woman expects him to pay for it. Even when, like that time, she wasn't working, it was there. Last night she came into the bar at the Hudson. She laid it on pretty thick, and the guys bought her drinks and played it up. She's very attractive and knows how to shine a spotlight on a man so he feels like he's something special. She asked me to take her home. She'd had a lot to drink, so I said yes."

"But she didn't ask for money?"

"Not in so many words. That's not how it's done. I didn't have much doubt that a figure would be named soon. Look, Molly, I don't want you to think I didn't sleep with her because she wanted me to pay for it. I didn't sleep with her because I am head over heels in love with another woman. And she gives me everything in the world I could possibly want."

"Another woman," Smith said the words slowly. "Anyone I know?"

"No."

She slapped his shoulder and they continued walking.

"She doesn't look like a hooker," Smith said, unlocking her door.

"You're thinking of the sad cases standing on street corners. That's the sort of hooker a beat cop or social worker sees."

"When I was in school, I did a placement at a shelter for street workers." She had been studying for her MSW, master of social work, when she quit the program after Graham's death. "Saddest bunch of people I ever did see."

"That's the underworld. Lowest of the low. Moving up the ladder you get women who work out of massage parlors, strip clubs, escort services, so-called gentlemen's clubs. And the escort services can get fancier and fancier. Better class of women, more money."

"Like Nicky?"

"I'd say your friend is at the top of the game. Now. There's no place for her to go but down. And in that world, it's a long way to the bottom."

Smith unlocked the door, and Norman greeted them with a long wet tongue and wagging tail.

"Should we do something about it?" Smith asked. She headed into the kitchen to put the kettle on. There was no prostitution in Trafalgar. Cases of sexual exploitation on occasion, but not prostitutes working the streets or the hotels. The town was too small, the community and the police too familiar with everything that went on.

"I've been thinking about that all day. I might mention it to John Winters, but what happened really? She didn't ask me for money. Easy enough to say she was captivated by my manly charm. She's in town for her father's funeral. Do you know if she's planning to leave once that's over?"

"She told me she lives in Vancouver. Where she owns an interior decorating business. I might tell her I'll drop into her store next time I'm in the city, see how she reacts. She did say she hates being in her mother's house. They don't get on, and she can't wait to get home."

"So that's it then. She can take her sordid business back to the big city. Leave us upright, decent citizens alone. Speaking of decent," he came up behind her and kissed the back of her neck. "I have to take Norman out for a sec. It would make me very happy if you were wearing that red nightgown when I get back. Keep the shoes on."

Chapter Thirty-one

May Chen didn't know why she couldn't be like Becky or Donna or any of the other girls in school. Her parents would have had a fit if they knew she'd gone to Big Eddie's with her friends on Friday. She told them they were walking the dogs. That hadn't been a lie; she'd just not mentioned they'd gone for coffee after.

She was almost the last one of the girls in her class to get a phone, and she'd had to beg and plead for it. It was only when Simon told them a cell phone was a good idea, so she could call in case of an emergency, they relented and bought one for her birthday. It wasn't even an iPhone like Donna had, just a cell, but it was better than nothing.

Saturday night and another dreary week lay ahead.

Monday was violin lessons. May hated the violin. Actually she didn't hate the violin, she loved the instrument, loved making music, loved the way it felt in her arms. She just hated Mr. Franklin, the teacher, and she hated having to sit in his stuffy back room after school while the other kids were riding bikes or going to Eddie's or hanging out, and she hated the hours and hours of practice her parents made her do.

She hated her parents.

There, she'd said it.

She hated them.

They were strict and old-fashioned and didn't understand that they lived in Canada, not some peasant village in China where a trip to the store was a three-day ride on a forty-year-old bus over unpaved roads. Her dad loved to tell stories about how hard life had been in China.

She didn't believe him.

Tuesday was Mandarin lessons. May hated Mandarin even more than the violin. At least her violin gave her pleasure (well, sometimes) but Mandarin was a waste of time. Her parents didn't speak English very well, her mom hardly at all. She didn't understand why she had to go to lessons when she could just talk to Mom, but Mom wanted her children to speak properly. Her own accent, apparently, was uncultured.

At least that was something to be thankful for. May's friends wouldn't know her parents were uncultured peasants.

May Chen wanted to be an actress. She loved watching movies and TV shows starring Asian women. Sandra Oh on *Gray's Anatomy*, Grace Park on *Battlestar Galactica*, Lucy Liu in *Charlie's Angels*. May had good skin, long silky black hair, big black eyes. Her friends told her she was pretty and there was that boy at school… No point thinking about him. Her parents wouldn't let her even think about dating.

Courtney had been going out with Trevor Saunderson for six months and she wasn't much older than May.

Courtney's parents were cool. They let her do what she wanted, when she wanted. Becky's dad was a cop, but he seemed like a nice guy and that was cool.

May's parents worked in a restaurant.

They owned the restaurant, and people worked there for them, but that didn't matter. All the kids at school knew was that the Chens were cooks and waiters.

Simon had been a fight a couple of months ago when a boy at his school had said Trafalgar Thai made "Chink" food. Donna's brother told Donna about it, and Donna told May. They said Simon really sorted that kid out. Simon didn't know judo or karate or anything, but the kid thought he did and ran away.

May would have liked to have seen that.

It was a Saturday night and May Chen was standing at the sink washing dishes. Becky and Donna were going to a movie. She'd asked if she could go, but Mom said no, she had to study. Dad had come home for dinner, which was unusual on a Saturday, but he had to get back soon. Simon stood up for his sister sometimes, but tonight he was getting ready to go out himself and wasn't paying any attention.

The one good thing in May's life was that her parents paid no attention to what she did on the computer. They couldn't read English well enough. Becky had said her dad checked her computer all the time to see who she was talking to. Cops were suspicious, she said.

May'd enjoyed having coffee at Eddie's on Friday, sitting out on the patio. They'd met a man there and he'd been nice, buying them drinks and asking questions about what they wanted to be when they finished school. May had hesitantly told him she wanted to act, and he'd gotten all excited. Said he worked film shoots in Vancouver, big Hollywood movies.

He Facebooked her later and said if she was ever in Vancouver he'd take her to work with him. Introduce her around. She had, he said, the look the camera loved. Asian girls were hot in show business right now.

She'd been on the phone with Becky while using Facebook. She told Becky she was thinking of going. Becky said the guy was just trying to sound important.

As if her parents would ever allow her to go to Vancouver, anyway. They didn't even want her to talk about acting. They wanted her to be a doctor, like her cousin Ellen who was in med school in Toronto. Simon hoped to go to UBC next year to study math and computer science. Maybe when Simon was at the university she'd be allowed to visit.

But that was a whole year away.

"May, violin," her mother said.

"Ah, Mom, no. It's Saturday."

Her phone rang, and she turned away from her mother's scowl to answer.

"Whatcha doin'?" Courtney asked.

Her parents didn't like Courtney much. Mom had been shocked the one time Courtney had come over during the summer because her T-shirt showed her bellybutton and the top of her breasts. Courtney had the biggest breasts in grade eight. Maybe that was why her boyfriend was Trevor Saunderson, who was in grade ten.

May's mother took May shopping for clothes.

"Hi, Becky," May said, loudly.

"It's not Becky, it's me, Courtney."

"Sleep-over. That would be fun. Hold on a sec and I'll ask. Mom, it's Becky. She wants me to come over and study for next week's history test. Can I can spend the night after? We'll probably study until really late."

Mom started to shake her head.

"You know Becky. Her father's a policeman, right? So it's okay?"

Dad finished his tea and stood up from the table.

"Dad can give me a ride to Becky's house. I really need help studying for that test and Becky's the best student in class."

"If studying, then okay," Dad said.

Mom didn't look happy, but she nodded.

"Great. Let me grab my stuff and I'll be right with you." She spoke into the phone as she ran to her bedroom. "It's okay, Becky. I can spend the night and everything."

"Cool," Courtney said.

Courtney was definitely not the best student in the class, and Becky had no intention of working on history homework. She'd contact that man and tell him she was ready to come to Vancouver.

Chapter Thirty-two

As Eliza didn't work regular hours and they didn't have children to worry about, Winters usually took the weekend shifts so Ray Lopez could spend the time with his family. Sunday morning, he was surprised to see Lopez in the office on his day off. He was even more surprised to see Ray's youngest daughter, thirteen-year-old Becky, crouched in the single visitor's chair. They both glanced up as Winters came in, the detective's face set in tight lines, the girl looking as though she wanted to bolt.

"Hi, Becky. Congratulations on winning the cup. Your dad told me all about it."

Becky mumbled something.

Winters glanced at his partner. Despite his surname, Lopez was blue-eyed and red-haired and had a splash of freckles across the bridge of his nose. He'd been adopted by a Spanish family, but the Irish in him came to the surface whenever he was angry.

He was angry now. "Becky has something to tell you, Sergeant."

Winters draped his jacket over the back of a chair. "I'm listening."

Becky studied her feet.

"Let me start then," Lopez said. "Becky met a man. In the park, is that right?"

"Yes," she mumbled.

Winters sat down. He could guess where this was heading. He said nothing, waited for the girl to speak.

"I took Scissors for a walk and he got away from me. He started barking at this couple sitting on a bench. When I went to get him, they said hi. Nothing happened, Sergeant Winters. We just talked for a few minutes, about dogs."

Winters glanced at Lopez. His color was high and his fists clenched. "You said a couple. What do you mean by that?"

"A man and a woman."

"Go on."

"Friday we didn't have school because it was a teacher's day, and I went out with some of my friends. Scissors is still a puppy so I have to give him lots of exercise. We took Scissors and Donna's dog Sammy to the park, and May came with us. Sammy is big and not very good so Donna took him home and then we went to Big Eddie's. We met Courtney on the way."

Winters glanced at Lopez. He was staring at Becky. Winters thought it would be a big mistake to mess with one of Ray Lopez's daughters.

"Go on."

"They were there, on the patio. That couple from the park. He bought us all drinks and we sat with them for a while. Look, Dad, I know I'm not supposed to be talking to men I don't know, but we were at Eddie's and there were all kinds of people around and he was with a woman. That means it's okay, right?"

Lopez and Winters exchanged glances. *Karla Homolka.* Girls, teenage girls, had gone with Paul Bernardo because Karla was with him, so he looked safe.

"It's not what happened at Eddie's, as you know," Lopez said. "Carry on."

She took a breath.

"The woman left. We stayed for a while and talked. The man was nice, friendly. Wanted to know where we went to school, what subjects we like. Stuff like that." She sighed. "He asked us if we're on Facebook. Of course we are. He said he'd like to be our friend, so we can keep in touch after he's gone back to Vancouver."

Becky shot her father a look. "I know the rules, Dad. You or Mom get to see all my Facebook friends and you can read what we post. I wasn't going to keep it secret."

"Good thing."

"We gave him our Facebook names, and yesterday he friended us."

"What's his name?" Winters asked.

"Joe McNally."

"Unlikely to be real. Go on, Becky."

She took a deep breath. "He told us he organizes movie shoots in Vancouver. Hollywood movies with big stars. He scouts locations, stuff like that. Said if we ever come to Vancouver, he'll show us around."

"I bet he will," Winters said.

"And then I came in," Lopez said.

Becky hung her head.

"As Becky said, we have rules. Madeleine and I access the girls' computers any time we want. We don't read notes to and from friends we know, but we do insist on knowing who they're in contact with and what web sites they're accessing. I looked over her shoulder and saw some adult male asking for her e-mail address and inviting her to Vancouver to meet movie stars."

"I wouldn't have gone, Dad!"

"I know that, Beck. It's not you I'm mad at."

"You'd never seen this man before you ran into him in the park?" Winters asked.

"No. Never."

"What about his Facebook picture. Does it look like him?"

"It's a shot of a man in front of movie set. Could be almost anyone." Lopez answered.

"Can you describe him?"

"Sort of normal-looking. Thin, shorter than you or Dad."

"Age?"

She shrugged. "Old?"

"The woman he was with?"

"She's pretty. Short, thin with long black hair and big boobs. I figured she might be one of the movie stars he's friends with. Oh, the man had a really strong accent."

"What kind of accent?"

She shrugged. "English, maybe?"

"Thanks for telling us, Becky," Winters said. "I'm sure this guy is harmless, but your dad's right about meeting men on the Internet."

"There is one other thing," she mumbled. "She told me not to tell, but…"

The men exchanged glances again.

"But what?" Winters asked.

"Becky…" Lopez said.

"It's my friend May. She's having a lot of trouble at home. Her parents are really strict. They don't let her go to dances and parties and stuff and they're always on at her about her marks at school and practicing the violin and stuff. They'd probably be mad if they found out she went to Big Eddie's, 'cause she's not allowed. She told them we were walking the dogs in the park, but didn't say we were hanging around in town after. She's been talking about running away, Dad. I texted her last night to say Donna and I were going to a movie. She asked if she could come, but her mom said no. She phoned me later and said she was thinking about going to Vancouver with this guy. He said he could get her a job in a movie."

"For heaven's sake, Becky, why didn't you tell me this last night?"

"She said to keep it secret," Becky mumbled. "She wouldn't actually run away, Dad. It was just talk."

"Do you have May's phone number on you?" Winters asked.

Becky pulled her phone out of her tiny pink purse. "Yes."

"Call her."

"Invite her around to our house for lunch," Lopez said. "I'll get your mom to talk to her. See how serious she is about this idea."

"Okay," Becky said.

Winters turned to his computer. The Nowak funeral was tomorrow and he intended to be there.

"No. She's not." He turned back at the sudden panic in Becky's voice. "I mean, I don't think…"

"Give me that," Lopez ordered his daughter.

He took the phone. Becky spoke to Winters. "May isn't home. She told her parents she was sleeping over at my house and they haven't seen her since dinnertime yesterday."

Chapter Thirty-three

Mr. and Mrs. Chen met the officers at the door. Their eyes were wide and their faces full of worry. Lopez and Winters had brought Becky. No point in trying to keep Becky out of it, Winters decided.

Mr. Chen's English was poor, his wife's worse. They owned and ran Trafalgar Thai, a popular restaurant on Front Street. Mr. Chen gave the visitors a small bow and led the way into the living room. It was immaculate, furnished in red and cream. Family pictures dotted the tabletops and hung over the gas fireplace in the center of the room.

A boy sat on the couch, iPod in his ears. He wore jeans and a BC/DC T-shirt. He pulled the white buds out of his ears. "I'm Simon," he said. His accent was Canadian. "I'll translate for you. My parents' English isn't too good." He got to his feet and gestured his mother into a chair. She sat, crossing her small hands in her lap. She stared at the police. She said nothing, yet Winters could almost smell her terror.

"Where May?" Mr. Chen said.

"Not at my house. I'm sorry," Lopez said, "May didn't spend the night with Becky. When did you see her last?"

Simon spoke to his parents. No one had offered the officers a seat. "I was out," he said when his mother and father stopped talking over each other. "I went to the movie with friends after dinner. May was here when I left, so that was around six-thirty.

Mom says she got a phone call just after that. She said she'd been invited to Becky's to study and then for a sleep-over. She packed a few things into her backpack and Dad took her."

"Took her where?"

"To your house, Mr. Lopez. He dropped her out front and drove away. I know he should have gone in, at least said hi, but May's embarrassed that our parents work in a restaurant and don't speak English and, I'm sorry to say, she does just about everything she can to keep them out of her life."

"Where did this phone call come in? The house phone?"

"No. May's cell. She only got it last month, for her birthday. The folks didn't think she should have one, but she put up such a fuss. All the other kids have one, don't you know?" He shook his head. "Poor May, she only wants to be like the other kids.

"When you told us, Detective Lopez, you hadn't seen May, I asked Mom to check her room. She took a lot more clothes and stuff than you'd expect for an overnight."

"Tell your parents we've begun a search," Winters said. "All of our officers have been alerted as well as the RCMP.

"Do you have a picture of May?" he asked Mrs. Chen directly.

"Picture?"

"To show police?"

She smiled. "Many." She picked a framed photograph off the side table. It showed a pretty Asian girl with long black hair and a big smile dressed in an orange and black soccer uniform. She looked at the picture for a very long time, before handing it to Winters. "May," she said.

"Thank you."

"May's on my team," Becky said.

"Good player," Mr. Chen added.

"Can I take this?" Winters asked.

The couple nodded. They were looking at him with so much faith, he was embarrassed. He wanted to tell them not to get their hopes up.

Instead, he turned to their son. "Simon, would you ask your parents to prepare a list of May's friends."

"I can help with that," Becky said. "I know her friends better than her parents do."

"Thanks, Becky. That'll help."

"What can I do?" Simon asked.

"You and Becky start phoning the friends. Kids at school, any teachers or group leaders she might be close to. Ask if they've seen her, of course, and tell them to let us know immediately if they hear anything from her."

"What do you think's happened to my sister, Sergeant Winters?"

Winters glanced at the parents, and then he looked at the photograph in his hand. The girl's face was wide open and innocent, her smile broad, her eyes clear. Breasts like rosebuds poked at the uniform shirt, her knees were scraped, and one long orange sock was crumpled around her left ankle.

"There's a good chance she's met someone here, in Trafalgar, who wants to her to come with him to Vancouver. We'll try to find her before they leave."

Simon let out a puff of air. "That's good then." He smiled at his parents and said something. Winters caught the word Trafalgar. Mr. and Mrs. Chen smiled and nodded.

Winters forced himself to smile in return. Highly unlikely this Mr. McNally would hang around Trafalgar once he had May. If she'd been taken to Vancouver, finding her would be a nightmare. Runaways disappeared into the city like water on a parched lawn.

◇◇◇

The funeral for Brian Nowak was held on a beautiful fall day. The sun shone in a startlingly blue sky, and the church grounds were redolent with the scent of falling leaves, freshly cut grass, and turned-over flower beds. The wind was cool, and people had put away summer sandals, short-sleeved shirts, colorful dresses.

Molly Smith accompanied her mother. She wasn't particularly well inclined toward Nicky any longer and had rebuffed her former friend's lunch invitation yesterday. Regardless of whether or not Nicky was a prostitute, that she would even attempt to seduce Adam, whom she'd met as Molly's boyfriend, would not be forgiven.

But she and Lucky had known Brian Nowak and wanted to pay their respects.

John Winters was there, on duty. So was the chief constable. Ray Lopez was in the office, working flat-out on the May Chen disappearance. Station gossip said Ray's youngest daughter was friends with the missing girl, and he was taking the case personally. There had been no sign of May since she'd left her parents' house after dinner on Saturday.

A lost cause, Smith thought. Girls that age did not show up, blushing and giggling about errors in communication, after being away for two nights. May was either raped and beaten and left in a ditch somewhere for the vultures and the wolves, or taken to Vancouver. For wolves and vultures of another kind to chew at a body that might be still breathing but otherwise wasn't much more than a corpse.

Molly Smith despaired, sometimes, at the depths to which humanity could plunge.

Pre-funeral conversation in front of the church was scattered with whispers about the missing girl. Dawn Solway was scheduled to give a talk to the students at May's school this afternoon. Something about predators and using the Internet safely. May hadn't been kidnapped, snatched off the street. She'd run away, leaving her home under her own power. Trying to convince themselves it would never happen to them, to their daughters, a lot of the gossip blamed the parents. Too strict, too lenient, spending too many hours at the restaurant, not involved enough in the community. Immigrants.

Smith saw the chief turn from whatever Winters was saying and give Lucky a smile and a wave. She crossed the lawn to join the men, leaving Smith standing alone.

"The love birds are looking quite happy." Christa said, giving her friend a hug.

"Spare me."

"Come on, Molly. I think it's sweet. They say Karen Keller is seeking a divorce. Do you think it's because of Lucky? Their house is going up for sale this week."

"Nonsense. Where'd you hear that?"

"Nancy at Alpine Meadows Reality. It's not a secret."

"It has nothing to do with Mom."

"Come on, Molly, give her a break. Not that I'd want to snuggle up in bed with the chief, but if she wants to let her go for it."

"They are not going to bed together."

"I didn't mean literally, but you obviously do. Your parents were happy, weren't they?"

"They sure were." It was the closeness of her parents' marriage that was, strangely enough, one of the reasons Smith feared committing to Adam. She just didn't know if she loved him in the all-encompassing way Lucky and Andy had loved each other.

"So, what's wrong with your mom wanting to be happy again? Don't you think your dad would want that for her?"

Smith looked at Christa, who said nothing more, simply put her hands on her hips and waited for an answer.

Smith shuffled her feet. "I guess he would."

"If he would be happy for her, why can't you be? She looks better, Mol. Her eyes are bright, her skin has more color, her smile is real and genuine. She looks like the Lucky I've always known, not as she's been this past year, going through the motions, holding herself together."

Smith looked across the lawn. Lucky laughed at something the chief had said, and he smiled down at her. John Winters had moved away, leaving Lucky Smith and Paul Keller in their own private world. Lucky wore a long blue dress decorated with silver beads that sparkled in the sun. She never wore dark colors to funerals, believing that a funeral should be a celebration of a life.

"Thank you for coming." Smith turned. Nicky was dressed in gray. A gray suit, skirt cut at the knees, well tailored jacket with a black blouse. Her jewelry was restrained, gold hoops through her ears and a small gold brooch. She wore large sunglasses. The heavy scent of cigarette smoke lay over her perfume.

Smith stared at the trees lining the lawn.

"Christa." Nicky held out one perfectly manicured hand, nails painted a pale pink. "It's been a long time."

"Nice to see you, Nicky. I'm sorry it's on such a sad occasion."

"Sad. Yes. But no sadder than the last fifteen years have been."

She took the glasses off and touched a tissue to her nose. Her eyes were red, and the pupils were very large.

Had Nicky had a hit of cocaine before coming to her father's funeral?

She saw Smith looking at her and quickly put the glasses back on. "I'd better join Kyle and Mom. Who now can proudly bask in the title of widow."

Nicky picked her way across the lawn. Mrs. Nowak wore a black dress about two sizes too big and a black straw hat more suited to gardening than church. Kyle slouched in a pair of paint-spotted jeans and a black T-shirt with lurid graphics advertising a heavy-metal band.

"Wow," Christa said. "Did you think that was a rather mean thing to say?"

"I'm beginning to think Nicky is a rather mean person. Let's go inside and find seats. It looks like it's going to be a full house."

Sacred Heart was an old church, built in Trafalgar's heyday of the 1880s when riches of forests and mines poured jobs and money into the area. The population was smaller then, but everyone went to Church on Sunday. The Catholics to Sacred Heart, the Anglicans to St. Peter and Paul, assorted other denominations to smaller houses of worship. Expecting the twentieth century to bring nothing but growth and prosperity, those early Catholic citizens built a large, proud church. The tall white steeple was still the first thing one saw, arriving in town from upriver. The stained glass windows were perfect examples of high religious art, the wooden pews and soaring rafters cut from ancient first-growth forest, the gardens lovingly attended year round.

All the building lacked in the early years of the twenty-first century was parishioners.

Sacred Heart was fuller today than it had been for a long, long time. Father O'Malley could only wish this many people would come to mass regularly, not just for a funeral with a mystery surrounding it.

He recognized the chief constable, the detective sergeant, the editor-in-chief of the Trafalgar *Gazette*, the news reporter. The MLA was in attendance, as were the mayor, members of the city council, and assorted prominent men and women.

Too bad they weren't in Church to hear the word of God.

The service droned on and Molly Smith tried not to think about the contents of the closed black casket at the front of the church. Instead she remembered Brian Nowak. She'd liked Mr. Nowak. Much as a thirteen-year-old girl could like the father of one of her friends. He was there for his children when he was wanted—driving them to parties or games—but not when he wasn't.

He didn't deserve to spend the last fifteen years on the mountainside. Alone. Forgotten.

No, not forgotten. His family never forgot him.

Almost impossible to believe Nicky would have become a prostitute if her father had lived. The Nowaks had been one of the few religious families young Moonlight had known. As a child Nicky hadn't rebelled against that religiosity. She'd accompanied her family to church without complaint and was active in its youth and sports groups. She seemed to be close to her dad in much the same way Molly was close to Andy.

They'd been good friends, Moonlight Smith and Nicky Nowak, talking on the phone for hours, sleep-overs at each other's houses, going to movies and school dances together, just hanging out watching TV, listening to music, and growing up. Nicky's family wasn't into the outdoors, and Andy Smith was training his kids to be wilderness guides, but Nicky liked to jump off the Smith's dock or lie on the beach on a hot summer's day. The only thing the girls didn't do together was ski. Nicky didn't ski. Molly had tried nagging her into it once and Lucky had sharply told her to stop it. Probably, Smith realized now, the family couldn't afford the expensive equipment and lift fees.

All that ended when Brian Nowak disappeared. She only ever saw Nicky at school, her attendance becoming increasingly sporadic. Lucky encouraged Molly to continue to invite Nicky to do things, and she did, but Nicky always said no, she had to go straight home. Then Molly found another best friend and she stopped even thinking about Nicky.

Nicky, who'd been a great student when her dad was around, quit school as soon as she turned sixteen. One day she simply wasn't there. It had made no difference at all in young Moonlight Smith's life.

Should she have tried harder to keep the friendship going? It wouldn't have helped.

Nicky's fate was sealed that April day along with her father's.

Look at Kyle. Couldn't even bother to put on clean pants or a decent shirt for his dad's funeral, slouching in the front pew, examining his fingernails as though he were bored. To young Molly, Kyle had been nothing but an older brother, vaguely present, usually with a sneer or a mocking laugh. He was a good bit thinner now than he'd been back then. Sallow-faced and hunched.

At every other funeral Smith had been to, including that of her own father, the family had clung to each other, arms round shoulders, heads bent together, hands clasping. The Nowaks sat so far apart, you could put another person between them and no one would have to shift over.

Mrs. Nowak had always been quiet. A small, nervous woman, constantly cooking or cleaning. A little mouse, particularly compared to Smith's own larger-than-life mother. She thought about the last time she'd seen Brian Nowak. The last time almost anyone had seen him. They'd been having pancakes, but he didn't want any.

A man got up to talk about Brian Nowak's devotion to his family, and the woman seated behind Smith stifled a sob.

John Winters paid no attention to the service. He sat at the back by himself and watched the congregation. Eliza had come, said a few words to Kyle and his mother. Greg Hunt was there, sitting alone. The priest had greeted Mrs. Nowak and her children at the door to the church. Kyle ignored the man's outstretched hand and pushed ahead of his mother and sister.

Kyle was clearly hostile to Father O'Malley, but Winters didn't know if it was personal or if Kyle had simply turned against the church.

The chief constable had looked pleased with himself, standing in the churchyard with a strangely demure Lucky Smith. They might as well have hung a sign around their necks advertising that they were now a couple. Instead, like everyone not willing to make their relationship public, they assumed they were protecting a big secret.

Winters realized people were standing. Pleased the service was over he also started to rise. He quickly dropped back down. Communion, and the faithful were preparing to be served the host.

Nicky Nowak looked sedate and modest in a gray suit. He wondered if, like the Queen, she travelled everywhere with suitable funeral attire.

He hoped she'd be heading out of town soon. He wasn't entirely sure what it was about her, but he sensed she was trouble.

Her brother wasn't a whole lot better. Eliza had spent most of last week raving about Kyle Nowak's art and the show he was going to have in Vancouver. Winters had been at the opening night reception of the current show at Eliza's Trafalgar gallery and liked the paintings. The prices were high but not unreasonable, and he thought she might actually be able to make some money at this. Why she assumed anyone with a lick of taste would be interested in Kyle's art was well beyond his understanding.

But Eliza was happy, and that made John Winters very happy, indeed.

At last the service came to an end. Mrs. Nowak and her children rose from their seats, and Father O'Malley preceded them down the aisle. Nicky had her hand on her mother's arm, but Kyle walked alone. Eyes fixed on the floor, he glanced at no one as they passed.

Winters was one of the last out the door. There would be no reception, and the service at the graveside was for family only. He stepped to one side of the carved oak doors and watched. People were gathering on the lawn, chatting in small groups. Mrs. Nowak and her children stood underneath a massive oak. It had probably not been her intention but a receiving line began to form, forcing Mrs. Nowak to shake hands and accept condolences.

Nicky was not playful and flirty now. She took her place beside her mother, close but not touching, back straight, head high. She had been perfectly made up when they entered the church, now tears carved rivers though her face and her mascara and eye shadow was rubbed almost off. Kyle studied his running shoes and stuck his hand out without looking at who stood in front of him. Mrs. Nowak said, "Thank you for coming," and "So nice to see you," with no inflection in her voice.

If he had been here in any role other than investigating detective, Winters would have told Father O'Malley to get the family out of here and end their torment.

Instead the priest was talking to Greg Hunt as the Realtor made his way down the line. As Winters watched, Hunt said something to Nicky. Then he reached for Mrs. Nowak's hand, but before he could touch her, Kyle shoved his mother out of the way. He stepped in front of her and faced Hunt. Nicky looked startled, her mother bewildered. Conversation in the receiving line died. Winters moved quickly away from the door and down the steps.

"Stay the hell away from my mother," Kyle said.

"I'm only wanting to extend my condolences," Hunt said.

"We don't want them or need them."

"Kyle," Nicky said.

"Shut up." Kyle stood firmly in front of his mother. Hunt lowered his head and walked away. Kyle turned to his mother and said something Winters couldn't catch. Then he stalked off. The people in line shifted in embarrassment and everyone began talking at the same time.

"Wonder what that was about." Molly Smith walked over to stand beside Winters.

"I'd like to know."

"I suspect Kyle's never grown up. He's trapped in a fifteen-year-old time warp. Whereas Nicky has gone way beyond where she was back then. This has got to be pretty hard on them all."

"Yes."

"Harder on Mr. Nowak, though. I wonder if he knew that day how badly his kids would turn out. He was so sad, as if he knew he was going to miss them."

"What did you say?"

"I said his kids turned out badly. Nicky looks…"

"I mean about Nowak."

"He was sad." Her blue eyes opened wide. "And he was. I'd forgotten how sad he was that morning."

"Tell me everything you remember."

She closed her eyes and was quiet for a long time. Around them birds sang, people murmured, car engines started up. "I'd been at Nicky's for a sleepover. You knew that, right? I had to go home right after breakfast because Nicky and her family were going to church, and Mom came to pick me up. Mr. Nowak was at breakfast. We had pancakes. They weren't very good and the syrup was corn syrup, not maple like my mom used. Mr. Nowak didn't have any. He snapped at Mrs. Nowak when she tried to get him to eat and told her to stop nagging him, he wasn't hungry. He sat there and drank coffee and watched us. No, that's wrong, he didn't watch *us.* He watched Nicky."

Smith's eyes flew open. She fixed them on Winters' face. "He watched her like he would never see her again. Like he was trying to memorize what she looked like. Oh, my gosh. I forgot all of that. I was sitting in church remembering the last time I saw him, and I guess that started things coming to the surface.

"Have you read the *Lord of the Rings*?"

"Let's talk about that later, what else do you remember?"

"That's it. *Lord of the Rings* was pretty much *de rigueur* reading in my house." She grimaced. "Which is why I am cursed with the middle name of Legolas. Anyway, in the book the young Hobbits know Bilbo is getting ready to leave the Shire even though he thinks he's keeping it secret because he's always muttering things like *I wonder if I will ever see such-and-such again*. That's the feeling I got from Mr. Nowak. He knew, that morning, nothing would ever be the same again."

Winters let out a long breath. "Are you sure?"

"Not at all. Would I go to court and swear to it? No. It was fifteen years ago and I was a kid. Kids don't pay much attention to their friends' parents. But I did like Mr. Nowak, more than a lot of the fathers I knew, and I think because I liked him I could tell he was sad. When he disappeared and the chief asked me about that morning, I didn't mention that. Adults were always having moods, so I didn't think it mattered. All that other stuff, about never being here again, really John, I've only thought about that now." She lifted her hands in the air. "Maybe I'm talking garbage."

The churchyard was emptying out. Most people had said their condolences and left. A few groups remained, chatting amongst themselves in low voices. One elderly lady stood in front of a fresh gravestone, head bowed. Lucky and Christa waited for Smith beside her car. The funeral home attendant, solemn in black, approached the Nowaks, and gestured toward the waiting limousine. He took Mrs. Nowak's arm and they began to move away. Nicky followed, tight butt swaying under the form-fitting skirt, sharp heels digging into the grass. Like most of the men remaining, Sergeant Winters glanced at her. He started to turn away, and then his head almost swiveled on his shoulders as he did a double-take. He started to move toward her, but stopped as the family reached the waiting limousine.

"John?"

"Something just occurred to me. I'll follow it up when we get back to the office. I don't think you're talking garbage at all. It's funny, the sort of memories we hold and how they can come popping to the surface when given the slightest nudge. Brian Nowak was sad that morning. Something very important was about to happen. Important enough that he wanted to pull memories of the family breakfast close. As if he knew it would never happen again." He gave Smith a lopsided smile. "Now all I have to do is find out what that something was."

Chapter Thirty-four

Smith hadn't stopped thinking about Brian Nowak and that last breakfast, but try as she might, she couldn't remember anything more. She couldn't even be sure if the memories she did have were authentic. It had been a long time, and so much had happened since an apparently normal Sunday morning in Trafalgar.

"Nicky's heading back to Vancouver first thing tomorrow," Lucky had said as Smith drove out of the church parking lot.

"Good riddance," Smith said.

"She's going to phone you later and see if you'd like to go to dinner."

"I'm working."

"I told her that."

"Good."

"Did something happen between you?" Lucky asked. In the backseat, Christa leaned forward.

"She only tried to seduce Adam, that's all. She knows he's my boyfriend."

"Oh," Lucky had said.

Smith's phone rang as she was heading out the door dressed for work. John Winters, asking her to come to his office as soon as she arrived.

Ray Lopez was there, not looking happy.

"We have a rough description of a woman of interest in the May Chen case," Winters said. "Very pretty. Small and thin."

"With big breasts and long black hair," Lopez interrupted.

"Don't know why I didn't think of it earlier, but when I saw her at the funeral... Sounds exactly like Nicky Nowak. See what you can find, Ray, about Nicky's acquaintances."

"Your friend Nicky..." Winters began.

"She's no friend of mine."

"May have been seen in the company of a man we suspect is attempting to lure young girls to Vancouver. For reasons we can only guess at. It's possible he contacted May Chen prior to her running away, and she might have gone to join him."

"Wow."

"Do you know anything about an Englishman Nicky might be traveling with?"

"She never mentioned anyone." Smith shifted her feet. "I wasn't going to say anything, John, but in light of what you've just told me... She tried to pick up Adam the other night. He was pretty sure she would have asked for money."

"Can't say I'm too surprised. I thought she looked like she might be not quite on the up-and-up, but I figured she'd have the good manners not to work around her father's funeral. I want to have a chat with our Nicky. And not where her mother's hovering over me, offering tea and cookies. Get her. Bring her to me."

Nicole did not like driving in the mountains at night. Too many wild animals out there—and only some of them had four legs. If it wasn't for the eight-hour drive back to Vancouver, she'd have left immediately after the funeral.

It had been tough, really tough. Mom had cried, but Kyle had sat there like he was carved out of stone. The only emotion he'd shown all day was when that man tried to shake Mom's hand. Nicky didn't even know who he was, but Kyle had shoved the guy out of the way.

Weird. Kyle was weird.

Living in the same house as their mother for the past fifteen years would have made anyone weird. He'd had plans, Kyle, big plans. When they were growing up all he talked about was being an artist. He was going to travel the world, painting everything he saw, being feted by rich and famous art collectors everywhere he went. He wanted to paint in the Impressionist style—like Renoir or Monet. He hoped to go to art college for grounding, and then study in Paris. Nicky had wanted to be a marine biologist and work with dolphins and whales. Her family had never had much money, but Dad always told Nicky and Kyle they would have whatever education they were capable of.

Dreams. What good were dreams, hopes, plans? Kyle had never seen the other side of these mountains, never mind Paris. And Nicky? Nicky and her childish fantasies died when her father did.

Only Nicole continued to live.

She wanted to go to dinner with Molly tonight. One last chance to talk about the old days and pretend they were innocent young girls again. Obviously that wasn't going to happen. Molly had refused an offer of lunch and then cut her dead when Nicky'd approached her at the church.

Adam must have told her what had happened.

Wasn't that sweet. They were in love.

Give it another year, and he'd keep quiet.

A year or two after that and she'd have his prick out in no time.

They were all the fucking same.

Too bad about Moonlight, though. It would have been nice to have a girl friend.

Not that Nicole ever intended to come back to Trafalgar. Maybe for her mother's funeral. Kyle's she wouldn't bother attending.

She needed a line, but she'd used the last of her coke before going to the funeral.

She wondered where Joey had gotten himself off to. If he was still around she might give him a call, see if he could get her another score.

"Can't we have some light in here?" she said, pulling herself out of the overstuffed couch. "Place is as dark as the freakin' grave."

Her mom began to cry. Again.

Nicky pulled back the front curtains in time to see a police car turn into the driveway, a uniformed officer at the wheel. She watched Molly get out of the car and walk up the sidewalk with strong purposeful steps. This looked to be an official visit.

Maybe they'd found something new about what happened to Dad.

Nicky hurried to open the door.

Molly Smith stood with her hand raised to knock. She did not smile at her long-time friend.

"Ms. Nowak. Sergeant Winters would like you to come down to the police station. He has some questions for you."

"What the hell?"

"Who is it, dear?" Nicky's mother croaked.

"Sergeant Winters suggests the station rather than your mother's home," Molly said. "For a private conversation."

"Has he found out who killed my dad?"

Molly's face was totally expressionless, her voice flat. "I believe this has nothing to do with the death of Mr. Nowak."

"I'll go and change."

"That's not necessary. Sergeant Winters is waiting."

Nicole put her hands on her hips. "When did you become such a power-hungry bitch?"

Something flickered in Molly's eyes.

"Unless you are arresting me, *constable*, you will wait while I change out of the clothes I wore to my father's funeral. I'd tell you to go and sit in the car, but you probably think I'm going to climb out the kitchen window." She turned her back and walked to her bedroom, satisfied at having put the cop in her place.

She slammed her door shut, and leaned against it. She tried to control her breathing. *What the hell was this about?* They couldn't be arresting her for prostitution. She'd hadn't gotten anywhere with Adam, which was the only time she'd tried. Good thing Joey had told her not to play with Winters; she had nothing to worry about on that score.

Joey.

This had to be about Joey.

What had the miserable bugger done? Why the hell had he come to her town anyway? After the fiasco with Adam Tocek, she'd told him she wasn't going to try again. This town was too darn small: she wasn't going to crap in her own backyard. Instead of arguing, he'd let it go. That in itself had been strange. Once Joey got an idea in his head, he stuck with it.

She'd last seen him sitting with four young girls under the awning on the coffee shop patio. What on earth had he done?

And more to the point, why had it led to her?

Chapter Thirty-five

Lucky Smith had forgotten that tonight was the monthly meeting of the marijuana legalization action group. They usually met in the Smith kitchen because most of the members were young and didn't have the space Lucky had around her kitchen table.

When Moonlight was living in the house, after having joined the police, the group decamped to various locations, but eventually they gravitated back to the Smith's. The enthusiasm of the group had been dying over the past year, but with the federal government now huffing and puffing and threatening to strengthen penalties for marijuana growing and use, they'd sprung back with fervor.

Lucky was assembling the ingredients for dinner. She'd planned linguini with a sauce of cherry tomatoes, arugula, and basil from her garden, tossed with goats' cheese. They'd have a glass of wine or two outside on the deck, and she'd slip into the kitchen to toss the ingredients together and cook the pasta. Then dinner, followed by coffee and apple pie. And then, she giggled to herself, who knows what might follow.

She heard a car and looked up. He was early.

Only when she recognized the battered old van belonging to Steve and Lynette did she remember the group meeting.

The pro-marijuana activists were here. More than just theoretical political organizers, they could be counted on to settle back in their chairs and light up.

The chief of police was coming for dinner. She'd changed her mind about continuing to see Paul Keller. Nothing wrong with a couple of single people getting together for a meal of an evening.

She ran for the phone and punched buttons.

Paul didn't answer.

She glanced at the clock. He was due to arrive in fifteen minutes.

Steve and Lynette had given a lift to a second couple. Lucky met them at the door.

"I'm so sorry," she shouted. She coughed and lowered her voice. "Sorry, I completely forgot. My… uh… my grandchildren are visiting. I won't be able to have the meeting here. Sorry."

"Hey, Lucky," Lynette said, patting her huge round belly. "That's okay. I'd love to meet your grandchildren."

"No. You can't. I mean, my grandson has allergies. Bad allergies. To smoke."

"Not a problem," Steve said. "We'll take it outside."

They edged toward her. She stood firm, blocking the door. "My son, he doesn't approve of pot. He might not let the children come again if he finds out you were here while his kids were."

"So, don't tell him," Lynette said. "The reading of that bill is next month in the House of Commons. We have to get to work on this."

"I'm sorry," Lucky said. "I can't have you here. Not tonight. Are Brad and Howie coming?"

"I think so."

Everyone turned at the sound of a car engine. Lucky's heart was in her mouth until she saw Brad's BMW turn the corner. He'd brought Howie.

Almost pushing and shoving, blathering excuses, Lucky got the group off her step. They climbed back into their cars, exchanging dubious looks, and drove away.

She went back into the kitchen and dropped into a chair.

Hadn't that made her look like a right fool. She could have just said she was sick.

Even Sylvester was looking at her as if she'd lost her mind.

Her political activities were important to her. They always had been. In the early years, Andy had stood firmly at her side, and she at his, but as they settled into comfortable middle age Andy had begun to seek the easy way. No more marches and demonstrations for him, no weekends around a kitchen table full of strangers painting posters and planning tactics, no more trips to Ottawa or Victoria in rusty vans armed with petitions.

Even on the one issue that should have mattered most to Andy, war and war resisters, he wasn't interested in doing more than looking up from the paper and insulting ignorant, strutting politicians.

They'd gone their separate ways, but Lucky had always known he was there for her, if only in spirit.

Could she say the same for Paul Keller, chief constable of Trafalgar?

They didn't talk politics, both suspecting they'd come up on opposite ends of some spectrums. For a senior police officer he was quite liberal, which was good, but it was unlikely he'd let his own views stand in the way of doing his job and enforcing the law.

Another car.

Paul would have passed the group heading back to town. No doubt he recognized Steve and Lynette's van. Hard not to, what with the giant marijuana plant entwined with a red Canadian maple leaf painted on both sides.

She put on a smile, tucked her hair into place, and once more went to greet her visitor.

Chapter Thirty-six

"Heard you got busted," Kyle said, stepping out from behind the bushes at the side of the house.

"I did not get busted." Nicky rummaged in her bag for a cigarette. She lit the match and sucked in smoke, watching the taxi drive away.

The miserable cops hadn't even offered her a ride home.

"What'd they want?"

She studied her brother. "What are you doing lurking in the dark?"

"I live here. If I want to stand outside, I will."

"Lurking," she said. "You've been waiting for me."

His eyes slid to one side. "I was sitting outside. Heard the cab pull up."

"I bet. An acquaintance of mine followed me here from Vancouver. He's been a naughty boy and the cops are looking for him. That's all."

"You were gone a long time. Mom knocked on my door, all upset, said you'd been arrested."

She blew out smoke. Miserable cops. Winters had had her brought in and stuck her in an interview room until he could be bothered to talk to her.

Hadn't Moonlight just loved it? Marching her into the station like she was about to be fingerprinted and locked up, looming over her like a Nazi storm trooper, fingering her gun, fantacizing about putting a bullet between Nicky's eyes.

Realizing she had no choice, she threw Joey under the bus. Winters and a red-headed plain-clothes cop showed her a picture of a Chinese girl, and Nicole's heart fell into her stomach. She'd overheard something in the churchyard earlier about a thirteen-year-old runaway; hadn't paid the slightest bit of attention.

The picture was of one of the kids they'd met at Eddie's. One of the ones Joey made friendly with and bought drinks for. And remained behind with when Nicole left.

One of the kids, probably the one with the dog, had described Nicole. Told her parents and they went screaming to the cops. The police knew Nicky Nowak well. Because she, she thought with a touch of satisfaction, did not blend into the hippie-skirted, yoga-attired, rugged outdoorswoman crowds in this pathetic town.

"You look pleased with yourself," Kyle said.

"I am always pleased with myself. I have a lot to be pleased about."

He snorted. "Hope that doesn't mean you'll be staying on."

"Don't worry, brother dear. It doesn't. I'm leaving tomorrow as planned."

Rather than order her to stay in town, Sergeant Winters had been happy to hear she was going to be on her way. She had no doubt he would be on the phone to the Vancouver police asking them to keep an eye on her.

Tough. She hadn't done anything to warrant the attention of the authorities, and she did not intend to start now. It wasn't she who blackmailed men stupid enough to screw around on their wives.

Time to get rid of Joey. Maybe move east, start again with a new name and a new partner.

If Joey was sniffing around underage girls, she wanted no part of it. Not because she cared what trouble small-town girls got themselves into, but she didn't need the attention.

And, sure enough, Joey had managed to attract police attention.

Idiot.

She'd told them he was a casual acquaintance. He'd come to Trafalgar after her when she heard about her father being found, saying he wanted to offer support. She said she suspected Joey wanted to be more than just friends, but she wasn't interested.

She gave them his name, at least the one she knew. Unfortunately she'd never been to his home and didn't know his address or his place of employment.

Nor did she know where he was staying in Trafalgar.

Sorry.

See how helpful I'm being.

Winters asked if Joey had been at the funeral earlier. No? Wasn't that strange, considering he'd come all this way to be supportive?

She'd dressed carefully, while Molly stood fuming on the front step, in jeans and a loose T-shirt under a sweater, and ballet-slipper shoes. She'd scrubbed her face clean of make-up, reapplying a touch of blush to her cheeks, and gathered her hair into a bouncy ponytail.

She looked sixteen, and as sweet and innocent as she had once been.

"I told him to go away, Sergeant," she said, focusing on his face. "He's been, well, following me. I'm starting to get uncomfortable. I hope he didn't turn to those young girls because I rebuffed him."

Eventually Winters stood up and told her she could go. He hadn't bought what she was selling, but he had no reason to hold her.

Kyle looked her up and down. "You're like a chameleon," he said.

"Don't you get sick of it? Living here. In this house. With her?"

"She's my mother, Nicky. What else am I supposed to do?"

"Mother. Smother. She's choking the life out of you. Do you have a girlfriend, Kyle? Have you ever had sex? Have you ever had an orgasm? With someone other than yourself, I mean." She read his face. "Thought not."

"There's more to life than sex."

"Sure there is. There's love." She laughed. "So people tell me."

She thought about the men who came to her. Their greed, their neediness. So overwhelming, they'd sacrifice everything to satisfy it. They cared, most of them, about nothing but their desires. Even the ones who expressed some fondness for her were only seeking her approval. Of them. They wanted her to moan and groan underneath them and grind her hips and tighten her cunt and cry out when she came. They had to know, every last one of them, that she wasn't really coming. It didn't matter. They needed to believe.

And so they did.

It didn't matter if they were so-called captains of industry or trust-fund babies, they wanted to be kings of Nicole Nolte's world, and she made them so.

And then it was over and they were faced, thanks to Joey and his pictures, with the truth. She felt nothing for them at all. Nothing for their pathetic wives and snot-nosed children.

Why should their world be any safer than hers had been?

Sometimes, in this life, you lose.

She looked at her brother. For the briefest flash of a moment she considered taking him by the hand, leading him to her room. He was as sad and weak as the men she saw in the Downtown Eastside trolling for hookers with child seats in the back of their cars. She'd had one, when she first arrived, who had an infant in the back. Nicky'd sucked his cock, pretending she liked it, while the kid snoozed and Daddy thrust and cried, "More, baby, more."

The silence of the night stretched between them. They watched each other, brother and sister, saying nothing. Feeling everything.

She flicked her cigarette butt into the rose bushes. "Have a nice life. I doubt we'll meet again."

"Do you ever wonder"—His voice followed her in the dark—"What things would be like if Dad hadn't died?"

"No."

Chapter Thirty-seven

"I expect to have that warrant tomorrow," Ray Lopez said to his boss.

"The grow-op?"

"Yup, the house on Cottonwood Street."

"Great. I want noise and activity, lots of it. Ask the Mounties for the dog and a couple of cars. Plenty of uniforms, them as well as us. We've been after these guys for a long time and I want everyone to know we've got them. Let's go in Thursday morning, first light."

"Got it."

"Any news?"

"You mean May? No. The artist will be arriving tomorrow afternoon. Becky's friend Donna seems to be able to give the best description of what this Joey creep looked like, and the artist'll work with Donna and the other girls to try and get a drawing we can use. Until then, we've got everyone looking for an average-sized, average-looking Englishman. Pretty useless description in a tourist town. I wish we could get more help with this, John."

"I know." May Chen had not been abducted. She had run away from home. She had lied to her parents about being invited to a friend's house for the night, packed her possessions, and allowed her father to drop her off. That she was only thirteen years old meant they could do something about searching for her, but the chief had refused to mount a full-scale investigation and bring in outside help.

"Ray's daughter is involved in this, John," Keller had said, "and most of our officers eat at Trafalgar Thai regularly. That makes it hard for everyone, but I cannot treat this as a kidnapping when it obviously was not."

"The girl was lured away…"

"That hasn't been determined. Yes, some man said he'd show her around if she came to Vancouver, but I don't consider that luring, and she was definitely not snatched. Have you and Ray contacted people in Vancouver?"

They had. Not only the police, but health and social agencies, anyone who might come into contact with a thirteen-year-old girl tricked into prostitution. Unlikely, Winters thought with a burst of acid in his gut, she'd be put to work on the street immediately. She'd be kept somewhere for a while. To be "broken in" before allowed out.

"Probably a waste of time, anyway," Lopez said. "Getting a description. It's been three days. He's not going to hang around here with May, is he?"

"Unlikely. But he might be known to the Vancouver police and if we can come up with a drawing that they recognize they can try to locate him. Joe Stewart's a damn common name, but I don't imagine that's his real one any more than McNally is."

"I had officers visit the hotels last night, after Nicky Nowak told us the guy's name. He was staying at the Mountain View, but they said he'd checked out. He paid cash, the address he put on the registration form doesn't exist, and his license plate number was an unreadable scrawl."

Lopez reached for the phone. "Speaking of Nowak, what's happening there?" he asked, punching buttons.

"Back to the basement. I haven't come up with anything new. I'm pretty sure the daughter, Nicky, is on the game, but once she's back in Vancouver that's no business of mine. She's a nasty piece of work, and I'm glad to see her skinny ass heading out of town. She should have left this morning. You can be sure I'll be asking my friends in Vancouver to keep an eye on her. She knows Joey Stewart, aka Joe McNally, a good deal better than she's letting on."

Lopez spoke to the Mounties and made arrangement for backup and the dog on Thursday morning. Then he pushed his chair back. "I'm getting a pop, want one?"

"Nope. Heading home. Eliza's off to Vancouver tomorrow to meet with her gallery manager. She's contracted Kyle Nowak to have a show next year."

The men walked down the hall together. "Do you have any suspects at all in the Nowak case?" Lopez asked.

He headed for the lunch room, and Winters followed. He'd never believed Nowak had come across something on his walk to buy cigarettes that meant he had to be snatched and eliminated. Certainly if Smith's memories were right and Nowak was facing an important decision, then it was even more unlikely he'd been the victim of random violence. Unless he was psychic. No one had suggested anything of the sort.

It was shift change, and Molly Smith and Dawn Solway were at the table, heads together.

"I haven't got a clue. Nowak," Winters explained to the women. "I'm sending the papers back to storage. I've uncovered absolutely nothing."

"What happened with Nicky yesterday?" Smith asked. "I felt like absolute crap dragging in my childhood friend. Despite the fact that she tried to steal my boyfriend."

Solway laughed. "That's a capital offence, isn't it?"

"She put on the sweet little me act and said that Joey Stewart, the man we're looking for, had been wanting to be more than just good friends but she'd told him no, so he left. She knew nothing about any penchant he might have for underage girls, or any businesses he might run. She pouted prettily and refused to budge from that line."

"What about the idea that Mr. Nowak might have been having an affair and ran away with the woman?" Lopez asked, dropping coins into the pop machine.

"Nothing came of it. Kyle Nowak insists his dad was a womanizer but no one else we spoke to backed that up. Everyone says he was a proper husband and family man. The woman in question, the one Kyle named, denied any impropriety. If another woman was in the picture, he kept it secret."

"For God's sake," Solway said. "Why does it have to have been a woman?"

"What?"

"You keep saying you're searching for the woman or women he was having an affair with." Solway looked around the room. "You people think you're so progressive, but you can't even see the blinkers you're wearing. With all due respect, Sarge, you've come up totally blank, but you can't look outside your own narrow box."

"Dawn," Winters said, "I don't understand…"

"A man," Smith interrupted. "He might have been having an affair with a man."

"Brilliant deduction, Constable Smith." Solway's tone was bitter. "You people call yourselves detectives." She got to her feet. "I'm off home. Catch you later, Molly."

Lopez and Winters stared after her. "What was that about?" Lopez said.

"She's right," Winters said. "We're only human and we bring our prejudices and preconceived notions with us. We do have blinkers sometimes.

"Okay, I'm going back to the case. First, I want to talk to Kyle Nowak. He was insistent that his father was a womanizer. The question is, did he suspect his father was fooling around and assume it was with a woman, or did he know and was not able to deal with it. For a fifteen-year-old straight kid, assuming Kyle is straight, the idea of men having sex can be pretty off-putting. Second, Greg Hunt. Nowak's good friend. I want to know what sort of friends they were that all these years later Hunt is hanging around the police station wanting to know what happened to his friend."

"The funeral," Smith said. "Hunt was at the funeral."

"That's right. And he had a confrontation with Kyle."

"What happened?" Lopez asked.

Smith was on her feet. Her face turning red with excitement. "Kyle shoved Hunt away from his mother. Everyone saw it."

"Time to have a chat with Mr. Hunt," Winters said. "I'll talk to Kyle later. Ray, you're still on the grow-op business and May Chen. Molly, I want a uniform presence when I speak to Hunt. I want him to know I'm serious."

"I'm supposed to be in a car."

"I'll square it with Al. It's three-thirty now. Chances are good Hunt's in his office. Phone first."

"Thought you were going home," Lopez said. "Something about a night with the wife."

"The wife," Winters said, "can wait. Hunt can not. Perhaps more to the point, I can not. If, and it's still a mighty big if, Hunt and Nowak were having a relationship, and Nowak, the good family man, decided to break it off, it's entirely possible Hunt took exception to that idea. Gay or straight, there's nothing like love thwarted to inspire murder."

Chapter Thirty-eight

Greg Hunt's assistant told Molly Smith he was in his office. Smith requested that he stay there, pending the arrival of Sergeant Winters. She hung up the phone without answering the woman's question: What can I say this is about?

"This might be a total waste of time," Winters said, fastening his seat belt in the patrol car. "But I've a feeling Dawn's onto something. As for Dawn herself," he glanced at Smith. "I've always assumed she's gay, but it's none of my business. You know anything about that?"

"Nothing I'm going to talk about."

"It's bothered me that I wasn't able to square Kyle's impression of his father with everyone else's. Something was missing. I never believed Kyle was lying outright, couldn't see why he would. Projecting teenage fantasies maybe, although in that case I'd have expected him to be more approving than scornful."

Construction on the big black bridge leading out of town had closed one lane, and traffic was backed up for a long way. "I wonder if the girl, Nicky, knew anything about it. Or Mrs. Nowak, for that matter." Winters talked to himself, not to Smith. It helped him, sometimes, to think out loud. Over the two years they'd worked together, Smith had finally realized that she was not expected to reply.

"Of course I might be totally out to lunch. But Dawn was right. I hadn't even considered that option. It's an avenue I need to explore. I don't know much about Hunt. A bit of trouble years ago, nothing since. He isn't married. That doesn't mean anything. Adam Tocek is in his thirties and lives alone with a dog, but it's rumored he's not gay."

The edges of Smith's mouth turned up. "So they say."

They reached the bridge. The sign-woman held the red "stop" facing them. Traffic coming from the other direction crawled slowly past. The sun was out, but the wind was high and the river was gray and choppy. A scattered handful of people walked along the beach, no one in the water.

"You know the chief's dating my mom?" Smith blurted out.

"Half the town knows, although the couple in question is under the impression it's a secret."

"I've decided I'm okay with it. It's her life, right? She deserves to be happy and if the chief makes her happy…"

The sign flipped to "slow" and the car edged forward.

"We can't run our parent's lives for them," Winters said. "Much as we might like to sometimes."

The mountain was steep on the other side of the river; a single road ran along the shore. A gardening center, a motel, a couple of small businesses spread out around the intersection with the highway. Alpine Meadows Reality was tucked into a small strip plaza, between a convenience store and a second-hand clothing outlet.

Greg Hunt waited for them outside, pacing up and down. He started talking before Winters had stepped out of the car.

"Sergeant, Nancy told me you want to speak to me. Is it about Brian? It must be, right?"

"Why don't we talk inside?" Winters said. Two young women, long-skirted, long-haired, came out of the convenience store pushing strollers. They stopped to stare.

"Good idea," Hunt said. "Come on in. Nancy, hold all my calls. Would you like coffee? Tea?"

"No, thank you," Winters said.

Nancy's face was a questioning blur as Hunt hustled the police past her desk and into the back.

Hunt's office was small and cramped. The desk piled with paper, walls covered with framed service awards, some of which went back to the 1950s. He plopped himself behind his desk. Winters took one of the two visitors' chairs, and Smith leaned against the door.

"Brian. Have you discovered something about Brian?"

John Winters tried not to jump to conclusions. It was his job to sift evidence, deal with facts, sort out lies from truth and sometimes from what lay in the nebulous area in between.

Nevertheless, he decided right there and then Greg Hunt had nothing to do with the death of Brian Nowak.

The man's eyes were bright, and he sat on the edge of his chair as if expecting good news. This was not a person in fear of being accused of committing murder.

"I would like you to tell me, openly and honestly, about your relationship with Mr. Nowak," Winters said.

Hunt blinked. He hadn't expected that.

"I can assure you that unless I am required to provide the information in court, or it involves the commission of a crime, anything you tell me will be strictly confidential."

Hunt's eyes shifted to the uniformed woman.

"Constable Smith will likewise remain silent."

Hunt took off his glasses. He pulled a tissue out of the box at his elbow and began cleaning them. Long thin fingers moved methodically, stroking the glass.

"We were in love," Greg Hunt said at last.

"I'm sorry," Winters said.

"Sorry? Sorry two men loved each other?"

"Sorry he died. Sorry I have to ask you about this."

Hunt pulled a set of keys out of his pocket. He unlocked his desk drawer, took out a photograph. He glanced at it before extending it to Winters.

Winters took it. Brian Nowak, laughing. He sat on a beige leather couch, arm across the back, right leg crossed over the left, ankle to knee.

Winters felt Smith behind him, peering over his shoulder. "That picture," she said, "was taken around the time I knew him."

"Two weeks before he disappeared." Hunt held out his hand. Winters returned the photograph. Hunt arranged it on his desk, standing. Brian Nowak watched them.

"My father was a strict man," Hunt said. "You no doubt are aware I had difficulties with the law when I lived in Toronto."

"Yes."

"I begged my father to have faith in me. To believe in me. To give me some money to invest, so I could show him how competent I was. Pride goeth before a fall, does it not? He gave me twenty thousand dollars, grudgingly. I should have been cautious with his money, instead I was reckless. I wanted to not just give him a good return, but a spectacular return. The stock was risky and it tanked. I lost almost all of it, almost overnight. I lied and told my father his money was doing well. One day, out of the blue, he wanted it back, plus all that had supposedly accrued. I panicked. I couldn't tell him I didn't have his money, and so I borrowed from other clients. I got caught. Convicted, lost my job, lost a respectable financial career. No money, no job, nowhere to live, I was forced to come home and beg my father to let me work for him. He had never approved of me and a criminal conviction didn't improve matters. I have spent my entire life deep in the closet. Hiding from my father's scorn."

Traffic sped past on the highway, and Nancy talked on the phone.

"Brian, obviously, was also firmly in the closet. He came from a deeply religious family, had a religious family of his own. He struggled every day of his life to reconcile who he was with who he was expected to be. We met at a city council meeting. I can't even remember what was under discussion. Brian sat down beside me. He said hello. And we fell in love. We went for a drink at the bar in the Hudson House Hotel. It wasn't as nice then as it is now. We didn't finish the drinks. He came home with me."

Hunt ran one index finger across the surface of the photograph. Tracing his lover's face. "Our affair went on for six months. We wanted, needed, to live our lives together, and finally decided we would do so, come what may. I would take my father's scorn. If he wanted to cut me out of the business, which he might well have done, I'd manage. As long as I could be with Brian.

"It was harder for him. He had a wife, children. He'd been told his whole life that the love he felt for me was a grievous sin. My father didn't have a religious objection to homosexuality. He thought it a weakness. A betrayal of what it meant to be a man, of masculinity. He was mortally afraid of being perceived as weak." Hunt looked at Smith. "He would have hated you, constable. Weak to my father meant women and what he called poofters. Police officers, like soldiers or firefighters, have no business being weak."

Winters said nothing. Let the man talk.

"As well as homosexuality, Brian's church is opposed to divorce. He was wracked with guilt over what this would do to his wife. He was determined to make the break as easy for her, and their children, as he could. We were going to move to Vancouver. I'd lose any hope of inheriting the family business, but I had a realtor's license and I'd proved, to my father's considerable surprise, to be a good salesman. Brian could get work anywhere. The plan was for my earnings to support the two of us, and Brian would give everything he made to his family. He didn't love his wife, he never had. He married her because it was expected of him to marry. He loved his children, particularly his daughter, Nicky. He simply adored that girl. Even though he was about to turn his back on his church, he prayed to God his children would find a way to forgive him someday."

Tears dripped slowly down the man's face. He did nothing to wipe them away.

"We made our plans. And then… nothing."

"Nothing?"

"Nothing came of it. He disappeared. I was completely destroyed, Sergeant Winters. Devastated. I had a breakdown and spent a month in hospital in Vancouver." He laughed, the sound bitter. Fifteen years of bitterness. "My father put it about that I'd had a manly heart attack. You see Sergeant, I assumed Brian had left without me. That he'd decided he didn't love me, but once he'd fully accepted himself as a gay man he wanted to change his life."

He looked at Smith once again. "You might think it strange I was so quick to believe the worst of the man I loved. I ask you to remember I had been taught that gay men, men like me, were perverse, warped, mentally deranged. I had no example of loving gay couples. Nothing to show me that they, and the people in them, can be the same as so-called normal relationships. Good and bad."

"You never told any of this to Sergeant Keller?" Winters asked.

"I considered myself to have been betrayed. I didn't think Brian had come to harm. I was… cowardly might be the word. How could I not only come blazing out of the closet by getting myself involved in a police investigation, but also reveal that my lover had decided I wasn't worth bothering about. At first everyone assumed Brian had simply walked away, needed some time on his own perhaps. By the time the police began a full investigation, I was in hospital. The police had no reason to send someone to question me. As far as everyone knew, Brian and I were nothing more than casual acquaintances."

Hunt pulled a tissue out of the box. He wiped at his face and blew his nose.

"For the past fifteen years, I've lived my life alone. I have few friends. My father is dead. I've never been close to my mother. I never wanted another lover. I would not chance having my heart broken again. I go to Vancouver every couple of months, visit the bars, meet the occasional man who's also looking for something brief. Love someone? Never again."

He gave Winters a sad smile. "Turns out I was wrong one more time. I don't have much of a track record in life. Brian never did leave me."

The floor creaked as Smith shifted her weight. Winters didn't dare look at her.

"Do you mind, Officers," Hunt asked. "If I ask you to leave? I need to be alone for a while."

"I have one more question, then we'll be on our way. Brian Nowak took ten thousand dollars out of his retirement account shortly before he disappeared. Do you know what happened to that money?"

"I do. It was for her, his wife. He didn't have many assets other than the house, which he planned to transfer into her name. She was from a family which insisted women didn't work outside the home, so she had no skills or experience, no way of supporting herself or her children. Brian wanted her to have some cash, in case it took him a while to find a new job. He gave the money to me to hold onto until he left her. When he never asked for it back, I assumed he felt too guilty to contact me. In my all-consuming grief and jealousy, I thought he'd met a man with money and didn't need it. When I got out of hospital, I gave the money to her."

"To who?"

"Mrs. Nowak. Brian's wife."

Chapter Thirty-nine

"When I decided to become a police officer I knew I'd have to deal with the hard side of life. Beaten children, raped women, accident victims, blood and gore. But that's not the hardest part, is it? It's the goddamn tragedy of people's lives."

They were once again sitting in traffic, waiting to cross the bridge. A few boats were on the river, moving fast, bright blue and white sails catching the wind.

Winters said nothing. He had nothing to say.

"Do you believe him?" Smith asked. Her hands were tight on the steering wheel, and they both knew she was fighting hard not to cry.

"Hunt? Yes, I believe him. I've yet to meet anyone who's that good an actor. Brian Nowak was going to leave his family. Abscond with another man. Who would care enough about that to kill him? Hunt's father, by the sound of it, but he's dead. The only other person I can think of is Mrs. Nowak. Humiliating enough for your husband to announce he's leaving you, but for a man?"

"Kyle Nowak." Smith said.

"You think so? He was sixteen at the time."

She shifted in her seat. She was nervous expressing her opinion. He knew that. Better a new officer be hesitant than butting in at every opportunity. "I was in an incident the other night. Outside the Potato Famine. A couple of out-of-town bikers got into a fight with two tourists."

"I read the shift report."

"The tourists were two guys. Just normal guys. What was funny was that it wasn't as you'd expect, bikers verses preppy tourists. Instead they came down on opposite sides. One of the bikers took offence at one of the tourists and everyone leapt in to join the fray." She hesitated. "Have you ever realized, John, that we'd have less work if women populated the bars?"

"Never considered that myself. I have, however sometimes suspected that where men will exchange punches before rhetorically kissing and making up, or at least going for a beer, women will take a fight to the grave."

"Touché," she said. "Anyway none of these *men* were prepared to sit back and take the insults."

"What does this have to do with Kyle Nowak?"

"He was there. Not one of the instigators, or the participants, but on the sidelines, shouting encouragement to the bikers. Stuff like let the fags have it. In stronger language. I've seen him around town on occasion. When Nicky and I were kids he was just an older brother. Not worth noticing."

Smith glanced out the car window. The vehicles ahead of them were disappearing off the far end of the bridge. The sign holder had an exasperated expression on her face as she beckoned them to proceed. No one behind had dared to honk at a police car. Smith put her foot on the gas and they rumbled across the bridge.

"I hadn't paid enough attention at the time of the bust-up to properly register that it was Kyle Nowak there, stirring the pot. You know what it's like when you're in a fight, it's all a frightening blur." She stopped and bit her tongue. Perhaps better not to mention she was frightened and not noticing everything around her.

"I remember the first time I got a punch in the face," Winters said. "I stood there for a couple of seconds, wondering why anyone would want to hit me. You're saying you think Kyle Nowak is a homophobe?"

She let out a long breath. "I guess that's what I'm saying. He's a bizarre character. Like Dracula, moving through the shadows at night, but he's never been in any trouble I've heard of and so we, the police, don't worry about him."

She pulled into the station parking lot. Winters did not unfasten his seat belt. "Mrs. Nowak," he said, choosing his words with care, "might also be considered strange. She showed surprisingly little curiosity when we told her that her husband's body had been located. I put it down to emotional numbness. After fifteen years of grief she couldn't find it in herself to care any more."

He spoke slowly and carefully. "Perhaps she wasn't curious because she didn't need to ask what happened to him. Let's pay a call on the Nowaks. I have a few questions for Mrs. Nowak and her son."

Chapter Forty

"Drop me around back," Winters said. "I'll knock on Kyle's door and bring him upstairs. You go to the main house and tell Mrs. Nowak I'll be along shortly to speak with her."

"Are you going to take them down to the station?"

"Not at this point. All I have is speculation based on peoples' behavior. I'll continue to treat them as family of the victim until I know more."

Smith turned into the alley and Winters jumped out at the back of the Nowak house. She circled around to the street. To her considerable surprise, Nicky answered the door.

"Not you again."

"I thought you'd left," Smith said.

"Don't I want to. My dear brother took my car last night and managed to plant it into a ditch. It had to be towed to a garage. You can be sure he'll be paying through the nose for the damage. It's supposed to be ready tomorrow. What the hell do you want anyway?"

Smith wanted to tell Nicky she was sorry. Sorry for having lost her father, sorry for all the pain she'd been through over the last fifteen years, sorry for forgetting about their friendship, sorry for not being there when Nicky's life went off the rails. Instead she said, "Sergeant Winters would like to speak to your mother. Is she at home?"

"Like she'd be anywhere else."

"I thought all this intrusion into our lives would finally be over." Kyle's complaining voice rounded the corner of the house. "This is an enormous strain on my mother."

"The gang's all here," Nicky said. She went into the living room. "Mom, we've got company."

Mrs. Nowak came out of the kitchen. Her face made Smith think of a bird. Blinking eyes, long sharp nose, no flesh beneath the folds of white skin. Her eyes flittered between the police officers, her son, her daughter. She twisted a tea towel in her fingers. Her nails were bitten, the cuticles torn, the skin on her hands as loose as on her face. She wore a housedress that might have once been colorful, but it had been washed to a faded gray dotted with anemic flowers.

"What's this about?" she asked.

Nicky tossed herself into a chair with a theatrical sigh. She was barefoot, dressed in jeans and a plain T-shirt. She made a display of studying her pedicure, but her eyes followed Winters. Her brother sat down, but remained perched on the edge of the seat, wary, watching.

The living room and dining room formed an L shape. Heavy red drapes, fading at the edges, were pulled across the back windows. Winters crossed the room in a few quick strides and yanked them open.

Mrs. Nowak blinked as sun poured in. A cloud of dust motes rose in the air, swirling and dancing in the light.

The windows were not windows but French doors, opening onto the deck. The glass was streaked and dirty. Outside, the wooden planks were cracked and broken, covered in dead and decaying leaves and bird droppings. Paint peeled off aluminum chairs in long strips and the table was thick with grime. Crumbled, shattered terra cotta pots were scattered around the floor, and the kettle barbeque was a rusty hulk.

"You don't sit outside much," Winters said. The contrast between the abandoned deck and the immaculately clean house and garden was startling.

No one replied.

"Looks to me as if this deck hasn't been used in, oh, fifteen years. That surprises me. It has a great view and must get a nice breeze on a hot day."

He turned and faced the family. "Nicky, did you use the deck when you were a child?"

She blinked in confusion. "Sure. Dad liked to barbeque and in the summer we ate out there almost every night."

"You don't barbeque, Mrs. Nowak?"

She threw a pleading glance at her son.

"No, she does not barbeque," Kyle said. "Not that that's any of your business."

"Just asking. Tell me about your marriage, Mrs. Nowak."

Another glance at Kyle.

"It was a good marriage," he said.

"It was a joke," Nicky said. She picked at the nail on her big toe. "They were roommates, not a married couple."

"Is that so?" Winters said.

"Lots of married couples live like that," Kyle said.

"You're very quiet, Mrs. Nowak," Winters said. "May I call you Marjorie? Did you and your husband not share a bedroom, Marjorie?"

She shook her head.

"Dad snored," Kyle said. "He disturbed her sleep."

Smith shifted her gunbelt and wondered why Winters was letting Kyle answer every question Winters aimed at his mother. She shot a quick glance at Nicky. The girl had stopped pretending to examine her feet and stared at her mother, mouth open in a round O, eyes wet with sudden tears. She shook her head slowly at Kyle's statement.

"No, Dad did not snore. He had the room next to mine. Kyle was across the hall and Mom's room next to that. They never visited each other's rooms at night. Why was that, Mom?"

"We had two children," Mrs. Nowak said. "That was all the family we wanted."

"As my brother said, some marriages are like that," Nicky told Winters. "They provide women like me with a nice income."

Her words were directed at the Sergeant, but Nicky turned her eyes toward Smith. It was a confession, of some sort. Perhaps even an apology. Mrs. Nowak appeared not to notice, nor to understand.

Kyle sneered. "You've uncovered my family's dirty laundry, pal. I hope you're satisfied. Don't let the door hit you or your Fascist buddy on the way out."

"Marjorie," Winters said. "Is there something you'd like to tell me?"

She hung her head. *In shame?* "I tried to make him happy. To be a good Catholic wife. The Church teaches that intimate relations are God's gift to a married couple. But Brian… Brian wasn't like other men. Brian told me he loved me, but… he preferred to sleep in his own room."

"Did you ever fear he might find someone with whom he would enjoy relations more?" Winters' voice was soft and very kind.

Kyle jumped to his feet. "I demand you stop this. You have absolutely no reason to be asking my mother these questions. She's the victim here. She's the widow. That fucking fag never…" He slammed his mouth shut.

Mrs. Nowak began to cry.

"So you knew," Winters said. "And you, Marjorie, did you also know your husband was gay?"

She shook her head.

"What the hell?" Nicky said. "Dad, gay? That's ridiculous. He was married. He had two kids."

"Surely, Ms. Nowak, you *of all people* are aware there are those who never are able to come to grips with their sexuality."

She didn't answer him, but tossed her Mother a pleading glance. "Mom?"

"He was going to leave us," Mrs. Nowak's voice was very small. "For… for a man."

"Shut up," Kyle shouted. "They're fishing. They don't know anything."

"But you do." Nicky jumped out of her chair, and ran at her brother. She flew into him, raking her long nails across his face. He stumbled backward and tripped over the curled edge of a rug. He crashed to the floor. Nicky fell on him, screaming. "You know. You knew. You've always known." She pounded his face with her fists.

Smith grabbed Nicky around the waist. Her childhood friend felt like a doll in her arms. "Leave it, Nicky, leave it," she said, staggering back, pulling the screaming woman with her. She felt Nicky's weight shift as Winters took one arm.

"It's okay," he said in a strong, composed voice. "Calm down."

Nicky pulled back her head and spat into her brother's face. Kyle scrambled to his feet. Two deep slashes across his cheek spurted blood. "You dirty whore," he shouted. "Keep your god-damned filthy hands off me. Your precious, saintly dad was a fag. Think he loved you so much? He loved his *boyfriend* more." He dropped into a chair.

Nicky shook the police officers off. Her chest rose and fell rapidly. She looked at her mother. "What happened to my father?" she asked. "Tell me."

"It was an accident," Mrs. Nowak replied.

Smith shot Winters a question. He motioned for her to stay silent.

"When Kyle and I got home from church, two suitcases were at the front door. Brian was on the deck, having a smoke. I asked him what was happening. Was he going on a business trip?

"He looked so sad, Mr. Winters, so sad. He told me he was leaving us. Going to Vancouver to live with his lover. I can't tell you how shocked I was. I never knew. I never had any idea. I told him I didn't believe he would leave his family for another woman."

Kyle laughed.

"Not a woman, he told me. Not a woman. Then I knew he was joking, so I went inside to start lunch."

"You didn't go inside with your mother, did you Kyle?" Winters asked.

"He was running away, running away with a fucking pervert. I hit him. He said he wasn't going to fight me. I said wasn't that exactly like a cowardly fag. So I hit him again. And again."

Nicky was crying hard, big deep sobs and great gulps of air. She made no move to blow her nose or wipe her eyes. She sat. And wept.

Mrs. Nowak stood up and walked toward the French doors. She stood there, staring out onto the abandoned deck.

"Third punch knocked him up against the railing. It broke. He stood on the edge for just a moment, looking at me. I didn't move fast enough, and next thing I knew he was on the ground. Lying very still."

"When I got home from the game, the curtains were drawn and you," Nicky said to her mother's back, "told me Kyle had been fooling around and had broken the railing so it wasn't safe to go out on the deck. The next morning the railing was fixed, but do you know, Sergeant Winters, I never questioned why we never went out there again."

"It was an accident," Mrs. Nowak said. "Kyle was defending our family. He didn't mean to kill Brian."

"Why didn't you go to the police?" Winters asked. "Tell them what happened."

"I wanted to, but Kyle said if we did that it would all come out. Everyone would *know*."

Winters looked at Kyle Nowak. The boy, now a man, stared back at him. And John Winters knew it had not been any accident.

"I came out to see what all the yelling was about," Marjorie Nowak continued. "The railing was broken and Brian was below. Lying there, on the concrete. I ran to him but he wasn't breathing. His neck was twisted. He shouldn't have been able to look at me, but he was. His eyes were empty, so blank. Kyle said no one had to know. I wanted to tell the police, Mr. Winters, really I did. I wanted to have a proper funeral for Brian. Even if my husband was a sinner, surely God would forgive him."

"You bastard," Nicky said to her brother. "You stuck my dad in a hole in the ground and you walked away. I've been looking for my father my whole life and you, you knew exactly where he was."

"Think your life would be any better once everyone in town knew you were the daughter of a pervert? That you were conceived in a duty fuck?"

"I think," Nicky said very slowly, "it couldn't have been a heck of a lot worse." She got to her feet, "I'm leaving now. I'll check into a hotel until my car's ready." She began to leave the room, back straight, head high. Then she turned and looked at her mother. Mrs. Nowak stared out the window. Smith could almost feel the rage emanating from Nicky's small body. "Kyle is a jerk, a macho posturing jerk. You however, are something so much worse."

Mrs. Nowak turned slowly and faced her daughter. "I tried to protect you, Nicky."

Nicky stared at her mother for a long time and then, with a shake of her head and a deep sigh, she left the room.

John Winters gestured to Smith to move in, and he said, "Kyle Nowak, I am arresting you for the murder of Brian Nowak."

Chapter Forty-one

It was late by the time they finished processing Kyle Nowak. A legal aid lawyer had been contacted, and Kyle would have a chance to talk to him over videoconferencing tomorrow, prior to the lawyer arriving in the next few days from the Coast.

Winters had asked one last question, before leaving Marjorie Nowak alone with her demons. "Ten thousand dollars. What happened to the ten thousand dollars Greg Hunt gave you?"

"Ten thousand? No one gave me any money. It disappeared when Brian did."

"No. Hunt gave you the money Brian had put away to help you out until he could start sending financial support."

She shook her head.

"He gave it to me," Kyle said. His hands were cuffed and Smith had hold of his arm and was leading him out the door. Winters signaled to her to let Kyle speak. "The *boyfriend* came around a couple of months later and gave me the blood money, said it was for Mom. I was to be the man of the house now, so I figured I'd look after it. If she told the welfare people she had it, they would have deducted it. It didn't last long. I needed to buy art supplies, a computer. When I bought that old car you never even asked how I could afford it. Totaled the damn car a year later, so that was a waste." He shook his head, and Winters had indicated for Smith to take him away.

"Think we'll get him?" she said as they climbed the stairs leading up from the cells.

"For murder? Probably not. He'll stick to his story about it being an accident. Probably believes it himself by now. I wouldn't be surprised if Mrs. Nowak muddies the waters by claiming she was the one who was there when Brian fell. We can try, and we will, to charge Kyle with lying to the police, for failing to report a death, for hiding evidence of a death, for offering indignity to a body. I'll hit him with everything I can. But murder? No.

"I can comfort myself to some small degree knowing that committing the act of patricide, and then carrying the body into the park and buying it, concealing the fact in the face of intense police inquires, pretty much destroyed his life."

"Mrs. Nowak?"

"She will be charged with being an accessory, but that won't go far. She's a mental wreck, and has almost completely shut down memories of her involvement. She had to have helped Kyle get rid of the body. They must have stuffed it into the trunk of their car and driven to Koola Park. The park would have been empty in early April. They unloaded it and carted it up the mountain and buried it. Hard to imagine."

"Kyle was bigger in those days. I think he worked out or something. Now he's a weedy little guy, but back then he had some muscle. Maybe they used a wheelbarrow." She shuddered. "Awful. And then Nicky comes home after church group. *Hi, Mom, what have you been up to today*? Mrs. Nowak has to be a total psychopath."

"Trying to protect her son, I'd guess. Instead, she destroyed him and her daughter as well. As for Kyle, it's down and out frightening how well he kept a cool head. He found some gay porn in his father's desk, replaced it with his own copies of *Playboy*. Probably burned other things like a letter of resignation to Steve Brooks, Brian's boss, and any other papers that indicated Nowak was planning on leaving. Scattered the ashes around the mountain no doubt."

In the front of the building, someone shouted, a man cheered, and people began to applaud. Smith and Winters hurried to see what the commotion was about.

Ray Lopez was coming through the front door, his grin about to split his face. His wife accompanied him, along with a beaming Mr. Chen, his son Simon, and a girl with her head planted firmly into her chest. May.

"Thank God," someone said.

"Where did you find her?" Winters asked Lopez, while he gave Mr. Chen's hand a hearty shake and slapped Simon on the back.

"I didn't. Madeleine was at the Chen's home, sitting with Mrs. Chen trying to give her comfort, when May walked through the door. Madeline called me, and thus I have the honor of bringing her in."

"Where's she been?"

"Hiding," Simon said. "Mom's at home now, crying her heart out. She didn't shed one tear before, but now she can't stop. May was hiding." His smile disappeared. "Some creep Facebooked her and said he could get her into the movies if she came to Vancouver. So she decided to go to Vancouver."

"Bad girl," Mr. Chen said. "Bad girl."

"She has a friend who lives on the outskirts of town. On a large piece of property with a garden shed in the back yard. Her name's Courtney, and it was this Courtney who phoned May Saturday after supper. Between them they came up with this plan. My folks don't like Courtney, and May knew they wouldn't let her go there for the night, so May said she was going to Becky's. Dad dropped her at Becky's, and May took off for Courtney's place. She's been living in the shed for three days, using the computer in the house during the day while Courtney's parents are at work, trying to contact the creep. Apparently he wasn't prepared to risk picking her up and driving with her to Vancouver. He told her to take a bus and he'd meet her at the bus station. Movie star, my ass. I can guess the kind of movies he was going to star her in."

"Bad girl," Mr. Chen repeated. Now that the child was back and everyone relieved, anger was settling in.

Winters didn't feel too sorry for May. She'd had a very lucky escape.

"As May didn't have bus fare to Vancouver," Madeleine Lopez added, "she came home."

"I'll be paying an official call on Courtney and her parents," Lopez said. "Everyone at her school knew we were searching for May."

"Take May home, Mr. Chen," Winters said. "We'll want to talk to her about this guy, but tonight I think she needs to be with her family."

Simon translated. Mr. Chen nodded, shook everyone's hand once again, and led his children out the door. May hadn't said a single word.

"A happy ending," Lopez said.

"For once," Winters added. And it was a happy ending. They didn't get many of those in this job. He took a deep breath. Enjoy it while it lasted.

"Now," he said, "I'm off home to tell my wife that I've ruined her gallery show."

She was sitting out on the deck when he drove up. It was dark and heavy clouds hid moon and stars. The bulb over the door threw a single beam of yellow light onto her, a small circle of humanity in the deep black forest. The rich voice of Sarah Brightman echoed off the mountains. A glass of wine sat on the table beside her and she was wrapped in a blue cashmere throw.

Eliza smiled as she watched him climb the steps. "It's a beautiful night and you look very pleased, John."

"May Chen, home safe and sound and untouched. She's been hiding out in a friend's backyard shed for three nights."

"I am so glad to hear that. Everyone was worried."

He reached out and plucked her book from her fingers. She was reading a historical mystery, iconic pictures of the Klondike gold rush sprinkled across the cover.

"We've made an arrest for the Brian Nowak murder." He put the book on the table beside her drink.

"That's wonderful, John. So it was murder, was it?"

"Yes, but I won't be able to prove it."

"You no longer look too pleased."

"I'm sorry, Eliza. It's Kyle Nowak I arrested."

"Why… Oh. Kyle." She unwrapped the throw, uncurled her legs and stood up. She put her arms around him and pulled him close. "You're afraid I'm going to be angry at you. For ruining my show." She smelled of vanilla hand lotion and good red wine. She tilted her head back and smiled up at him. His heart almost stopped beating.

"Rather, I'd say Kyle Nowak ruined my show. It would be worse, wouldn't it, if he hadn't been caught? Are you sure?"

"Positive. But don't give up hope. He committed the crime when he was sixteen, and we're not going to be able to prove murder. I don't expect he'll get much jail time, if any. It's a sensational case and will get a lot of press. The notoriety might do your gallery good."

She chucked, low in her throat. "Notoriety, I can do without. No, John, I'll be cancelling the show. It might cost me something to get out of the contract, but I suspect Kyle has other things on his mind. I've prepared a stew for dinner. It's in the oven and the last time I peeked it wasn't burned too terribly badly. Are you hungry?"

"How about a glass of wine first? You should probably take the stew out of the oven. I know we shouldn't be buying up your stock for ourselves, but I did like that painting of the house with the yellow roof. It would look nice in the landing."

The CD clicked off and the only sound for miles was the tinkle of her laugh.

Chapter Forty-two

On a Wednesday evening Flavours was largely empty. The black-clad waiter escorted them to an alcove at the back with an obsequious smile. He took the highly starched apron off the table and fluffed it in the air before settling it into her lap. He lit the candles on the table, and said, "Good evening, sir, madam. I'll let you look over the wine menu and be back shortly."

His name was Tim Croft and he was six foot three with a buzz cut, a row of rings through his right ear, and tattoos, hidden by the formal shirt, covering his arms. He was a student at Kootenay School of the Arts, studying jewelry and small metal design. Lucky Smith had known him when he was in diapers and when he was an awkward pre-pubescent boy hanging around the youth center. She settled into her chair and said, "That would be lovely, thank you."

Paul Keller smiled at her. "You look beautiful tonight, Lucky."

She returned his smile. She'd treated herself to a new dress, flowing navy blue with matching jacket, and wore shoes with heels. The shoes she'd dug out of the back of her closet. It had been necessary to wipe layers of dust off them. She hadn't worn heels for years and felt quite risqué slipping her feet into them. She knew Paul was taking her to Flavours and wanted to make the effort to look nice.

He looked nice too, in a gray business suit with perfectly knotted tie.

He opened the wine menu and consulted it, humming and hawing about what would be good. She didn't much care. Wine was wine. Some bottles more expensive than others.

"You made an arrest in the Nowak case, I hear."

He pulled a face. "Sad, sad story. Marjorie and Kyle both knew where Brian was all these years. I'd say they led us a happy dance, but believe me, Lucky, it wasn't happy for anyone. Of course I can't comment further until the matter is settled."

"And May Chen?"

"The worst cases of them all. Missing children. It made everyone darn happy to see her walking into the station, healthy and whole and mighty embarrassed."

"What was she thinking?"

"She ran off. Heading for the bright lights and big city. If she'd gotten there she would have been like a minnow in a shark tank. Gosh, Lucky, I'm sorry. I didn't bring you here to talk business and that's a heck of a downer. Can we forget about it and have ourselves a nice dinner?"

"Don't worry about upsetting me, Paul. In my work at the women's support center and the battered women's shelter, I do see some of what goes on the world. What May was in danger of getting herself into simply boggles my mind. Why some men can possibly think it's acceptable to pay for sex with a child who's obviously been coerced at best and out-and-out beaten at worst, I cannot…" The man across the table was watching her with a look of such adoration she stopped talking in mid-sentence.

"Of course," she mumbled, "you know that."

"It's nice to be able to talk to you, Lucky, about things like that. Karen wasn't interested. She doesn't want to know about the ugliness of the world."

"Sometimes I think I know more than I want to. Paul…"

"The specials today are…" Tim began to recite them.

Paul consulted with the waiter and Lucky and then ordered a bottle of Cabernet Sauvignon from B.C. Lucky always liked to eat locally, when she could.

They buried their heads in their menus for a while and when Tim returned, flourishing the bottle and a cork screw, they were ready to order.

Over dinner they talked about prostitution. Paul was a cop, with a bit of an old style approach, but Lucky was pleased to realize he didn't regard the women, the younger ones at any rate, as criminals but as victims. Lucky thought every man who used an underage prostitute, should be strung up by his thumbs in the town square.

Tim cleared the main course plates and asked if they would like dessert.

"Just coffee," Lucky said, and Paul agreed.

"I had some news today," he said, and Lucky suspected he'd been leading up to that statement all evening. She clutched her napkin. "We've had an offer on the house."

"That was quick."

"It was. It's a good offer, so we have no reason to turn it down."

"Are you wanting to?"

"No. Not at all. It's just that… the closing date is only a month away. They want to move in as soon as possible. Means I'll be homeless. Imagine, the chief constable sleeping under a bridge." He laughed.

Lucky sensed a chasm opening up in front of her. She grabbed her wine glass and chugged what remained. She'd once again promised herself she wasn't going to see Paul any more. But they were having fun. He so obviously enjoyed being with her that she enjoyed being with him. It was fun to have a man again. Not just the sex, although that was fun too, but a companion. Someone to talk to. Lucky had lots of friends. She talked politics with her friends, organized campaigns, went to movies and the theater, to Trafalgar Thai or the Sunshine Grill for a meal. But not to *Feuilles de Menthe* for lunch or to Flavours for dinner. She didn't buy new dresses to wear for her friends or dig around in the closet for sexy shoes.

"Lucky," he said. "I have loved you since the moment I first set eyes on you."

She was genuinely shocked. "You have not!"

"I remember where it was. You were sitting in the city hall park. You were wearing a yellow skirt, the color of daffodils, and it was spread all around you and you were refusing to move because you were protesting… something. I don't remember what. The sun shone on your hair and it looked like it was on fire. I'd been married to Karen for ten years, we had two kids, and I realized at that moment that I did not love my wife."

"Please, Paul, don't."

"I respected Andy. I respected your marriage. But now, all these years later things have changed. Why, I don't even have a home any more. Lucky, I…"

With great care she placed the white linen napkin on the table. The candle was low, flickering, almost out. Tim hovered in the background. He had the coffee but sensed this was not a good time to approach. Lucky stood up.

"No, Paul. You say your marriage is over, but nevertheless I will not be responsible for breaking it up."

"Karen and I…"

"Things can change. People change. People change their minds. If your wife changes her mind, decides she wants to save her marriage, house or no house, I will not be the one in her way."

"It's over, Lucky."

"And so it may seem, but you have to give it more time. Give her more time. I'm sorry, Paul. Karen needs more time. I need more time. I'm… I'm sorry. It's just not right. Please don't call me again."

She ran out of the restaurant. Tim stepped out of her way, clutching coffee cups. Startled patrons watched her go.

Chapter Forty-three

On his way home from work, Ray Lopez stopped at the video rental store. The girls were out tonight and he and Madeline would have a rare evening alone. Madeline wanted to spend it curled up on the couch watching a chick flick. He had a list of suggested titles in his pocket, romantic comedies most of them. Personally he'd rather spend the night at the dentist than watching one of those movies. He considered telling her the ones she wanted were out, and all that was left was *District Nine*, which he still hadn't had the opportunity to see.

But, he realized, Madeleine spent far more time with the girls than he did. Let her enjoy her night off. He handed his list to the teenage boy behind the counter.

"Lame," the kid said, and Lopez laughed.

"The lot of a married man."

The boy shook his head in disbelief. "Most of these are in. How many do you want?"

"Two, I guess."

While the clerk fetched his selection, Lopez chose a big bag of popcorn and another of Doritos.

The boy rang up the charges and Lopez handed over the money.

"Is, uh, Marlene doing anything tonight?" the boy asked, his face turning bright red underneath his greasy skin and collection of pimples. Marlene was the Lopez's third daughter, starting Grade Eleven with plans to become a cop, just like her dad.

She was at a friend's house, studying. Lopez had absolutely no intention of letting this kid know anything about that.

"Watching movies with her mother," Lopez said.

"Lame."

The video store was in a small strip plaza not far from his house. Lopez took a short cut around the back rather than walk the extra distance on the sidewalk. Away from the streetlights it was dark, traffic only a background buzz. He was about to round the corner to cut through a weed-choked field which would get him back to the road when he heard voices ahead.

"Is this good stuff?"

"Guaranteed the best."

Very quietly, Lopez placed the bag of videos and chips on the ground.

"I'd like…"

Lopez rounded the corner. Two men were standing beside a dumpster. A single light burned above the back door to the pizza shop and the air was heavy with the scent of garbage, tomatoes, cheese, and yeast.

"Ronnie Kilpatrick. I heard you were back in town."

The men whirled around, startled.

"I'm not doin' nothing, Mr. Lopez, really." He was young with a shaved head and numerous piercings and tattoos.

The second man, older, shoved his hand into his pocket and started to edge away.

"Police," Lopez said. "Stay right where you are. Take your hands out of your pockets."

Ronnie Kilpatrick had lost weight in prison and looked like he'd put on some muscle. The other man was in his mid-thirties, small and thin. He glanced over Lopez's shoulder, looking for the road. Unfortunately, for him, he'd stood in the shadows of the dumpster to conduct business and was blocked in. He looked at Ronnie's face and saw no help there. He lifted his hands to chest height. "No problem," he said.

"What you got in your pocket?" Lopez asked.

"Nothing."

"Turn your right pant pocket out. Use your left hand and keep the right hand where it is."

"I donna have ta do that." The Scottish accent was strong.

"You do. I am arresting you on suspicion of possession of narcotics." Lopez pushed his jacket aside so his badge and gun were visible.

The Scotsman looked at Ronnie. "Tell him, mate. We're talking about getting some movies, right."

Ronnie's face was as blank as normal. "Don't know nothin' about no movies, Mr. Lopez." Every cop in Trafalgar knew Ronnie. Ronnie had ambitions to be a big time drug dealer. Unlikely to happen, as he was as dumb as a bag of pot.

Lopez flipped his phone open and called for a car. He kept his eyes on the Scotsman, aware Ronnie was edging away.

"Stay where you are, Ronnie," Lopez ordered. "You know the drill."

The back door to the pizza shop opened with a burst of loud music and warm air. A man gave them one startled look and slammed the door shut.

Ronnie Kilpatrick bolted.

For a flash of a moment Lopez considered going after him. But Ronnie was twenty-one years old and in good shape after his stint in jail. Chase Ronnie and this other guy would get away. Lopez knew where Ronnie lived; the other guy would disappear into the mountains.

"Name?"

"What the hell? Aren't you going to go after him?"

"I know him. Don't know you. Name?"

"Stewart. Joe Stewart."

Lopez sucked in a breath and his heart skipped a beat. He hoped he managed to keep his face impassive. *Joe Stewart. Facebook user and friend to teenage girls. Handed to Ray Lopez on a platter.*

"Mr. Stewart, where do you live?"

"Vancouver."

"What brings you to Trafalgar?"

His eyes shifted to one side. "Visiting a friend."

"Your friend in the drug business?"

"No. And neither am I. You've made a mistake."

"Mr. Kilpatrick is a well known drug dealer. Want to tell me why you're meeting with him in a dark alley at night?"

"Dinna ken he were a druggie, did I?"

"If that's the case you will be allowed to go once you've showed me the contents of your pockets."

Stewart shifted his feet and glanced toward the road.

"I advise you not to attempt to run, Joe," Lopez said. "This is a small town. Isolated. There are only three roads out. They can be blocked off before you even get to your car."

A siren sounded and lights washed the alley.

"Fuck it," Stewart said.

Lopez let out a breath he hadn't known he was holding. He'd almost considered cancelling the call for a uniform. *A dark alley. No one around. An unfortunate accident.*

He'd come closer than he liked to crossing the line.

The car pulled up and Dawn Solway got out. She stood back and watched as Lopez told Stewart to turn around and snapped handcuffs on him. The detective patted the man down and found a wallet, keys, cigarettes. And a crumpled lottery ticket, wrapped around a soft material.

"Tsk, tsk," Lopez said.

Solway handed him a plastic bag, and he dropped the items into it.

"Okay, Mr. Stewart, time for a trip to the station."

"You're going to charge me with that little bit of powder, while the other guy gets away?"

"Don't worry about Mr. Kilpatrick. We know where we can find him. Did he sell you that stuff?"

Stewart's eyes moved as he calculated. "Yeah," he said at last.

"Thanks. Let's go."

Solway drove the car into the secure parking bay and the door closed. Only then did she and Lopez get out. Solway assisted Stewart.

She processed him through the computer while Lopez watched.

"If you do not have a lawyer of your own, you may contact a legal aid lawyer in the morning," Solway said.

Stewart grumbled.

"You don't look like a user," Lopez said. "Are you buying for someone else?"

"No. And even if I was, you think I'd confess to trafficking?"

"Not trafficking in that quantity," Lopez said. "Just wondering. You said you have friends in town."

"I lied. I don't have any friends."

"Come on. Time for beddy-bye." Solway grabbed his arm to take him to a cell.

Stewart offered no resistance.

Unlikely a judge would order him to be held. White powder was wrapped in the lottery ticket. Cocaine, probably less than a gram. Stewart didn't show signs of being a long-time user and the amount was too small to be able to charge him with trafficking.

Kilpatrick was a fool, but he wasn't harmless, and Ray Lopez was not happy to see him back in town. Stewart had readily admitted he'd bought the stuff from Kilpatrick. Better if they caught the dealer red-handed, but a buyer's testimony would go a long way toward obtaining a conviction. With Kilpatrick's record hopefully this time he could be sent away for a nice long stay at Her Majesty's Pleasure.

But that was of little important to Ray Lopez tonight.

"Hold on a minute. Ever been to Big Eddie's Coffee Emporium?"

Stewart eyed the detective. "Might have."

"How about the park? We have a nice park, high over town. You get a great view from up there."

"Might have."

"You said you don't have friends in town?"

"No."

"You sure about that? How about a woman friend? The sort of friend you might have coffee with now and again."

"I said no."

"Do you like girls?"

"What kind of a question's that? Sure I like girls, don't you?" His eyes flicked to Solway, who looked confused, not knowing where this was going.

"Young girls, I mean. Little girls. Underage girls."

Understanding moved behind Stewart's beady black eyes. A single drop of sweat trickled down his right cheek. He wiped it away. His fingernails were chewed into the quick. His glance slid to one side. "Of course not."

"Constable Solway, get a camera and take a photograph of Mr. Stewart. I want to show it to a potential witness. I think we might have more charges to lay before the judge tomorrow."

Chapter Forty-four

Nicky Nowak had taken a room in a cheap motels where she spent the entire day sitting and stewing and waiting for her car to be fixed. Then they phoned and told her it would it would be another day.

She'd finished reaming them out for the delay when her cell phone rang. She took the call, listened, and phoned a car rental company.

She had to get out of here, now. She threw her toiletries into the suitcases she'd hadn't bothered to unpack and walked the few short blocks to collect the car. Back to the motel to toss her cases into the trunk.

She sat in the car for a few minutes, staring at the line of motel room doors. Then she took a deep breath and pulled out her phone.

In Big Eddie's Coffee Emporium chairs were stacked on tables. A man ran a broom energetically across the floor as Nicky walked in. Only one table, in the center of the room, was occupied.

"Thanks for seeing me."

"It's okay."

"I guess you're mad at me for coming on to Adam, eh."

Molly Smith shrugged. "Why would I be mad about something like that?"

Nicky did not sit down. "It's who I am, Molly. I fuck for a living. It's like if you saw me not putting money in a parking meter you wouldn't just walk away."

"First of all, I would just walk away because that's what the bylaw officers are for. And secondly, it's hardly the same. But most of all that might be what you do. It's not who you are. It's not you, Nicky."

Semantics. "Joey Stewart used his one phone call to tell me he's been arrested. He was caught making a drug deal and they're going after him for trying to lure girls to Vancouver. I don't want anything to do with that, so I'm outa here. I thought... I guess I wanted to say good-bye, Moonlight. To thank you for being my friend."

Molly gave her a long look.

"What do you think might happen to Joey?"

"They can hold him on the narcotics charge while they dig nice and deep into his background. If he's ever been seen in the company of underage hookers or handling kiddie porn, he's toast."

"Not my problem. I'm cutting him loose. I'm thinking of going to Toronto. Start over." Ironically, Joey had hung around Trafalgar in case Nicky needed him, and he'd been buying drugs for her when he got pinched. After fleeing her mother's house, sitting in a crummy motel all the next day staring at the walls and consuming two bottles of wine, Nicky phoned Joey to say she was desperate. Joey never touched the stuff.

Maybe he really did like her after all.

Fool.

"You know you should think about getting into a new line of work?" Molly said.

"Yeah, I know. You might not want me to be your friend, but I'm glad you're mine." She held out her hand. Molly hesitated, just for a moment, and then she stood up and wrapped her arms around her friend.

They held each other close. Nicky broke away first. "Thanks. Keep in touch, eh?"

"Sure."

Nicole Nolte drove out of Trafalgar. Molly Smith would not keep in touch, and Nicole would never see this town again. She'd arrange for someone to bring her car to Vancouver, never mind the cost.

It was late and the sun had long ago disappeared behind the hills. Clouds were gathering in the west. It would rain soon, snow on the mountains perhaps, and the wind was high, tossing the river into waves, tips crowned white. It would be morning before Nicole pulled into Vancouver.

Molly Smith had been wrong. Nicky Nowak was gone, and she would not be coming back. Being a hooker was more than what Nicole Nolte did, it was who she was. It was all she had.

A no-smoking sticker was stuck to the dashboard. Nicole pulled up at a red light, dug in her purse for a cigarette and light. She flicked the lighter; flame broke the dark inside the car. She lit the cigarette, breathed in deeply, and felt the smoke move into her lungs. The traffic light changed from red to green as Nicole took one last glance at the night-covered mountains. The car behind her beeped its horn, telling her to hurry it up. She drove out of town.

To receive a free catalog of Poisoned Pen Press titles, please contact us in one of the following ways:

Phone: 1-800-421-3976
Facsimile: 1-480-949-1707
Email: info@poisonedpenpress.com
Website: www.poisonedpenpress.com

Poisoned Pen Press
6962 E. First Ave. Ste. 103
Scottsdale, AZ 85251